The World At Large

Cody Punter

The World at Large by Cody Punter
Copyright © 2013 Cody Punter
All rights reserved.
Cover by Andrew McTavish of McTavish Associates
ISBN-13: 978-1494317560

"Be sure the safest rule is that we should not dare to live in any scene in which we dare not die."

Lewis Carroll, Preface to *Sylvie and Bruno*

One

I flagged down the bartender and ordered another beer. "That'll be 9.69." No smile. Not even a nod or a glance. I couldn't blame her. We were both doing our best not to draw attention from the nervous go-getters scattered across the bar. The only difference was she was being paid to do it. Her lifeless routine was so entrenched in her burgundy painted lips that it was hard to tell whether she had just been laid off from her job in the city or been born and raised with 3 kids and no pension before crawling to the suburbs on her hands and knees. It didn't really matter either way.

She stared at me with her matted lips without saying a word. Not that I had anything to say. But how was she supposed to know that. She wrapped her knobbled fingers around an empty glass and topped it off with an undrinkable froth before sliding it onto the bar. The foam spilled carelessly over the rim, glistening in the fluorescent light as it made its way towards the cardboard coaster that was busy soaking up the last few rounds. I didn't need another one, and it was 8 dollars more than the stale swill was worth, but there was no arguing with routine.

The TV above the bar hummed along while the speakers in the corner dribbled out the kind of monotonous jazz classics that you only hear at corporate Christmas parties and funerals. The 10 O'clock news was on but I couldn't make out what the silicone silhouette was saying above the bellowing of some mediocre Ella Fitzgerald impersonator. I kept focussing on the screen, if only to avoid another mindless conversation. The camera flashed to footage of the recent protests in New York. In the past few days the situation had deteriorated as peaceful demonstrations escalated into violent clashes with police. After a quick shot of the carnage they flashed through similar scenes from across the country. The movement was rallying and it was spreading like wild fire. They panned across the entire nation, covering every major city from coast to coast until they reached a sullen outpost of desert villages, which had recently been reduced to rubble *'amidst the renewed outbreak of hostilities'*.

It wasn't long before I was ready for another one, and even less time before it was overflowing over the rim and onto my hand. I looked down at my ticket then up at the clock. The minute hand continued to move dutifully over the white background leaving me with little choice. She caught me reaching for my credit card and scowled. She was right. I didn't have the time for that anyway. I finished the beer and left enough money to pay for my drinks, along with whatever change was left in my pocket.

There were still a few stragglers making their way up to the gate. I walked up to the desk and smiled, flashing my passport as I made my way down the tunnel with my head down. The plane was almost full but when I got to the back I was relieved to see that the two seats beside the window were empty. I stuffed my bags in the overhead compartment and pushed past the man in the grey suit that was occupying the aisle seat. He was clean-shaven and he had his hair parted to one side in the same way I would have done if I had been wearing the same grey suit he was – three quarters to one side one quarter to the other. I probably wouldn't have it cut so short. But then again I couldn't afford to have my suits fitted by a tailor. Maybe if I had a suit in that warm shade of grey, and if my skin had that healthy glow, I'd probably make sure to shave as closely as he did.

I ran my fingers across the gristle on my face. It had only been a month since I'd had to shave and at least a few more since I'd had to wear anything resembling a suit. It had certainly been long enough that I was ready to settle for a bit of stability and some cash; at least enough for me to escape every once in a while so that I could pretend that I still had some sort of control over my life.

There was a light rain falling on the tarmac. Down below, the baggage handlers were busy chucking the neatly packaged lives' of passengers onto the moistened conveyor belt. The grey suit next to me shuffled his thumbs nervously over the edges of his paper as he tried to get the attention of the attendant. His seat was stuck in the upright position. I checked to see if mine worked but it was stuck too. He started to grumble to himself. He'd had enough. He dropped his newspaper and pushed the panic button and a woman in a baby blue knee high suit and a faux-silk scarf appeared out of the back of the plane.

"May I help you sir?"

"Yes," he replied firmly. "There seems to be a problem with my seat." He pushed the button and tried to shove the seat back with his shoulders, "It won't go back any further than this."

"I'm sorry about that sir." She clasped her hand in front of the scarf that was modestly covering up her neck while leaving the perfectly rounded crest of her chest exposed.

"Isn't there anything you can do?" he blurted out before she was able to give him an offer. "There's barely anyone on this damn thing."

"Yes sir, I most certainly can. If you like I can move you to a new seat once we are in the air."

He frowned at her, "Isn't there anything you can do right now?"

"I'm sorry sir, the engines are running and the captain has turned on the fasten seatbelt sign." She paused, intent on seeing his reaction. "You'll have to wait until we're in the air."

Her hair was being pulled from all sides towards a single point on the back of her head. A feigned smile crept out from behind her lavender blush and I shuddered. I was waiting for her to pull a pin out of her tightly wound bun and shove it in his eye, but he replied before she got the opportunity.

"Ok, thank you." he said, leering facetiously at her as she walked away before registering his complaint under his breath, "Fucking ridiculous!"

He mumbled just loud enough for me to hear, before returning to the greyish pink pages of his newspaper.

He had no intention of following me to the end of the line. He was probably getting off when the plane stopped to refuel in Japan. He'd spend a few days there, take care of business and get back on the plane before I was even settled in. A few sleeping pills and some fresh coffee and it would all be over before his wife even noticed he was ever missing.

The rain slowed to a light mist. The few drops that clung to the wings evaporated before they had the chance roll off their polished surface. The engine hummed quietly underneath and the captain's voice crackled over top of the loudspeaker reassuring us with meaningless numbers and facts. No one really gave a shit whether we were going to be flying 35,000 feet above the Rocky Mountains or whether we were going to cross into the Arctic circle at 600 miles an hour in order to use the earth's magnetic field to slingshot us to our destination in record time; so long as we made it there in one piece with less than a couple trips to the bathroom and a few Adam Sandler movies. When the monologue was over we were asked to observe a moment of silence as the attendants nervously repeated the company sermon in the event that our bodies were never to be found.

The engine's hum grew to a rumble as the plane prepared to take off. The vibrations trickled down the wing and up my spine as my head rattled against the thick pane of double glazed plexi-glass. The plane bounced down the runway. The man in the grey suit clenched the corrugated edges of his jaundiced paper into balled up fists. The roar of the engines mounted and the plane kicked back like a mechanical bull. We pulled back further with no intention of bucking forward as we lifted into the mist soaked sky. The pressure outside began to build, attempting to crush the fuselage as we pulled off the ground. But we just kept rising effortlessly into the air. The plane flattened out and the attendant returned. She bent over to address the grey suit with her hands clasped together in front of her chest. She smiled at him as he gathered his things. He handed her his newspaper and she directed him to his new seat before retreating out of sight.

I swallowed two Robaxacet, kicked off my shoes off and lay across all three seats. My mind raced ahead for a few minutes but the haze soon started to cloud my mind. I could feel my stomach starting to soak up my tired thoughts and I began to feel warm inside. The weight started to lift from my fingers and toes and I began to drift off at 580 miles an hour, 27,000 feet above the ground and climbing.

...

As soon as I walked off the plane I was hit by the recycled tropical fumes that had managed to slip through the security checkpoints. I took my place behind the army of white sneakers who were slumped over their luggage and waited my turn. When I got to the end of the line I handed my passport to the security agent. He took my picture, handed me back my documents, and waved me through without even looking me in the eye.

I had only booked my flight a few days ago, and all I had in my pocket was my wallet and an old receipt with the name of a train station and a phone number scribbled on the back of it. It took me 45 minutes of sweating and cursing at an automated computer voice before I gave up and slammed the receiver against the hook.

The stale tropical air followed me out of the airport as I staggered through the automatic sliding doors. I was immediately shoved into the back of a cab with the piece of scribbled paper in my hand. I looked at the flashing clock radio on the dash. It was almost midnight. I tried to haggle the driver into giving me a fixed rate. He spoke just enough English for me to flash the amount of money with my fingers and make a deal.

We pulled onto the highway and I rolled down the window. The road was lined with hulking billboards that blocked out the glow of the polluted skyline in the distance. We weaved through endless figure-eights of on-ramps, off-ramps, bypasses and exits as we floated effortlessly over industrial shanties and barren slums. After driving for half an hour, we were surrounded by endless rows of brightly lit high-rises that dwarfed everything in sight. Every single building over 20 stories was equipped with industrial strength casino lights and helicopter landing pads that lit up the sky in a toxic shade of green and pink. We continued to twist through the streets the city, guarded by concrete apartment complexes and chain linked fences, as we were slowly digested by the never-ending maze of the city.

After a while I began to wonder where we were heading, "You sure you know where we're going?"

The driver hesitated.

"You know?" I repeated emphatically.

"Yehhss, I take you," he grinned.

I slumped back in my seat. There was no use arguing. He picked up on my resignation and repeated himself in an attempt to reassure me, "Yes, we go. We go…" Other than occasionally blurting out the mispronounced destination, all I could do was wait until the car stopped before re-evaluating the situation.

We finally came to a stop underneath two concrete pillars that were holding up an overpass. There was no way this could be right. Based on the brief exchanges I'd had with Sam, I had been expecting a busy square, with lots of bars and people, maybe a temple or a palace, or a post office – at least some kind of identifiable government building.

The driver insisted that this was the right place. After protesting for a while I decided to get out and see if I could figure out where I was. The overpass was outfitted with sets of tracks on either side but at this hour the trains were no longer running. The bus station across the street was littered with drunks and homeless people passed out under glass shelters and on top of benches. There was a brightly lit McDonald's right beside it. Sam probably would have bet on meeting me there but it was closed now.

I walked down to an open-air bar on the street corner. It was Friday night, or maybe it was Saturday now, and the place was dead except for a group of 20 some-odd local students, all crowded around a big screen that was broadcasting a football game being played live on the other side of the world.

It must have been about one in the morning now but the air was still ripe with moisture. The water seeped out of my skin before making a prompt re-entry as it soaked right back into my clothes. All I wanted was a clean bed and a cold shower but I had to settle for a lukewarm beer, and a football game that was taking place more than 12 hours and 10,000 miles away.

I sat down at a table in front of one of the screens. The home team was controlling the play without effort. The visitors showed great bursts of speed down the wing. Each time they made a run, the home team would pinch them off along the sidelines until they had nowhere left to go. Once they retrieved possession they would hold onto the ball. They spread wide across the field, outmaneuvering any man that approached them by passing the ball along the ground or chipping it to the far line leaving the visitors with nothing to do except retreat and hope for an interception. They took a shot on goal and the ball deflected off the defender. The midfielder jogged down the field to take the corner kick when I caught Sam panning across the patio.

The wispy hair of his father was cut shorter than usual and his crisp stubble was old enough to show recent signs of his ginger heritage, which he had been lucky enough to escape in its entirety. He clocked me and I watched as the shit-eating grin danced onto his face. He marched up and threw his arms around me.

"Dravott, you creepy bastard!"

"Good to see you too!" he said, as he patted me on the back.

"It's been a while…"

He pulled back and looked at me. His cheeks were flush and sweaty. "Too long!"

I smiled back and pulled out a chair, "Who cares, we're here now. Grab a seat, I just ordered. I figured I'd get some food in me in case you didn't show up."

As I spoke, a gaunt looking Brit stepped out from behind Sam.

"Austin, this is Russell. He works at the firm."

"He was my boss back in London," said Sam in an attempt to jog the conversation.

"Pleased to meet you," I said, shaking his hand vigorously.

He smiled back, "Pleasure indeed."

I stared at his face. His cheeks were tickled pink. I was sure I'd seen that same childish grin somewhere before. "I'm sure we've met before," I suggested. I kept staring, waiting for Sam to interject, but he had already turned his attention to the TV.

"It's certainly possible," he replied.

I scratched my head to show that I was at least making an effort but I soon lost my train of thought, "Oh well, I guess it doesn't matter."

He nodded.

"Thanks again for having us. And my apologies in advance for taking advantage of your hospitality."

He cocked his head to the side and chuckled, "You're quite welcome. But there's no need to apologise."

"Don't worry. It's just a precaution. In case something were to go wrong while we're under your care."

Sam shuffled embarrassingly, "Don't mind him."

"No, no, it's fine. I'm sure you'll be no trouble at all," he insisted with a fresh smile.

"We don't plan on sticking around very long anyways," I said.

"22 days to be exact," Sam said reassuringly.

Russell sighed, "It's a shame you're only here for such a short time. There's so much to do here, it could take you years do everything."

"We're not too worried about that. But I don't know if I can speak for Sam," I said as I gripped him on the shoulder.

"The important thing is that we're here," said Sam. "And to get out of this town as quickly as possible," he added, laughing nervously as he fell back into his seat

He looked around for a waiter and signalled for more beers to be brought to the table. The waiter brought over three large bottles and some rubbery squid cooked in garlic and basil. The sun was long gone but the sky was still sweating down upon us. As soon as my fingers touched the bottle, they sapped whatever coolness had been preserved on the trip from the fridge to the table and I was left trying to throw back the beers as soon as they were brought to us, to keep my hands cool and the beer cold enough to swallow.

"We just went to some kind of deranged Oriental cabaret staged in a German beer hall," said Sam. "You've never seen anything so obscene."

He smacked his hand on the table as he described the flying trapeze acts and the sword fighting opera singers doing Celine Dion impersonations, and the Shakespearean burlesque dancers fighting off papier-mâché dragons, before concluding that it was something that you had to see it for yourself to believe it.

"I tell you, I've never seen something so demented in my life."

After a few drinks the initial flurry of conversation came to a lull and I sat back in my chair staring across the table at Sam.

"So you finally decided to quit," I said smugly.

"Quit, fired, repurposed, what's the fucking difference? I just had to get out of there. I was losing my fucking mind!" He held his beer up to his lips but held back for a second "I don't know how people do it." He looked sheepishly to his side, "No offence Russell."

Russell smiled and put up his hand to show that no offence was taken.

Sam took a large sip from his beer and shook his head, "I just couldn't take it anymore! You spend 6 years of your life studying all these lofty ideas, then you end up spending 8 hours a day writing contracts for coked out monkeys who couldn't give a fuck about anything, unless you can sue it or shove it up your nose. And the rain… That fucking rain – all day, everyday, non-stop, fucking rain. I just couldn't take another day of it."

I winced and forced a smile, "You don't need to remind me."

"The sad thing is I'll probably just end up begging for them to take me back. It was either that or jump down the stairs and hope for a severance package. " He took a sip of his beer and stared at Russell. "I can't even imagine what they've got you doing down here."

Russell smiled at Sam, "At least it doesn't rain."

The manager come over to our table and interjected politely with a bow, "We ar closing soon… No mor…We close…"

Sam looked up and flashed with his fingers, "Three more of your coldest beers please."

He smiled and dipped his head, inching slowly back from the table. He returned seconds later with three large bottles that perspired heavily in his hands.

"What about you? Any news yet?"

"Nothing yet. I should know in the next few days."

Sam laughed out loud "Sounds promising."

"I'd say my chances are pretty slim, but I guess it's better than nothing." My mind flipped a switch for a moment and I paused, "Actually, that reminds me. Do you mind if I check my emails when we get back to the apartment?"

"Of course," Russell replied calmly.

The building was outfitted with a doorman in a creamy khaki suit and a matching cap. His body went limp as we approached. He proceeded to fold in half like a cheap Japanese knockoff as he pressed his palms flat against one another and pointed his fingers hopelessly towards the sky. He tried to put on a brave face but you could tell exactly what he was thinking.

We took the elevator up to the apartment. I threw my bag down and collapsed on the sofa. It was almost 2 a.m. and Russell was noticeably more drunk than Sam. Sam urged him to come out but he insisted that he had to get up early in the morning.

"I'm actually trying to plan a trip of my own at the end of the month. I was thinking of going up north to do a bit of exploring."

"What about the floods?"

"Oh, its fine now. The news makes it out to be much worse than it actually is. You know, it's supposed to be the most beautiful part of the country," he said, wiping his face with a towel, "It's a shame you don't have enough time to make it up there."

Sam smiled to humour him, "Maybe. But it's probably for the best."

Russell stood in his bedroom doorway, stripped down to his loose-fitting boxer shorts with his ribs tempting to snap through his flaccid skin at any given moment,

"I'll be heading to visit the National Monument with a friend first thing tomorrow morning so I might not see you before you leave. Unless of course, you decide to extend your trip."

"Greater men than us have been swallowed up by this circus," said Sam with a serious look on his face, "And we don't need to run that risk."

Russell looked at us cock-eyed and laughed, "Well, the world is your oyster…"

And with that Russell signed off on our trip as Sam and I marched off into the night, looking for a drink.

Two

I woke up wearing considerably less clothing than when I went to bed. I must have shed it in the middle of the night amidst the strange dreams and profuse sweating that accompanied them. It didn't help that it was now midday and the sun was making its best efforts to cook me as I lay in front of the window with the A/C turned all the way up. Sam was already awake and making preparations to leave. He saw me lift my head up and turned around.

"What a night!" sighed Sam. "I've never seen so many straight-faced suits desperately looking for love at 5 in the morning."

I laughed, "I think we got out of that place just in time."

We left the apartment in shorts and flip-flops but no precaution was sufficient enough to repel the sweaty cloud that rose mercilessly from the asphalt. We spent a few hours pacing up and down sidewalks, ducking in and out of small shopping complexes that looked like they had been freshly imported from northern Detroit. There was nothing even remotely resembling a restaurant in sight, and I was relived when we ended up scarfing back cheeseburgers at the McDonalds across the street.

We spent our lunchtime thumbing through a Vacant Universe guidebook that Sam had bought at the airport. After skimming over it we decided that we should probably head for the coast on an overnight train. Sam flipped to the schedule in the back of the book. The next one left in a few hours.

We hurried back to the apartment to grab our bags and the doorman bowed insincerely as we left the building. We grabbed a taxi and headed for the train station. After a brief ride through the maze of soviet-style slums we came to a stop. The white plaster of the station across the street shone brightly in the lingering sunlight. The tired building was capped with an elongated semi-dome that sprawled across the decrepit skyline. Underneath it was the varnished portrait of the king, which glistened in the yellow haze. The entire weight of it all rested on rows of plastic double columns capped with ionic scrolls. It was perfectly sturdy but bland, and in the setting sun it looked like a sanitised Roman temple imported from the local IKEA.

A man with a thick carpet of black hair and a freshly pressed dress shirt tucked into a pair of baggy khakis hurried up to the cab and ushered us into the building. He rushed us past the bedraggled mix of tired workers and anxious travellers that crowded the unimpressive station, and crammed us into a dingy travel agency the size of a phone booth. The room reeked of desperation and exhaustion. We booked a first class cabin as quickly as possible then rushed out and went back into the streets.

We had a few hours to kill before our train left so we walked around, watching people hurry past the shuttered buildings on either side of the street. I tried to picture the animated chaos that would be taking place if the entire city hadn't just been wiped out by torrential flooding. There was a river running beside the street and you could see a thick line of green scum where the flood had left its mark. The signs of a recent disaster were strewn across the banks: dishevelled bits of rotting clothing, rusty shopping carts mangled from being sucked by the currents into jagged rocks, and mountains of plastic containers and jugs covered in a pungent green film.

The fishermen on the bridge remained undeterred by the site as they continued to cast their lines into the water. The lines would inevitably get intertwined, leaving the fishermen spending the majority of their time untangling the knots, while the fish escaped up the murky stream. As we were leaving one of them pulled back hard on his line. The metal rod bent into a triumphant arc, but when he pulled the line out of the water the only thing attached to the hook was a rotting carcass that could barely be mistaken for a fish.

The sun sunk behind Greco-Swedish dome as we walked back

towards the station. We stopped for curry at a small restaurant across the street as backpacks and yoga mats scurried in and out of the station, strapped firmly to the backs of their loyal masters.

We shuffled frantically down the platform and into one of the cars. The pious faces in the second-class carriage grimaced at us as we walked past them. Two American couples were busy giving hell to an usher over the state of their bunks. "These are so small!" ... "And they're dirty! Look at this Kleenex in the sink!" ... "And we have to share a bathroom?" "How can you call this first-class? We paid good money for this…"

I looked back at the gloomy faces of the proud travellers and tired farmers who were crammed on top of one another in the lower class carriage and breathed a sigh of relief. Our compartment was no bigger than two porto-potties flipped sideways but it had two beds a sink, and a window.

The train pushed slowly ahead, passing through the barren slums on the outskirts of town as they flattened out into a dense jungle of trees.

"I still can't believe I let you drag me here," I said.

He laughed sarcastically and pointed at me with his index finger, "No one forced you to come."

"Maybe not. But what am I supposed to do when I get a message from a manic depressive lawyer, telling me he's prepared to throw his life away on a whim."

He cracked open a beer and took a sip. "You could start by getting a job."

I took a big swig of my beer and laughed. "We'll see who gets the last laugh."

My nerves started to loosen their grip as we chugged further into the night. Every time I looked out the window the same scene kept repeating itself. Abandoned train yard after abandoned train yard passed by, overgrown with tall blades of tropical grass and thick jungle vines. The vegetation crawled over the concrete walls and electrical towers engulfing any sign of civilization in its path. Once in a while a group of corrugated steel huts would creep out of the background before being sucked back into the green monster that surrounded them. After a while I stopped trying to keep track of the crumbling monuments, and fell I back into my bunk with my eyes fixed on the darkness outside my window.

...

I could feel the heat seeping in through the window and into the crown of my head as we pulled into the station. I rolled my eyes into the back of my skull and looked outside. I could just about make out the rusted shapes of the derelict train depot that had carried us through the night. A crackling voice came over the loudspeaker to announce that this was the end of the line as the train jolted to a stop.

We stumbled onto the platform and into the streets. The town spilled out from the station in the shade of abandoned warehouses and a few malnourished palm trees. Everything was covered in a chalky film that shimmered in light shades of red and brown in the morning light. Even the group of mangy dogs that was busy scavenging for their first meal of the day behind a dumpster was painted in a golden brown dust. Aside from the polished advertisement on the side of the bus that was pulling out across the road, there was no sign that this haggard outpost had ever been visited before.

We went across the street and waited for the next bus at a small kiosk that doubled as a restaurant. We ordered bacon and eggs and took turns rushing to the back to manoeuvre our way around the muddy hole in the ground. The sun continued to rise over the angular buildings through clouds of dust that wafted through the air like an eerie morning fog every time a car passed by. The bus pulled up as we finished our meal and we all marched onto it single file. The engine rumbled underneath as we wobbled across the pot-holed streets to the tune of a worn out clutch and the international grumblings of sleepless travellers. We drove south past endless grassy deserts. They were protected by primitive mountains that pierced the sky covered in a thick green flesh. There were small clusters of concrete villages at regular intervals along the side of the road. Old women and children were selling a collection of gas, rice and booze as motorcycles zipped back and forth along the gravel.

A wild pack of taxi drivers was waiting for us when we got to the next town. They snatched our arms and bags and clambered over one another's for the chance to get our business. We brushed them off and wandered down the road looking for a way to the coast. It was the middle of the day but there was no traffic. Every second building was an electronics shop and all the other ones were either foreign currency exchanges or boarded up. Sam pulled out the guidebook and looked around, "This can't be right."

We went into one of the banks and asked for directions but the tellers simply mimed at us without understanding what we were trying to say. An Indian man with thinning hair standing behind picked up on our frustration.

"You are looking for the beach?" he asked with a charming colonial twang.

"Anywhere but here…"

He smiled sympathetically and waved us over, "Follow me. I'm on my way there right now."

We followed him down the street and turned the corner. He pointed to a truck with a white vinyl canopy and a row of rusty benches welded onto the flatbed. "This will take you where you want to go."

We bought a couple of beers from a small convenience store and sat next to our new friend. He explained that he was on a three-day escape from Mumbai. It seemed like a dubiously short tour of duty. Then again, it wasn't as if India was halfway around the world. He had travelled here half a dozen times, and he was an authority on everything from cheap suits and local wild life to fine wines and hookers. He explained the country to us and gave us a list of the places to visit and the people to avoid. "Especially the Russians. Make sure you stay away from them. They can be a nasty lot indeed."

After 40 minutes of driving we finally started to see some signs of civilisation. Terraces with young couples in neatly pressed shorts trying to enjoy espressos around small rectangular tables spilled into the street and motorcycles dipped in and out of the shoulder so that the pale skinned women covered in bleached white dresses and wide-brimmed sun hats had to skip from the side of the road like frogs.

We pulled down one last hill and stopped at the edge of the ocean and the Indian informed us that we had reached our destination. We jumped off the back of the truck and made our way up from the beach, looking for somewhere to lay our heads. Pedestrian streets shot off the main road at regular intervals. Each one seemed to open up into a large square. We turned down one of the alleyways and into a plaza that was lined with aging white signs, covered in faded flags from across the world. The first place we walked up to was called the Kangaroo Inn. A short woman in a dark blue dress greeted us outside the front door. After exchanging a few unnecessary pleasantries, she took us upstairs to a room outfitted with air conditioning, a fridge, a 27-inch TV and single king-sized bed. It had everything we needed to survive for the night.

We paid for the room and dropped our bags in the corner, before heading down to the beach to get some food. Most of the restaurants were closed, so we settled for drinking beer and eating overpriced thin-crust pizza at one of the white plaster hotels across from the beach. The sand on the other side of the road flattened out towards the ocean in a gently sloping crescent that hugged the shoreline for about ten miles, before carving up towards the sky into a pair of jagged peaks on either side of the beach. We wanted to come here because the Vacant Universe had said it was one of the only places in the country where you could surf. But the ocean was dead, and the only signs of misspent youth on the beach were the ageing oligarchs that trudged along in the sand with their chubby children and loathsome devotchkas in tow. Some of the balding fat men had decided to leave their misery behind, opting instead for a leggy trophy, which replaced all sense of Napoleonic shortcomings with a cocktail induced swagger. We watched on as they funnelled back and forth between the powdered styrofoam beach and the corporate resorts that cut pristine geometric shapes into the horizon.

After we were finished eating we made our way down to the water to wash off the stench of our travels. Even with the tide coming in, there wasn't a single ripple in the ocean, and the hopes of a swell coming in the next few days were slim.

The boardwalk back to the hotel was lined with large white signs on metal posts stuck into the ground at regular intervals. Each one had a diagram of a large wave crushing a family of stick figures, accompanied by some illegible local script, with English subtitles underneath: "Tsunami Evacuation Route: In case of tsunami, follow the signs". It hadn't dawned on me until then that this was one of the places worst hit by the storm.

It was only a few years ago that the wave broke over these shores, wiping out half the country's coastline. I remembered watching it hit. It was the day after Christmas and we were all busy going through the motions of another depressing holiday shouting match. When we heard what had happened, we turned on the TV and planted ourselves in front of it, unable to blink. It was the first time in days that the room had been silent. Everyone tried their best to look horrified and indignant as the counts of dead and missing foreigners were updated every few minutes.

Everyone asked the same question: 'how could such an ungodly thing happen under the watch of such an unvengeful god?' There was no shortage of answers as everyone poured out a toxic mix of rationalisation and sympathy until the entire room was subdued with sadness. At around 7 o'clock dinner was ready, and we all sat down to a feast and we ate for days until there wasn't even a bone left for the dogs to pick on.

We spent the rest of the afternoon sitting in our hotel room with the A/C cranked all the way up. It was so cold that I had to pull out my only sweater and a thick scarf to keep me warm. We drank beers while we watched a television that was no larger than a computer screen. The only channels that were in English were the BBC and CNN, and we flipped back and forth between the two to avoid commercials.

The BBC had propped up a greying reporter in front of an elegantly bound bookshelf. He was scolding the Minister of the Interior of some distant country for not resigning, even though he had supported the old regime. But no matter how much he was prodded, the minister resisted the pathetic arm-twisting of his interrogator and reaffirmed his dedication to changing the ways of the old guard.

Then we were off to the desert, where a young man with milk chocolate skin was condemning the audience on the other side of the screen. "You say you support us – that you understand, but you lie!" The clean-shaven journalist interviewing him tried to assure him that he understood his plight and that he was there to help, but the young man in the black and white Afghan fought back, "If you understand, then why do you call us rebels? We are not rebels; we are revolutionaries. The blood of our people is being spilt and we want justice. This is a revolution!"

We finished the beer and went to get some food from the small hole in the wall that sat back from the square under our guesthouse. It was the kind of square that you might expect to be decorated with stalls selling fresh vegetables and knock off designer clothing had it been anywhere but here. Instead there were tattered flags of every major capital in the

Western hemisphere standing still in the stale and starless night.

The same five Germans that had been there when we checked in were still sitting around smoking pipes and drinking small bottles of Heineken on the terrace. There wasn't a single one of them that was under 40. They were typical sex tourists – it didn't matter to them whether it was low season or high. If anything it just meant a greater supply for their twisted demands.

The stockiest of the quintet was telling the others a story. He alternated between emitting enthusiastic grunts and whimpers. You could tell from his accent that he wasn't German; maybe Swiss or Austrian. His audience bellowed loudly in between inhaling and sipping from green bottles. The one doing most of the talking was bracing himself for the big moment. He motioned with his hands as he spoke, occasionally using the table as a prop. He grabbed it and rattled it violently until finally he came to the climax.

"Ich woll makt, und das untergloben war suchen eine grosse schweine hunden." He pounded the table in unison with his staccato delivery and the rest of the table erupted in laughter. They kepy lauginhg until streams of sweaty tears rolled down their pudgy cheeks. When they were done the German man in the apron left the entourage and came to our table.

He looked like he was in his mid 40s, and he ran the bar on his own except for a local woman who stayed the kitchen, leaving him to hobble slowly back and forth between the bar, the kitchen and the tables, with a right knee that he had blown out, most likely in a skiing accident in the French Alps, long before he decided to move here to open his own abandoned café in an abandoned seaside town.

His hair was thick and greasy, and it glistened in the halogen light as he shifted across the room. It parted into a rolling coif on the front of his head, so that it was just barely out of his eyes. Sam turned to me with a slightly concerned look on his face, "It's Slippery Pete."

I stared blankly at him.

"You know…" said Sam trying to jog my memory, "Slippery Pete… from that Coen brothers movie …"

I watched him as he brushed his hair out of his eyes. They were dead and sunken into his head and they were balanced treacherously over his well-hung jaw. He looked more depraved than menacing, but I couldn't be certain that he might not have a wood-chipper set up in the back of the kitchen.

"Of course," I nodded, "Slippery Pete."

He returned 15 minutes later with two plates of rice and curry. After we were finished we sat around drinking beer on the patio. I wondered what had happened to all the people we had seen earlier in the afternoon. Eventually Slippery Pete jumped into the conversation: "All those people you see, they go out during the days and then live on the resorts at night. They have everything the need there, why should they ever leave?" You could sense the bitterness in his voice. It was hard to know whether he was right, but you could tell that he was at the end of his tether. He was counting the days until the end of the low season, like a pensioner who believes that if he only wishes hard enough, the snow will melt before spring comes.

He flicked his hair out of his eyes and turned his head awkwardly to the side, "I've been here 16 years now; and for many years it was good. Some years are good, some not so good."

It wasn't long until his stress gave way to nostalgia, "Before the wave hit, we had many more young people. When they rebuilt the town they decided they would make it bigger and better with nice white fancy hotels and white sand to match. Now there are resorts everywhere but they are mostly empty and no one ever leaves at night. It's still early in the season but it just hasn't been the same since then."

We allowed a moment of silence while he brooded over his fate.

"So where can you go out in this town?" interrupted Sam. "We've only been in the country a few days and we're feeling a little antsy. We need some action."

"It's very quiet still a few weeks until the season begins. But there are still many places. Do you like ladies?"

"Of course!"

His eyebrows twitched upwards, "Local ladies?"

Sam looked at me and we both and shook our heads. I tried to divert the conversation.

"We don't need ladies," I said, cutting him off, "just somewhere where we can get drink."

"You can drink here!" he said resignedly, before running through a few selections, all of which seemed less appealing than the next. "You could always go to The Coconut Grove. It's just up from the beach, a few miles south of here. They have a very good band that plays nice music. It's very good really. If you mention it to a taxi driver, he should be able to take you there."

Given the circumstances, it seemed like the best solution. We paid our bill and gave our regards to Slippery Pete.

"And don't forget the ladies," he said as we walked off.

The taxi sped over a series of hills that overlooked the ocean before doubling back again. It was clear that our driver had no idea where he was going. Sam told him to pull over on the side of the road and handed him a fistful of bills. When we got out and we were greeted by a blast of repetitive radio hits coming from the oversized speakers of street vendors that were selling an assortment of frozen ice cream and glow in the dark cocktails. We bought a couple of drinks and stumbled around, searching for Pete's bar. After walking for a few blocks Sam dipped into a pharmacy to ask for directions.

"She says it's that way," said Sam, as he pointed down a street lined with flashing lights and aggressive looking women.

We made our way through the gauntlet, keeping our heads low and our eyes fixed on our feet. Every bar on the strip had a half dozen feminine looking Demi Moore impersonators wrapped up in tinsel and vinyl, with painted boyish faces that looked like they'd been blasted on with a shotgun. They blew kisses to no one in particular and some of them pretended to fondle one another to keep the clientele guessing.

They weren't picky. At the end of the day it was just a job. And other than working in an abandoned rubber factory, it was the only way for them to put food on the table. They'd memorized every Asian fetish cliché from every Full Metal Jacket sequel and skin flick ever made. It was a struggle not to be distracted as we tried to swat away the prying fingers. I could hear the high-pitched rattle of live music that Slippery Pete had promised coming from a bar at the end of the street. We rushed to the end of the road and lunged through the doors to the roaring crescendo of the solo from Free Bird. Apart from the five guys on stage, there were 3 people in the bar, including a stout bartender with a mullet and a couple of tired hookers that had come in to rest their feet. We ordered a couple of beers drank them in peace as the lead singer continued to finger the neck of the guitar with unbridled enthusiasm.

The band continued to go through the motions of a soulless repertoire as we sat down. The only one who seemed to care about the performance was the mysterious frontman who wailed away on his guitar as if he were spilling his soul in front of hundreds of thousands of people. The band strummed along with mathematical precision in the background as they rattled through each tune, from Zeppelin to Bowie, with unnerving accuracy. The music was almost refreshing amidst the sex and humidity that surrounded us. But after a few songs I started to notice that something wasn't quite right. I listened carefully to the next song as the drums kicked in, followed by the bass, as the band's leader broke into the opening riff to Sultans of Swing. Sam and I bobbed our heads and tapped our coasters in approval to his Mark Knopfler impersonation, while the two ladies in black nylon boots sitting next to us tried to talk above the music.

A few bars into the chorus I realised what was wrong: "Johnny, don't mind, he's on the telephone tonight, making a call to make it right." I looked over at Sam. He raised his eyebrow as the front man carried on. "She don't give a damn, about that American country man, he don't know how she play rock and roll" The lead guitarist winked at us like an ageing talk-show host, as he sang the last line and launched into an impressive rendition of Knopfler's solo. He hit every note emphatically as he made his way up and down the scales without so much as glancing at his fingers. His playing was flawless; almost to the point of being cold and inhuman. The band looked bored as hell. They kept trying to fake it, as they played along in the background like robotic mannequins at a kid's birthday party. They knew their job was to just stand there and pretend like nothing was wrong. They rattled through classics like Prince's "Hurtful Pain", and Guns and Roses' "Carrazzzy City". Halfway through an agonizing rendition of Axel Rose's chorus Sam looked over at me and laughed. "This has to be some kind of joke." But they were dead serious. We ordered a couple more beers and drank slowly, until the gimmicks and sleazy looks from our fearless leader started to wear thin. We got up during a unintelligible version of the Rolling Stone's "Pay it back" and left without saying a word to the black velvet ladies sitting next to us.

On our way back the girls were far more aggressive than they had been a few hours earlier. With no one to give them business, they had spent the early hours of the morning throwing back cheap whisky and waiting for some kind of saviour. In my drunken stupor I let them cling to my arm more than I had a few hours earlier.

"Are you out of your fucking mind?" Sam asked as he pulled me by the arm. The girls pulled on the other, resulting in a heated game of tug of war over my limp body. In the end Sam always managed to pull me out.

It was a depressingly failed sate of affairs. It was just past 2 a.m. and the only man in sight was a balding Santa Claus with a gut and a half dozen girls on his lap. It was clear that the girls were just as desperate as Slippery Pete for the sad parade of deep-pocketed tourists to start marching on the town. For them the impending perverted thaw could never come too soon. They latched on to us, promising to fulfill our wildest dreams if only we'd give them 30 minutes of our precious time. I felt like a cheap whore that had been paid to get down on her knees but refused to swallow. I shrunk away from their grip, and stuffed my hands back into my pockets. I felt disgusted and embarrassed. As I broke free one last time I started to feel sick to my stomach.

We turned onto the plaza with the tattered flags and the fading signs. I stopped outside the door to fumble for the keys. We climbed up the stairs and into our double bed in the safety of our air-conditioned room. Sam went to turn off the light before crawling onto the other side of the bed. He looked over at me as if he was about to say something but I stopped him just in time. There was really only one thing for us to say before we went to sleep. "We need to get the fuck out of here!"

Three

Slippery Pete cooked us a full American breakfast in the morning. A white van came to pick us up before we were able to finish eating, and Pete waved us off as we loaded our bags into the trunk. We drove on for hours back through the lush mountain landscapes that had brought us here in the first place. We stopped off at a few gas stations along the way and when the minivan dropped us off at our final destination, it was three times as full as when we left the coast.

    We stopped at a dockyard where we hoped to catch a ferry to take us off the mainland. It was still early, and the landing was already crowded with fresh-faces draped in sunglasses and canvas shoes, doing their best to look like dogged sherpas. Friends and strangers stood around exchanging excited glances, as sweat-stained men in baggy trousers unloaded crates and canvas bags full of rice and frozen goods, with cigarettes pinched between their lips. We cut through the crowds to get tickets for the ride and bought beers on the way to wash away the taste of stale bread and greasy eggs we'd had for breakfast. Looking around, there was no doubt that we were all here for the same reason. All we wanted was a secluded beach in the middle of the ocean where we could be left to our childish devices. No fucking around with dictionaries, or maps, or translators, or cultural acclimatisation. Nothing but the universal language of anxious indifference.

    The boat was overbooked, and the smell of stale diesel filled the air as it laboured to pull off the dock. It was still morning, but most of the crowd were either drunk or stoned, and now that they were on a boat they had gained confidence, with each of them taking turns rushing to the front of the boat to proclaim themselves 'The King of the World!'

Halfway into the crossing the wind picked up. It wasn't long until the waves followed. They rose gradually higher and higher, rocking the boat back and forth like an antique cradle, while limbs and heads bobbed listlessly over the side. A mousy woman in an odd fitting naval outfit ran out of the wheelhouse and screamed at the eager photographers and aspiring actors "Seet down! Or tah boat flip over n' sink!" She mimed the motion of the boat flipping over with her hands and repeated herself in clear English, but her funny looking outfit made it easy to mistake her as part of the show.

I started to plan an escape route in the event than it all went wrong. I explained it to Sam, pointing to a life ring behind a girl in a yellow bikini top while making blatant gestures with my fist and elbows. He smiled and nodded in approval before pulling a towel over his head and drifting off again.

We continued past dozens of cookie-cutter islands until we turned south around a luscious mountain and headed towards the greenest of them all. The boat hugged the shadows of the creeping rock face until the mountains parted before us. All of a sudden the boat stopped swaying. The smell of lightly salted coral and rotting fish mixed with the rich burn of the well-oiled traffic that filled the bay. It felt like we were drifting into a manic Jurassic wonderland.

The scene at the dock was ugly. Morning commuters with slumped shoulders and bags under their eyes dragged their luggage across the ground. They tried to squeeze their way onto the boat before giving us the chance to get off. They'd had enough and they'd forgotten the petty customs that had been drilled into them at boarding school. Either that or they just didn't give a shit anymore.

We pushed through the damp army of bodies and continued down the dock without stopping. There were dozens of young men in baggy dress shirts waiting for our business at the end of the gangway. We allowed ourselves to be dragged over to a small booth, where we picked out a bungalow based on a faded Polaroid picture taken over a decade ago. We stood under the roof of the decrepit shack, while a man in a Hawaiian dress shirt made arrangements for us to be shown to our room.

"This doesn't seem too bad," I said.

"It'll certainly do for a few nights," Sam added.

I let out a comfortable laugh, "I was getting worried for a while there. I was almost beginning to hope that the boat was going to go over, just to give us something to do."

Sam laughed, "I'm just glad you didn't end up having to elbow that poor girl in the face."

We hung around on the corner waiting for someone to take us to our room. All of a sudden, I felt a chunky finger tap me on the shoulder. "Hey mate, couldn't help but hearing that you guys are staying at the Bamboo Bungalows."

"Ya."

"Mate, you don't want to stay there, it's a fucking hell hole and it's horribly over-priced."

Sam and I looked at one another and sized him up. He was pudgy and pale and he had a distinct Northern accent.

"We're just waiting for some guy to show up and take us to our rooms."

The pudgy Brit let out a sigh and a laugh simultaneously, "Ha, don't wait for those lazy bastards, we're staying up that way if you want to follow us. It's half the price and it's only a few minutes from the beach. Besides it's a great place to meet ladies."

It wouldn't be fair to just take off but he was making a convincing case.

"You haven't given them any money yet have you?" he asked.

I shook my head.

"Well then follow us, we're heading to our place up the hill. It's a little bit of a trek compared to those damn bungalows but it's still only 10 minutes from the party."

The other one nodded. "Trust him, you'll thank us later."

I looked at Sam, "What's the worst thing that could happen?" We were both antsy and desperate to get to anywhere where we could finally rest our heads so we decided to follow them.

"So what's your deal?" asked the tall one as we left the dock.

"I'm Dave," said the fat one before either of us had the chance to ask. "And this is Charlie." He pointed to his friend who was slightly taller but equally aloof. Side by side, they looked like a pair of mismatched hobbits setting out on a futile quest.

"Where are you lads from?"

"We're from Toronto... Canada," said Sam.

"Thank god! We were worried you might be Sepos!"

They both stared at us waiting for a response.

"Sorry," chimed in the other one. "That's what we call the Yanks. It's cockney rhyming slang. You know, like in the movies. Yank – rhymes with septic tank, but that's a bit of a mouthful, so it just gets shortened to Sepo."

It was a wonderfully roundabout way of shortening a word that had already been abbreviated, but it was a nice way of showing their hatred for the big bad Yanks while coming off as lower class poets.

Sam took the lull in the conversation as an opportunity to feign solidarity, "Fucking Sepos!"

"I thought you might like that," laughed the pudgy one.

The rows of shops ended as the path narrowed and sloped up along the southern escarpment. It wound past weathered guesthouses and empty cafes on either side of the dirt road. On the way up the hill, there was a sign marking out the Tsunami escape route, which was conveniently located in the same place as the scenic lookout point that towered over the island. I had no idea where the hobbits were dragging us to but I was relieved to know that at least we were on high ground.

"I worked in finance for a year," said Dave as we walked on. "When shit started to hit the fan they decided it wouldn't be worth their money to keep me around so they gave me a severance package. Couldn't have worked out any better if you ask me. I'm getting paid off to go spend 'the best fucking year of my life in seeing the world'", as he liked to put it.

Charlie had been less fortunate. He was a marine biologist. He was supposed to be working for the government on a sustainable fishing project in the North Sea, but spending cuts were introduced and the project got cancelled before it even began. No job, no severance, just a golden ticket to freedom.

"I was lucky enough to have my grandfather die a few months ago though. He left me a bit of money and I paid off a few debts, but once I I got those out of the way I figured I might as well put the money to good use. I'm hoping to make my way to Australia. I know someone there who might be able to get me a job studying the migratory patterns of penguins. Until then, I'm just going to keep spending 'the best fucking year of my life' with my mate."

It all seemed a bit morbid; then again I'd never really known anyone who'd died before. As far as I was concerned dying was something people did on TV.

They asked how long we were staying as we started up a steep incline. When I told them a couple of days they both burst out laughing.

"What's so funny?" I asked.

Charlie looked over at Dave and they let out a chorus of boisterous laughter. "We said the exact same thing when we showed up. That was eight days ago…"

We finally go to the top of the hill and Charlie pointed to a row of bamboo bungalows perched on metal stilts across from of a rectangular lagoon. "Welcome to paradise," he said.

"You can check in over here. That's where we meet for beers most afternoons. Feel free to join us later on. We usually go down and meet up sometime after dinner then head to the beach."

"Thanks," I said as I scanned the hillside. "We might just do that."

"We'll see you at the bar then…"

We shook hands and they retreated to their cabin. Sam went to the front desk and arranged for a room with a balcony. We trekked up the concrete stairs grasping on to the worn steel railing for balance. I dropped my bag off between the double beds in the room and hung my sweaty t-shirt on the balcony to dry. I stood there, dripping with sweat, squinting at the island down below. It was overgrown with thick forests of dishevelled trees that shimmered like clumps of melting plastic bags melting on top of the rocks. The only exception was the pristine gash of white sand that spread out between the rocky peaks on either side of the island.

Sam came out to the balcony. "Let's get a drink. We've earned it."

We certainly hadn't done much to earn anything, but I was too dizzy and thirsty from the hike to disagree.

We went back down the hill and bought a bottle of gin. We came back and sat on the balcony that overlooked a rectangular reservoir of stagnant water. At first I thought that it was a pond or a lagoon. But the more I looked at the more I realised it was probably part of an overly ambitious plan to build a swimming pool, which had been abandoned due to a lack of funds. Now it was just a breeding ground for mosquitoes and other harmless parasites. On the other side of the pool, local families gathered in front of makeshift shelters covered with bamboo shoots and palm leaves. Older women with their hair cut short were preparing large portions of fish and rice in the dying afternoon light, while the men sat around impatiently smoking cheap cigarettes.

A pair of dirty blondes walked out onto the balcony next door and interrupted my train of thought. Sam and I greeted both of them together. They glanced at us briefly and each took turns eking out a 'Hallo', before rushing down the steps.

"Swedes…" Sam said as they went off.

"Danes" I said instinctively.

"What's the difference?"

"Danes are taller and their hair isn't as blonde."

Sam shrugged his shoulders, "Who cares, more gin for us!"

The jungle laboured under the weight of the sweaty dew, which gathered on its extremities in the dying light. Down by the water a few longtail boats were belatedly being dragged up and anchored onto mounds of sand that stuck out in the low tide. The only sound that could be made out above the evening breeze was the noise of mosquitoes slowly rising from the stagnant pool below. They were too small to see, but the faint buzz-saw humming of their wings made sure their presence was known. After the mosquitoes came the crickets – always invisible, always present, endlessly chirping. The island twitched with anticipation as it prepared itself for the international broadcast of its regularly scheduled program. Then, at the flick of a switch, the rolling thunder of sand-filled speakers started to roll up the mountainside; and in a flash of darkness, the sun was gone.

We polished off the bottle and headed into town for some food. We ended up at a run down restaurant down a quiet alleyway off the main drag. The air outside filled with the thick smell of sun-kissed skin and burnt chilli peppers. The restaurant was listed as one of island's hidden gems in the Vacant Universe and it was packed. We managed to squeeze onto a small table beside a glowing Irish couple. Their 3-month tans looked awkward on their pale skin. The girl was slight and energetic with sandy blonde hair that wrapped around her neck in tight curls and her boyfriend had rounded shoulders that made him look like a semi-professional surfer. It wasn't long until we were taking turns filling in the blanks.

"We just came here for a bit of a laugh before we decide to pack it all in for good," said the surfer. "I'm gonna make her teh luckiest girl on earth."

He laughed and puckered his lips against her cheek.

"Fuck off," she said as she pushed him away "Don't mind that eedjit."

"We actually met in Ireland," I said. I looked over at Sam and smiled, "But that was a long time ago."

Along with a casual drug habit and damp afternoons spent in dingy pubs with greying drunks in heavy knitted sweaters, Samuel Dravott was one of the unexpected hazards one comes into contact with when going to university in a county with a severe religious hangover. The fact that we were from the same city and ended up in the same program thousands of miles away only made matters worse. We'd both left home with the best intentions. But after 4 years of trying to find an excuse to get out of bed we had both become accustomed to absurd three day binges and the neurotic early morning heart to hearts in dimly lit basements that came along with them.

He wouldn't admit it to anyone else and there was no way in hell he would admit it to me; and if you had asked him if any of it was true, he would probably have to deny it all – not out of shame, or embarrassment, or even pride. But rather out of fear that those fleeting moments were the only times when he felt like anything mattered.

"Ahn wad' jah tink of it?" asked the surfer.

"It was great," I said. "But I'm glad it's over."

"Jayzus. Tanks for the vote of confidence!"

"It's not you, it's the rain."

The couple invited us to join them to watch a boxing match after dinner. We couldn't think of an excuse not to go so we paid the bill and followed them into town. It was muggy, but you could catch an occasional whiff of the salty breeze floating up from the water. We got to the end of the street and walked into a bar to the sound of a ringing bell. A faint cheer rose from the dozen or so drunks that were lined up on rows of long wooden benches as the two snarling masochists returned to their respective corners. Then theme song from Rocky came on over the speakers and everyone in the room went back to talking as if nothing had happened.

A sluggish looking lout slung himself over the turnbuckle. He was panting and the steady flow of sweat rolled off his chin like a leaky faucet. He struggled to undo the lid on a bottle of water that had been handed to him by the prepubescent janitor who was attending to him. When he finally got it off he poured it over his face and shoulders, with very little making it into his yawning jaw. He hadn't even finished catching his breath when the bell rang again. The music stopped and the lout staggered to the centre of the ring to meet his fate. A few sarcastic cheers rose from the crowds but for the most they just carried on sipping their drinks through their teeth. The two men touched gloves and the onslaught resumed. The bout was unimpressive. Neither of them was sober enough to throw a proper punch and both men looked tired and at the ends of their wits as they alternated between trading blows and stumbling around the ring.

"Don't wurry it gets better," said the girl. "Dis is just tha warmup. Tha main event comes later on, once they've let all the backpackers beat the piss outta each other."

"Don't listen to her. These eedjits don't have anything to lose. Dhey're dessprate and drunk, and there's nuttin more entertainin den watching a desprate man trade blows wid an even drunker and more desprate opponent."

The lout finally got caught off guard. He left his chin wide open and his rival had smashed him clean to the floor. He lay there for a few seconds before peeling himself off the mat and heading to his corner in drunken shame. "See what I mean. You just can't make this shit up."

The bell rung again and the two drunks came back to the centre of the ring. The bald one with the baby face was throwing more and more punches but they struggled to make it through the air. Occasionally they would glance off his target before being met by the recoil of his opponent, at which point he would fall backwards and reach for the ropes. He had a disturbing gut and you could tell from the naïve confidence in his blows that he wasn't just drunk; he was horribly out of shape. At this rate he wasn't going to last much longer. The bell went after only a few minutes. The round hadn't ended but the referee had decided to call the fight out of mercy.

We sat through a few more fights. Each was just as painful to watch as the next. In the middle of one of the bouts, a stocky Eastern European came up to our table. He was at least 6'2 and his arms were almost as thick as my waist.

"So," he said in thick accent. "Which one of you sissies wants to fight?" He glared at Sam and the Irishman. "I need a challenge to defend my title."

The Irishman sized him up for a bit. He had a glint in his eyes. You could tell from the hook in his nose that he'd seen his fair share of action in and out of the ring. But he choked back his pride and put his arm around his girlfriend "Sorry," he said. "We're just here to watch."

"Too bad for you," he chuckled. He looked over at Sam and patted him hard on the back. "And what about you... You want to come and have boxing match. No fancy kicking like these sissies, just punching like a real man."

Sam shook his head. The Pole stood over him with a childish grimace. "Come on, we make a good fight. It will be finished before you know it."

"That's what I'm worried about," said Sam.

"Don't be a little sissy man."

He stood up and flexed his biceps and triceps at the same time, "Men must fight! Are you not a man?"

Sam just kept looking at the table, "Not today."

The giant recoiled in disgust. "When you are ready I will be here waiting."

He walked away and went over flexing to another table.

"That could have been interesting," I said to Sam.

"I could have taken him you know," mumbled the Irishman in disgust.

"I know hun. But Ah don't need to be bringin you home in a coffin."

The Irishman opened his mouth as if he was about to say something, then put his arm around her and gave her a kiss on the cheek.

I turned to Sam and smiled, "Maybe we should get up there."

"You're out of your fucking mind," he laughed. "Maybe we should just have another drink."

We had another round before leaving the lovers behind in search of the party. I could hear the mob submitting itself to the awkward rhythm of the music as we made our way to the ocean. We followed the noise until we came to a clearing. There were a dozen or so bars bunched along the edge of the sand. Each bar was selling the same amphetamine riddled concoctions poured into child-sized sand buckets and everyone congregated around the stacks of weathered speakers that stood in front of them. Colourful bursts of flesh rose amongst the shadows. The flashing lights flickered over the glistening bodies and sun-kissed cheeks in waves, crashing every so often in an explosion of pink and yellow and green. You could see the terrifying energy in their bodies as they twitched and turned, groping one another to stop themselves from falling over.

"This is more like it," said Sam as he charged into the thick of it. I followed closely behind, bouncing of errant breasts and thighs that fell over one another in unison with the noise. We danced around, drinking anything that was put in front of us as quickly as possible. Everywhere I turned I could see groping and thrusting and well-lubricated orifices strung up on the skeletons of middle class skin and bones. It didn't matter where you looked; they were everywhere, each one with their own calculated routine, contorting their bodies in spastic thrusts in the hopes of keeping time with the beat.

The music got louder over time and the gin made it harder to tell the difference between the beginning and ending of a song. Eventually it all became a continuous barrage of dull thuds and repetitive screeches. I felt like my head had become unhinged from my neck as I tried to keep myself upright. We kept our feet moving, kicking sand up in the air and jostling with girls in cut-off shorts any time they came near. The bronzed packs stalked one another in a frantic daze, snapping and clawing at the moist bodies that were paraded around them, oblivious to the impending attacks. Their nostrils flared as they sucked in the suffocating humidity that seethed with the violent smell of freedom. They were like well-bred dogs that had become so domesticated from years of being force-fed their daily allowance of repackaged horsemeat that they had forgotten the sublime taste of raw flesh.

I let my head sway from side to side to keep me cool. The lights tugged my eyes in all different directions as I tried to pull the flash of colours into focus. The pack moved closer and we spun around in circles, laughing uncontrollably. I could make out faces, ankles, breasts and shambles of tattered clothing. It was impossible to keep track of it all and soon I gave up.

I pried my eyes open my to look for Sam but he was nowhere to be seen. I straightened my posture to make sure that I wasn't seeing double but he was gone.

"That slimy bastard. He must have run off with one of those girls."

"Good for him," I thought to myself. That's probably just what he needed. I wondered which one he stole but by my count the girls were all still there. "I should probably go look for him," I thought. "But that would probably just lead to trouble."

My eyes were pulsating, throbbing in time with the music. I kept moving my arms and legs to keep up the appearances of dancing. The girls danced circles around me, tip-toeing across the sand like sexually charged nymphs. Out of the dim light, one of them started to drift nearer. When she reached me, she grabbed my arm and guided my hand down her back. I could feel her limp nipples pressed against my chest and her yellow hair swept across my face as she swayed back and forth in front of me. She held herself close to me and I could just about make her rosy cheeks against the dark night sky.

The next thing I knew the girl was gone and the music had stopped. The lights from the bars were flashing and the stars were still hanging over the water. I walked up to the bar and found her perched on a bar stool beside one of the DJs. I started to feel dizzy and I pressed my hand firmly on her shoulder to keep my balance. "So you've found a friend?" I slurred. "How nice…" I was doing my best to not to vomit every time I opened my mouth.

She introduced me and I shook his hand. I leaned over and whispered into her ear. "He seems great but I don't think he speaks English." She turned away and kept talking with him, ignoring my interjections. I thought about asking her back to my room for a drink, but I couldn't think how I was going to drag her back there.

I convinced myself that a swim would be a good idea. If nothing else it would sober me up. I grabbed her hand and headed towards the water. The tide had retreated, and the beach now extended into the ocean for half a mile. There were a few stragglers dancing on the water-logged sand and I thought I could make out our Danish neighbours lying on their backs with their eyes fixed on the stars. The palm of her hand felt warm and clammy against my skin as we waded into the ocean. The water rose higher, past my ankles, knees and thighs until my feet finally left the ground for good.

I floated out towards the opening of the lagoon, propelling myself with my hands. The water was warm and the thick jungle mountains toward upwards, protecting us on all sides. We were all alone in the middle of the ocean, and as I drifted out further I could make out a school of girls skimming on top of the water with their faces pointed at the stars. They pulsed through the water like majestic pink jellyfish with their breasts concealed below the surface, each one topped off with a fleshy pink dot that punctuated their ivory skin and smiles to match. They were timid but they didn't seem to mind my presence as I swam in between their bodies. I reached out to touch one of them but she pulled away and disappeared underwater. I could feel the water rushing under me as she kicked her legs back and forth. She wrapped her legs around mine and tried to pull me down. She had a strong grip, and I fumbled around trying break free. I watched her breasts float effortlessly in front of her. I reached for them in a desperate attempt to pull myself up but I couldn't manage to break free. I could feel the tide rushing underneath me. I was running out of breath. I kicked off once more and pulled myself up to the surface. But when I looked around there was no one there. I was alone in the middle of the bay, except for the stars, which continued to dance delicately between the ripples on the water.

The water began to grow heavy all around me. I could feel myself starting to sweat. I was panicking, getting too excited. I worried that my limbs might cramp and seize up. Once that happened I was done for. I could feel the ocean flowing gently between my legs. I took deep breaths and focussed my attention on the flickering lights between the waves. All I had to do was get back to shore. My mouth began to feel dry and I started to worry that I had swallowed too much salt water. I was thirsty and my mouth was dry. I looked around but I couldn't find her. I tried to call out her name but my tongue was stuck to the roof of my mouth.

I rolled over onto my stomach. My eyes were closed and my face was pressed against the bottom. I put my fingers up to my mouth and felt the surface around them. It was too thick to be salt water and too soft to be sand. My face was in a shallow puddle. The sun felt hot on my skin and my pores were clogged with a grainy mixture of water and salt.

I heard a deep grown. I shot up off the bed and scanned the room before falling back down and wrapping the sheets around me. The door was open and I was alone. I heard another loud groan followed by a more pronounced grunt.

"Sam, is that you?"

Another grunt then a pause.

"What do you want?" I looked out the door and saw a pair of feet wrapped in a sheet.

"What are you doing out there?"

"You came home with that girl last night," he sighed, "so I did us both a favour and kicked myself out."

"But…" I paused to made sure I was in still the room. My thoughts were tangled up and flaky, and my head felt like a VHS tape being pulled off the reel by a petulant child "What happened to you? I thought you had run off with someone."

"Shit! How mangled were you?" He paused but I didn't give him the satisfaction of an answer. "I came home and left you with that broad. You seemed pretty content at the time."

I pulled my tongue off the roof of my mouth and the stale taste of vomit wafted up the back of my throat. I looked around the room. "Where did she go?"

Sam sighed again and rolled over onto his side. "She ran off about an hour ago."

"Well, at least she had the manners to leave before I woke up."

I rolled over and rubbed my eyes to try and relieve the pressure that was building behind them. I lay back and felt something jab my side.

"Looks like she even left me a souvenir." I picked up the black bra and threw it out the door onto Sam's feet.

"Jesus, what did you do to the poor girl?"

"By the sounds of it, you probably know better than I do."

Errant visions crept into my head as I tried to push distant memories of the starry night into the back of my mind. I got out of bed and stepped over Sam. I stood there, leaning over the balcony in my underwear. Sam hid under his sheet to avoid the advancing heat as the sun flickered in the stagnant pool below. Our neighbours came out dressed in white t-shirts that barely concealed their tan lines. They slammed the door and shook their heads before running down the stairs.

After lunch we made our way down to the beach. The street leading down from the main road was full of bronzed specimens buying slices of pizza and fruit smoothies. In between the pizza shops there were tattoo parlours with the occasional local artist smoking grass and cigarettes and playing downloadable video games on their cell phones. The streets reeked of desperation and it was impossible to go more than a few shops without being asked to spend money.

The dive shops were the worst. They were all guarded by half naked men with hairy chests and bald heads. They were either French or Australian, and they all chain smoked constantly, as if the air above ground just wasn't good enough for their finely tuned lungs. They all had the same story to tell. They fell in love with diving during a summer holiday with their family in Egypt; all it took was one breath under water and they were hooked. And now they were glorified street merchants selling a few hours of uninspired adventure a day to pay for their filthy habit.

Every time they tried to coax us into joining them, we'd come up with a half-assed excuse just to see them squirm.

"Sharks!"

"More afraid of you than you are of them. You're more likely to die in a plane crash than in a diving accident."

"Breathing underwater..."

"It's fine we'll teach you everything you need to know. And we'll make sure you're always in a controlled environment. There's nothing to be afraid of."

"What about the bends! I don't want my goddamn ears to explode. My balance is suspect enough as it is."

"You'll be fine, just take your time and stay close to your diving instructor."

"But what if something goes wrong and I panic?"

"What could possibly go wrong? I've done 451 dives. Nothing to be afraid of."

"You arrogant prick!"

It didn't matter what kind of excuse you came up with. As long as you could slap a dollar sign on its face and drag it underwater for a few hours, nothing could possibly ever go wrong.

During one of our daily exchanges we were picked out by a desperate voice from across the street.

"You guys are Canadian?"

I looked over my shoulder fearing another proposition. I caught the eye of the greasy haired kid across the way and admitted reluctantly, "Ya, we're Canadian. How did you know?

His face filled with excitement. He was wearing a pair of worn out khaki shorts and a grey tank-top with a low cut collar exposed a few overgrown hairs on his chest. "Call it a lucky guess," he paused and smile. "I'm actually from Toronto."

"No shit! So are we," Sam said

He cracked a smile, "Really? I go to law school there."

"He's the lawyer, you'll have to talk to him about that," he said.

"I guess you guys are probably wondering what the hell I'm doing here?"

I couldn't have cared less. I was more interested in knowing if he would sell us whatever it was that was making him sweat so much.

"I'm taking a year off, you know, seeing the world." He fidgeted with his hands as he swayed back and forth, shifting his weight between from one foot to the other. "I've actually only been here for about 5 months. Before this I was in Europe. I ended up running out of money and getting stuck in Rome. I had to get my girlfriend back home to bail me out and send me some money."

"So where is she?" I interrupted.

He rubbed his face with the palm of his hand. "She's back home waiting for me. She's a great girl. Love her to death! She really got me out of a tight squeeze there. If it wasn't for her I'd be screwed"

"It must be nice to have someone like that waiting for you," said Sam.

"Sure is, sometime I just can't get over how lucky I am. What about you two?"

Sam fed him a few lines about seeing the world before it was too late.

"Well if you like getting drunk and you like boats, then you should come on this cruise." He stepped back in a sweeping motion and presented the sign behind him. "It's all the beer you can drink and you get to visit the beach where they shot that movie."

"Which one?" I asked.

"The one based on that book. Have you read it?" He didn't wait for us to answer.

"Oh well, doesn't really matter. People used to want to go to the island where they shot that James Bond movie but that was a long time ago. The Cold War's over. No one gives a shit about dapper spies with martinis and nuclear warfare anymore. These days everyone wants to save the planet and get laid one last time before they're six feet under. Besides, this island was practically built around that movie. Ten years ago this place was nothing more than a heap of jungle in the middle of the ocean."

"They should put that in the guide book," said Sam.

"I'm pretty sure that movie is the reason they made a guide book in the first place," he said smugly.

"Well, we like to drink and it certainly wouldn't hurt to take a trip," I said.

"Ya, and it's run by a Canadian guy who sailed his boat down from Vancouver. He's real laid back. And when I say all you can drink, I mean all you can drink."

"Is he the one who got you this job?" I asked.

He shifted his weight from his heels to his toes. "I didn't know him before I came down, but it's not like it's a big island. There's a couple other kids working for him too, an American and another Canadian and there's even a local guy who works on the ship."

I smiled at him, "At least there's plenty of work to go around."

"Ya, we get by." He slid his fingers up the side of his face and into his dark brown hair. "I also work for a bar at night, handing out flyers and making sure tourists are buying drinks. The owners find they sell more drinks when white people hustle the tourists. It's not the most glamorous job in the world, but it's honest work."

He scratched his head and gave us a friendly look. "Come down to the Barracuda tonight and I'll get you guys some cheap drinks. It's the big bar with the green sign in the middle of the beach"

"Ya, we know the one," I said. There was a lull in the conversation and I started to turn towards the beach. "We'll probably see you down there."

He stepped forward and threw his arm towards us as we walked away. "You're not heading down to that beach are you?"

Sam and I turned around and looked at each other, "Ya, we need to go and cool off."

He shook his head.

"Don't go down there. All the sewage from the hostels gets pumped out into that bay. It's full of shit and vomit and used condoms. You should check out One Mile Beach on the West side of the island, it 's much more civilised and less crowded."

Sam and I smiled to acknowledge the tip. As we were leaving he extended his hand to each of us. "My name's Patrick by the way. Just let me know if you need anything."

We shook hands and I walked away, unsure of what to make of the kid. I looked over at Sam, "What do you think?"

"I don't know. I guess he seems harmless."

Down on the beach all the signs from last night's party had all but disappeared. The few bottles that were strewn across the sand were leftover from people trying to drink the morning away. The shoddy bars were still there, propped up with thick wooden beams and bamboo shoots. At best they could have been called run down and at worst derelict. Each one had a unique collection of clunky Japanese electronic equipment and neon signs advertising European beers. They looked like the kind of rundown antique shops that flourish in ethnic suburbs, which are under threat of being paved over by mild-mannered yuppies.

We found a clearing on the beach and threw our towels on the sand. The sun stood high above the rocky fortresses at the end of the bay. The tide was still coming in and the water was too shallow to go for a swim. It was uncomfortably hot and I went to get some beers to cool us off. Sam had already started to medicate himself. When I came with a beer he pulled out another Tramodol and swallowed it with a big gulp. I couldn't understand why he had wanted to come here in the first place. He had spent the last two years of his life waiting for this moment. He had spent every waking hour sitting at his desk dreaming about lying on a beach and doing nothing. Now that he was here, the only way he could make it through the day was by popping a few prescription pills and waiting for the day to end. I should have known better than to follow him here but I didn't have much of choice. Sam knew I had nothing better to do and as much as I resented him for saying it, he was right.

"Maybe we should go for a walk," I suggested.

"Why would we want to do that? We've got everything we need right here."

"Well we can't go swimming, there's no fucking water."

"It'll come," he answered. "Just give it some time."

He pulled his sunglasses down over his eyes.

"Well I'm going for a walk," I exclaimed stubbornly.

"Where are you going to go?"

"I don't know, maybe I'll go check out that beach that kid was talking about."

"Why would you want to do that? The sun's just going to set in a few hours anyways."

There was no point arguing with him. I went over to the corner store and bought more beers. I drank slowly while I waited for the tide to come back in. When the water finally got to the edge of the sand, I was so parched from the sun that I couldn't care less whether or not the water was filled with shit and sewage. I left Sam passed out the beach and dove in headfirst. It felt good to be off dry land, even if the water was only up to my chest. I swam around for a while, trying to tire myself out. Soon enough I was joined by Sam. Once he hit the water, he came back to life. We both swam out towards the mouth of the bay until we couldn't see the bottom anymore. Once we got out far enough we let the tide carry us back to shore as it pushed further up the beach.

Later that night we went into town to look for somewhere to eat. We wandered around for a while peaking through windows and patios before ending up at the same restaurant as the night before. The night was sticky and the weight of the air made it hard to swallow anything you put into your mouth. The only way to stop myself from sweating was to drink three times as much as I ate, which only made me feel worse.

We finished up our food and went back to hide in our room as we waited for the night to begin. The mosquitoes floated up from the stagnant pool. We tried swatting them but they danced around our open palms and continued to prick us. We polished off the last few ounces of gin between scratching and swatting blindly at the air, before we gave up and escaped down to the safety of the beach.

The air hanging over the sand was drenched with an intoxicating mixture of sex and innocence. Half naked girls flung their bodies around with reckless abandon. Every night they congregated in hordes of internationally geographic tribes, as they banged away in impromptu drum and bass circles. Their faces were painted in primal detail in the most unnatural shades of pink, yellow and green and their eyes flickered with terrifying energy. Their contorted bodies and sun-kissed cheeks shook vigorously in the night, and I could feel my pupils starting to dilate as my brain struggled to make sense of what was happening.

This wasn't just any beachfront paradise. It was a third world playground for an entire generation that had been raised on the second-hand morals of failed sexual revolutionaries and disillusioned poets.

I looked over at Sam. His hair was flattened across his forehead by the dense sexual stench that lingered in the air. His face was lit up with delight at the pornographic spectacle that was unfolding all around us. It wasn't long until we were joining in the ritual, shedding clothing and painting out faces like savages. Flashes of abstract silhouettes glistened in the darkness, while drunks whistled and roared as they chased after anything with a pulse. Occasionally you would catch two of them together, mid-thrust, accompanied by a mixture of squealing and grunting. We were descending into a hellish bacchanalian dress rehearsal with enough amphetamines and home made liquor to keep an army on the march for months.

The music was harsh and loud. We were being constantly bombarded by the neurotic pounding of the sandblasted speakers, which repeated the same static melodies in the same static order. I recognised most of the songs from the night before. After a while I realised I had been listening to the same songs in the same order for the last three hours. It was barely music at all. It was just a glamorous tribute to the depressing soundtracks that accompany infomercials with brightly painted SUVs and flashes of jello-fed body parts jiggling in and out of focus on TV.

Every so often, the noise would fade out and the void would be filled with the ethereal sting of a feminine soprano uttering something mundane about 'feeling good'. Then an overly aggressive Alpha male would take over and shout at the crowds to 'just do it'. Each time this happened the garbled chorus would rise from the crowd as they sung along. When they had finished singing their parts, the music would come roaring back and the crowd would start shuffling aggressively with their mouths open, as they pumped their fists violently at the empty space around them.

We kept drinking, round after round, without stopping. I could feel my stomach sinking deeper and deeper but the flashing neon lights and hordes of palm-olive skin showed no signs of giving up. The mountains of flesh howled like wild packs of family dogs as the moon began to disappear. As the sun crept up from under the horizon, a group of Spanish girls flocked towards Sam. By the time he caught on to what was happening, they had retreated into the shadows. The music went on and we kept dancing, moving our hips and feet and shaking our fists at the sky, until we were finally drunk enough to not give a shit about where we were or why we were here.

Four

By the time we made it downstairs for breakfast, the sun was already burning a bright red hole in the sky. We both ordered the American breakfast with all the trimmings. The eggs were bland and the sausages were just hot dogs cut in half but they did the trick. It was a relief to know no matter where you are in the world, you can always get fried eggs and bacon.

After breakfast we went to the beach for a swim. The ocean had been replaced by a festering patch of swampy sand. All I wanted to do was go for a swim and now that the water had disappeared, it was all that I could think about. I watched the ocean at the end of the bay, trying to figure out whether it was coming or going. There was no way I could just sit on the beach all day waiting for the tide to come back in. Sam was too medicated to care but I couldn't bear the though of wasting away in the sun all day.

"We should go to find that beach that kid was telling us about," I told Sam.

"Why? I'm pretty happy right here." Sam barely even moved his lips to mumble.

"Fine, but I'm going to find a place to swim."

"What's the difference? The tide's going out."

"How do you know? Maybe it's on its way back in. Besides it wouldn't kill us to check out another part of the island."

"What does that kid know anyways, he's just a college drop out."

I was surprised Sam was even bothering to put up a fight, "Get off you ass and let's get out of here. You can take another dose when we get somewhere worth being."

Sam realised that it wasn't worth his effort to keep arguing and gave up. I peeled him off the sand and we headed towards the other side of the island. We followed Patrick's directions up the hill and past our cabin, until we were walking up a steep dirt road. I tried to convince myself that it would be worth it once we got there but it didn't take long until the soupy air had me ready to give up.

"We must have passed it," said Sam as he doubled over.

I didn't want to admit that I'd already lost interest. I noticed an expedition of veteran backpackers in their early thirties came towards us from the top of the path. They smiled as they walked past us and we lifted our hands to acknowledge them. They must know the way, I thought to myself. But by the time I had thought to ask, they were already at the bottom of the hill.

"It seems a shame to have come this far for nothing," I said.

There was a narrow dirt path cutting through the jungle that looked like it led down the hill toward the ocean. I pointed at the trail and urged Sam to follow me.

"That doesn't look like it leads anywhere," Sam protested

"What's the worst thing that can," I said as I stepped into the bush.

The path twisted awkwardly across the slope. I could make out drapes of white linen drying on a thin piece of wire through the trees. There were brick houses and piles of plastic toys covered in dirt behind them. As we got closer, I could see families standing in the clearing. I could just about make out the whites of their eyes and the short mops of dark hair that covered their heads. They stared at us without moving. As we passed their houses they shook their heads and went back to hanging their laundry in the shade. We headed towards a clearing at the bottom of the hill. The trees began to fade behind us as the dirt gave way to perfectly manicured grounds with freshly cut grass that felt like velvet under my naked toes. There were small houses on stilts and a swimming pool bordered by an elongated bar with champagne flutes hanging delicately over top of the rail. By the time we got to the beach it was clear that we had walked into a trap.

"Look!" said Sam, "That's where we pulled in yesterday."

Sam pointed towards the ferries that were shipping fresh blood in and out of the harbour, "And there's the next batch of precious cargo."

"So much for shortcuts," I groaned.

The crescent stretch of sand looked the same as on the other side, except for the gaping mouth at the end of the bay that was receiving the incoming traffic. The water was clear and the smell of diesel wafted up from the port. The trees exploded into an endless sprawl, enveloping the highest peaks of the island in green plastic. The higher the mountains climbed into the sky the thicker the vegetation grew, as it fought for precious real estate on the cluttered escarpment.

We were alone on the beach except for a few casual sunbathers basking in the sun that was moving slowly over to the other side of the island. A girl in a white bikini was drying her hair as at the edge of the water. When she was done she laid her towel down beside a gap-toothed redhead and pulled out a beaten up copy of Crime and Punishment. She looked perfect lying there in the sun as she propped herself up on her elbows to read. I was sweating uncontrollably. I wanted desperately to say something to her but my brain was melting away in the heat.

I watched as made his way into the water. He slipped and cut his foot a piece of coral. "Goddamnit!" He pulled his bloody foot out of the water to examine it.

"It's probably there to keep the tourists from scaring the fish away," I laughed.

He shook his head, "I doubt it. Look at this shit. There's no fish in here and the coral's rotten!"

The coral was dead: a brownish grey pile of moldy rubble. The tide soon sucked all the water back out to sea and Sam and I were reduced to sitting on the dry sand while we waited for the day to end. I woke up in the cool shade of two shadows extended across my face. I opened my eyes slowly hoping to see the girl in the white bikini.

"Hey do you guys have the time?"

I lifted my bare wrist up to my face to show that I wasn't just trying to get rid of them. "I'm afraid we don't."

"We try not to concern ourselves with such matters," Sam added.

They were suspiciously handsome for a pair of average beach bums. They both looked at Sam for a while before turning around. They were just about to walk away, before Sam spoke up. "Where you boys from?"

"Canada..." said one.

"Edmonton..." added the other.

"Prairie boys eh?"

"So you're familiar with our neck of the woods!" They were both about the same height. One of them had jet-black hair and a grizzly beard to match it. The other was fair skinned with short sun bleached hair and long eyelashes. Neither of them was particularly big, but they each looked like the kind of guys you'd want to have on your side if shit hit the fan.

"We can't really compete with that. We're just a couple of city slickers," said Sam.

The bearded one tried to put on a heavy Western accent that sounded more Texan than Canadian. "What are you doing around these parts?"

"Some guy told us about a beach where we could go swimming without any crowds. But we got lost along the way and we ended up here."

The bearded one spoke up again.

"So you've found the perfect beach and you don't want us to know your secret?" He pretended to be insulted "Are you going to have to kill us?"

Sam laughed, "We've got nothing to hide. I think it's just down that way where all those boats are going. I don't even know why we bothered, every beach here seems the same to me."

I threw my hands in the air, "I just wanted somewhere where I could swim without cutting my feet open," I laughed, "What's the point of being stranded on a desert island if you can't swim in the ocean?"

"I guess we'll let you off the hook," said the bearded one.

"What about you two?" I asked.

"We're travelling together. We've only been in the country for a few weeks but we've still got a long ways to go."

"We only flew in a few days ago," I said.

"You sure made it down here pretty quick."

"We checked into a few places along the coastline on our way down but there was nothing worth sticking around for," said Sam.

I wasn't going to let them get off that easy. "We managed to end in up the asshole of the world. It was full of Russian oligarchs and cheap hookers. I swear some of those oil barons must sneak out a night to keep that place in business." I shook my head as I remembered the town, "They must come here to escape Putin and his friends down at the KGB. I don't think take too kindly to the poor bum-fuckers."

The two of them looked at each other and smiled awkwardly.

"You know we're gay right..." said the bearded one.

Sam's face turned red. This was exactly the kind of mishap he feared most, but I jumped in before he could start apologising.

"I figured that's why you had the matching rings. Besides asking for the time has to be the worst pick up line possible in a place like this."

"We really did want to know what time it was," the bearded one said with a chuckle.

"So are you two together?" I asked.

The fair-haired one spoke up for the first time.

"That's what the rings are for..."

"The plan is to get married when we get back," added the other, "So long as that faggot Prime Minister doesn't change the law and make it illegal by the time we get back."

We all burst out laughing. We hadn't been expecting company but it was refreshing to meet people who weren't afraid to mix things up a bit.

"So what are you two doing here?" I asked.

"You mean other than being fags?" the bearded one added with a smile. "We decided to put life on hold for a year."

His fiancé concurred with a boyish smile, "Kile works as primary school teacher. He managed to trick the school board into giving him a sabbatical. I didn't have much going on, so I just quit my job and followed him here."

"At least you know it'll be waiting for you when you get back," answered Sam.

"Yeah! That's a huge relief!" joked Kile.

Kile was determined to use a connection he had in China to get a job teaching English. He said it was guaranteed to get him a pay raise when he got back. He admitted there were better ways he could spend his time but all that really mattered to them was that they got to spend it together.

"So does that make this your honey-moon?" I asked.

They looked at each other and smiled, and James spoke up through his lumberjack beard, "Well... Kile wants to have the wedding in sunny

Edmonton."

"And James wants to have a bachelor party in Vegas and a ceremony in Mexico," countered Kile.

"Sounds pretty extravagant."

"A bit excessive," said Kile, before flashing a sly smile at James, "But we'll see who gets the last laugh."

"There's nothing wrong with a little excessiveness!" said Sam emphatically. "You only get to do it once, so you might as well do it right."

They looked at one another and laughed.

"We'll see what happens. Who knows, maybe we'll never go home, just stay on the road forever. Keep living the dream... Does that count?"

"I don't know. I've never been engaged but it sounds like a damn fine way to spend a year," I said.

The happy couple was just the kind of distraction we needed to keep us out of trouble for a few days. We spent the afternoon sipping large bottles of beer from the nearest bar, halfway down the beach. The island glowed in the twilight as the sun climbed over our heads. It wasn't long until the madness of another night would start up again. The few people that were lying on the sand began to slowly disappear back through the thinning jungle. We finished our beers under the orange glow of the sun, then walked our new friends back to their bungalow. The black bra was still hanging on the back of a chair outside our room when we got back. It was hot, almost too hot to be anywhere but in an air-conditioned basement with the lights off, and I lay in bed, sweating slowly on top of the sheets until I drifted off to sleep.

I took a long cold shower when I woke up, and after mixing a few drinks we headed down to meet the happy couple at their room. We ended up going for dinner at the same Vacant Universe restaurant we had been eating at every night since we arrived. The happy couple kept us in stitches throughout the entire meal. Whenever anything resembling an awkward silence threatened to ruin the atmosphere, one of them would step in with an outrageous statement that would reduce the rest us to tears. After enough drinks nothing was off limits.

"So, when did you two know you were gay?" asked Sam.

"Haha!" James laughed as he stared at Sam, then quickly back at Kile, "You really want to know?"

"Sure, I've always wondered about that. I mean I don't think I'm gay. At least I've never thought about a man that way. But how the hell am I supposed to know?"

"Believe me, you would know."

"What do you mean?"

"Have you ever dreamt of sucking a man off?" James said with a straight-faced grin.

Sam laughed and shook his head, then James looked over at me.

"Don't look at me..." I said. There was a pause and then we all broke into laughter.

"I knew when I was four," Kile blurted out.

"Four?" I stuttered as I choked back on my drink.

"Ya, I just knew," he said with a smile.

"I didn't even know I could get an erection until I was 12,"," said Sam. "I mean the only thing I can even remember before the age of 5 is Barney the Dinosaur."

"Well, there's nothing gayer than a talking purple dinosaur!" Kile joked, before continuing on, "I just had a feeling. It's kind of hard to describe. I could just feel it in the pit of my stomach."

"They don't come much gayer than him," smiled James. "That's why I love him."

"What about you?" Sam asked James.

"It took my a while to figure out. I had to fumble with a few dry pussies until I really knew..."

"You still do!" Kile said with a grin.

"Only when I'm drunk," he said with a loving look in his eyes. "But I didn't really know for sure until I was about 15 or 16. The real moment of revelation was when I would start jerking off to the Spice Girls and before I could finish I would be thinking about the Backstreet Boys."

"Well, I guess we're safe then," I said with a shrug of the shoulders.

"You know... You never know until you try..." said James. "I actually have a pretty good track record."

"Of what?" I asked.

"Turning boys like you to the dark side. Everyone's got a little gay in them. It just takes the right person to fuck them out of the closet," he blurted out and we all burst out laughing.

It was refreshing to be around someone who was willing to speak their mind without worrying about the repercussions. We sat around after we were finished, drinking beers until the restaurant started to close then headed back to our room for more gin. By the time we got down to the beach, the exotic after-hours marathon was already well under way. I was relieved to be back in the wilderness. I let myself get carried away by the parade as we made our way towards the front of one of the stages. We marched and stomped like giants, making as much noise as possible as we passed in front of the wilting jungle trees.

Swarms of breasts and legs and unruly tuffs of hair flung themselves in our path. I felt my heart throbbing heavily in my chest. Their bodies writhed in ecstasy as they were dragged along by the stars like high-strung puppet. Sam was standing right in front of one of the speakers with his shirt off and his mouth wide open. James had his arms wrapped around Kile's waist. He slid his lips up and down his neck and Kile tilted his head towards the sky in a dull show of excitement as the music pounded on.

By now the entire beach had descended into a wild frenzy. All around us the same depraved scene was unfolding. Girls were being bent over like folding chairs and pummelled from behind by faceless strangers. They inevitably responded by wrapping their legs around unsuspecting victims and attacking them with wild sensual thrusts. Their faces twitched and grimaced with pornographic detail under the heat of the lights. Their nostrils flared and their eyes filled with a terrifying look of shock and awe with each violent gyration. Each one looked more deranged and excited than the next.

After a few hours of dancing I was feeling drunk and confused. My stomach bottomed out and I thought I was going to retch. I could feel the booze and promiscuity gnawing away at my insides. The next thing I knew, I found myself smothered against the salty humidity of an under-developed bust. I started to panic. Part of me wanted to sink my teeth into her sweaty neck and the other part wanted to shove her out of the way and keep flailing around like a madman. I tossed my head around looking for a way out. I swept back across her face and saw my reflection in her glazed over eyes. She stared at me and batted her eyelashes. I was frozen for a moment, locked into the empty abyss of her pupils. My heart stuttered all of sudden and I dug my fingers into her back. My hips mashed against her delicate frame as my hands slid further down her spine. I could feel myself smiling and she looked like she was smiling back at me. Then I realized she probably hadn't stopped smiling in months and she was just going through the motions like everyone else. She eventually broke free and I went to get another round of drinks. When I came back Sam had disappeared again. I looked over at the happy couple. Kile had now lost his shirt and they were both mauling each other vigorously on the dance floor.

"Where's Sam?" I asked.

They pointed up to the stage without taking their hands off one another. He was doing a mediocre Mick Jagger impersonation, strutting violently back and forth on top of a wooden platform, surrounded by a group of well-lubricated brunettes. I jumped up beside him and started moving my hips and arms around in wild spasms. Sam was practically foaming at the mouth, and the brightly coloured paint that some girl had splattered under his eyes was now running down his face in blotches, making him look like a muscle bound sex-craved clown. I stared down at the rabid train wreck that was unfolding before our eyes. They might as well have had us on our hands and knees drinking from long wooden troughs, recycling our piss and vomit back into them when we were too full to drink anymore, so as not to waste a single drop. There was something comforting about the constant fits of vomiting and fucking and obnoxious mind-numbing music. It certainly wasn't glamorous but for a few hours each night, the island felt alive and the repetition and the drinking and the never-ending tease of sexual frustration made sure that it was all over before you could say you'd had enough.

I turned around and saw Kile flailing around uncontrollably. It looked like he was trying to dance but he was just too drunk to stand up. James tried to prop him up as he kept moving back and forth across the sand but Kile's body fell limp against his shoulders. We offered to help him drag his lifeless corpse home but James insisted that it would insulting to drag us away from the party on account of his boyfriend not being able to handle his liquor. I wanted to tell him that we felt like leaving but too but we couldn't let them down, so we kept dancing as the happy couple disappeared into the crowd. When the music finally stopped we were both too wasted to talk. On the way back up the hill Sam stopped outside a pharmacy.

"You buying more Valium?"

"Just wait here," he said. I stood outside and watched girls in string bikinis being carried into the night by topless firemen. A lone couple sat across on the curb across the road, sticking their vomit-covered tongues down one another's throat. It seemed almost romantic in a twisted indifferent way. By the time I fell into bed, the thought of having to perform any kind of bodily function, mutual or otherwise, made me feel dizzy. I tried to look at the ceiling to keep my stomach settled but it just made matters worse. I turned over and gripped my pillow tight, andwaited anxiously for my brain to stop working.

Five

I woke up the next morning with a splitting headache and an empty bed. It had only been two nights but the knockoff booze and legal speed was already beginning to take its toll. I was in rough shape but I'd seen worse, and I managed to convince myself that there were worse things than being hungover on a tropical island in the middle of nowhere. When Sam woke up we decided it would be best to stay for a few more nights. The newlyweds had given us the shot in the arm that we needed and we agreed that it would be a shame to leave with everyone getting along so well.

    I left Sam sweating away in the bathroom and crawled down the stairs, gripping the handrail as firmly as possible to keep my hand from shaking. The man behind the bamboo desk was smoking a pack of local cigarettes and watching a DVD of some ancient British sketch comedy. It hadn't even occurred to me that we didn't have a TV in our room until now, and I was somewhat relieved that we didn't have a bunch of perfectly tanned strangers waiting to greet us every time we went back to our room. The attendant looked like he was in his early 30s and he sported a thick black handle bar moustache to match his shaved head. I stopped myself from asking how long he'd been here or how he ended up running this place, if only because I was afraid to find out just how easy it was to get stuck here. It was clear that he didn't want to be bothered with wasteful small talk, and I couldn't really blame him. I got straight to the point. "We've decided that we'd like to stay a few extra nights."

He looked down at a scrappy pad of paper marked up in pencil and different coloured pens.

"Let's see," he hummed as he flipped through his notebook. "You booked in for two nights on Tuesday."

He dragged his pencil across the pad of paper before continuing on in a thick Manchester accent, "And now it's Saturday… You've been here five nights, and paid for two," he paused and held the pencil up to his lips, "Which leaves three nights."

I scratched my head and started going through the nights and days on my fingers. Five nights seemed like an awful long time. Was I going crazy? There was no way we'd been there for five nights. This would never have happened if we had a TV to tell us what day it was.

"Are you sure about that?" I felt almost ashamed to have to ask.

He looked up at me and cocked his eyebrow like he was about to use it to push a bullet through the back of my head.

He made a mark on the page. "So would you like to settle up for the three remaining nights. You still have time to check out today if you like. I won't even charge you for interest for the nights you owe."

I started counting on my fingers again and hesitated for a second. "No, that's ok." I reached into my pocket and pulled out everything I had, "Here's the money for the nights we owe. And that should be enough to cover two more."

I should have gone to ask Sam but that would have just been a waste of everyone's time. We were staying here for better or for worse. He took the money and went back to scribbling on the pad. I tried to apologise for not having paid for the nights we had already stayed but he didn't care. "No, worries mate."

I tried to look embarrassed and smiled. "This sort of shit must happen all the time." I regretted saying it as soon as the words came out of my mouth, but it was too late. He flashed his teeth from under his moustache and mustered the kind of everyday laugh you develop from spending months on end being surrounded by rioting brain-dead drunks.

"All the time."

Sam was just getting out of the shower when I came back in. When I explained what had happened he started counting on his fingers and mumbling to himself. There was a brief pause before he looked up at me, "I guess that sounds about right."

I fell back into bed and closed my eyes. My head was pounding and my body was craving something, anything. I just needed to get out of this sweatbox. I felt less lightheaded after a full American breakfast. After Sam finished his third cup of coffee we went to find the happy couple and headed down to the beach. Patrick was waiting for us at the end of the path. He was strung out. His shirt was worn out and wrinkled and it looked like he hadn't been to sleep for days.

"Hey guys, how's it going?" He hadn't lost any of his enthusiasm and he managed to eek out an honest smile. We introduced him to our new companions. He extended his hand and acknowledged the couple's presence before returning to his train of thought.

"So what do you think? You going to come on the cruise? We've still got a few spots left for this afternoon. The Captain's setting sail in just under an hour."

We talked it over amongst ourselves with a few well-timed interjections from Patrick. Despite all the handshaking and laughs, you could tell that he really just wanted someone to talk to. In the end we promised him we would think about it.

"Don't worry buddy, we'll be back," Sam reassured him as we walked away.

Down on the beach, bare-chested locals in skinny jeans were still cleaning up last night's mess. Every day was the same. They would drink and smoke and put on a fantastic act, in between putting away the rickety scaffolding and aging speakers that kept the all night parties afloat. They kicked footballs at groups of girls in bikinis, and did cartwheels and backflips on the sand. In just a few hours they would be putting the stages back together and getting on with their double lives as DJs, bartenders and fire-eaters.

It was a scam – they were as local as the shitty reggae they blasted during the day. They probably would have been just at home on a campus in some small American town as they were on this half-secluded beach. All the flexing and back-flips were just a teaser for the girls who were eager to bring home an exotic memory of their adventure in paradise. After all it was one thing to sleep with a black man with a college degree, it was quite another to sleep with a dark and mysterious man whose working knowledge of English was refined just enough to get one of them into bed. After a few too many late afternoon cocktails, you could occasionally hear a whisper rise to a cackle as a group of girls with peeling skin toyed with the idea. Most of them tended to keep to themselves. But occasionally a girl would be confronted with the opportunity to exploit her penchant for liberated sexual experimentation and her post-colonial idealism in one foul swoop. It was a good way to keep the diary full and it made sure that the box of condoms her mom bought her – 'just as a precaution' – didn't go to waste.

The sun was too hot to bear, and we made our way to the glistening pool of turquoise sewage to cool off. The tide was almost at its peak, and I dove down six feet and skimmed the bottom, swimming under the wooden hulls that were overgrown with thick layers of mossy algae for 50 yards at a time before coming back up for air. When we were done swimming we headed back to our room. Patrick managed to catch us off guard on our way. His hair was already spread out of the way of his eyes but he combed his fingers through it anyways.

"Hey, I was hoping you guys would come back. The boat's almost all booked up for tomorrow, it should be a good one!"

We talked it over quickly as we dried off in the sun and agreed that it would be a good idea to get off the island for an afternoon.

"How many more spots do you have left?" I asked.

Patrick shuffled back to a cluttered desk. He rustled through a pile of paper before pulling out a bright red notepad. "We've got 11, signed up, so…" he looked up and did the math in his head, "Room for three more."

"But there's four of us," Sam protested.

He scratched his head and considered the repercussions of sending a bunch of half-sober tourists to an unfortunate end in the middle of the ocean. "I'm sure we can make room."

We handed over half the cash and Patrick crammed the bills into a brown folder tucked under some of the clutter on his desk.

"You can pay the rest when you board the ship tomorrow," he said with a grin before shaking all our hands. "Don't worry. You won't be disappointed."

Six

I woke up later in the evening to the sound of Sam struggling in the bathroom.

"It smells like death in here," I shouted through the door.

"I don't think I'm going to make it to dinner…" he mumbled between retches.

I laughed. "You probably just need a drink."

I waited for a response. Sam took a deep breath as if he was about to speak. Then came the splash of water being forced into the porcelain bowl.

"I guess Patrick was right about the water being an infested pool of shit," I said as I reached for the bottle. Sam muttered something about showing me a pool of shit through the wall but I was too focussed on pouring the gin to hear exactly what he said.

"Ok, well I'll head down and meet the boys and leave you to it."

He moaned before another violent retch drowned him out for good. I slammed back both the gin and tonics and left him alone in the room. I went down and knocked on the boy's door. Kile answered in his underwear. He popped his head out the door and looked around, "Where's Sam?" he asked.

"Sick."

"Oh!"

He seemed surprised, "That's too bad," he sighed. "James is feeling pretty rough too."

I tried to throw out my joke about swimming in shit, and he was polite enough to try and force a giggle.

"What are you up to then?" he asked

I didn't really have an appropriate answer. The sight of me alone must have looked as strange as it felt.

"I was going to go to dinner," I hesitated for a bit hoping he would say something before continuing on. "What about you?"

He looked back into the room and paused for a moment, "I think I'm going to take care of James, he's not feeling so well."

I didn't want it to seem like I was relieved to not have to make small talk without James and Sam around, so I asked him to join me.

"No, thanks. I'm not that hungry and James could probably use someone to take care of him."

Maybe I should have been back at the bungalow taking care of Sam. I was hungry though and I needed to eat. For some reason I decided to prod him one more time.

"Are you sure?"

"Ya, I'm sure. But we'll meet you at the dock in the morning."

I pulled myself together and refrained from asking a third time, "Ok, well I hope he feels better. See you tomorrow."

The night felt cool under the weight of the clouds. It was the first time the stars had disappeared since we arrived. I walked down the side streets flipping through menus and staring at the clientele hoping that something would catch me eye. In the end I settled for the comfort of a trashy pub that advertised greasy over-priced food on postcard-sized photos. I grabbed a table near the street and held the menu up to my face so that I could stare at the traffic in the street. When the waitress came I ordered a cheeseburger and chips, with a coke and a large beer.

The constant flow of white-smiled girls passing in front of the patio kept me amused while I waited for my food. I'd only been on the island for a few days but I already recognized most of the faces that passed by. The waitress returned with my drinks and I sipped the coke and beer in turns trying to cleanse my palette.

I looked up and saw an old man with thinning white hair slicked across his sunspotted scalp. He was walking down the street with his arm around a fair skinned pansy, who couldn't have been more than a day over 18. The boy didn't have any make-up on and aside from his elegant stride was obviously a man. *"What a sick fuck!"* I thought to myself. *"How could a dirty old man take advantage of an innocent boy like that!"* I stared at them as they got closer but my anger subsided as they passed. Maybe they made each other happy, I thought to myself. Maybe I just needed to loosen up. But as soon as they were out of sight my rage returned. *"What a sick fuck! How dare that filthy bastard take advantage of that innocent old man!"*

The thick vapour in the air began condensing into drops of rain that fell increasingly fast and heavy. It came down harder and harder and the streets cleared out, as people ran for cover anywhere they could find it. I continued to sit stubbornly under the awning on the patio, drinking my beer while I waited for my food to come. The wind started to pick up, until it carried the rain sideways into my face. I was determined not to move but I didn't want to have to eat a soggy burger, so I finished my coke and carried my beer inside.

I squeezed in between two tables, with pairs of girls picking away at their food on either side. I had been eyeing them from the terrace and the rain gave me the perfect excuse to intrude. One of the girls at the table next to me looked familiar. It was the one in the white bikini that I saw reading on the sand just a few days ago. She was now dressed in a lace summer dress with frilly cuffs that barely covered her shoulders. A pair of leather thongs wound round her ankles and up her calves like aging vines on a fence post. I twisted my ear so I could I hear what she was saying to the girl with the small hoop earrings that was sitting across from her. She had a smoky Chelsea lisp that rolled softly through the air under the noise of the rain. I turned towards her and paid close attention to her sensually obstructing lips.

"Just another lonely rainy night in Soho…Perhaps, but it never hurt anyone… Shit… I didn't think of that…"

"No, I'm just waiting for my cheeseburger… Really?… That sounds great… No, but he's at home … Sick. Must be something in the water… That too…It certainly doesn't help. "

"He's a lawyer for a shipping company. At least he used to be… Something like that… No, I'm just waiting to hear back from them… Exactly…"

"What about you?.. London?… What are you talking about?... Oh, that sounds nice…Excuse me? … No no, it's ok. Don't worry I get it all the time."

"...Really?... You mean Myanmar?... Exactly, same same but different... I didn't know he was buried there... No, but five years can still feel like an eternity. Just ask Dostoyevsky... Is that so?... Seems like heavy reading for the beach... Me too, at least three times... I don't know. Call it a lucky guess..."

I looked her in the eye. She didn't recognise me. I was just another stranger to her.

"...I doubt it... At this rate we'll never even leave this god-forsaken island..."

"...Jesus! That must be nice. How long is that going to take you? ... If I had enough money I might... If that were the case I'd never work another day in my life! Hell, I'd never have a reason to leave home ever again... Ya it happens, I'm sure you'll get over it though... Don't say that... You'll be back before you know it. It'll be like you never even left in the first place..."

She smiled and looked over at me.

"What's that?... Oh, I'd love to but I should go and check in on my friend... Really?... No, I really shouldn't... I actually think I'm coming down with something myself..."

"I really would but... That too. And I'm still waiting for my food to come..."

Just then my food arrived. Before I could open my mouth, the girls got up from their table and made their way into the rain. It was a tropical monsoon now and the soaking crowds ran through the darkness looking for cover. A blonde girl to my right was contemplating her escape while her friend slumped her head over her folded arms. Her tattered hair partially covered a tattoo of a colourful map on the back of her shoulder. It was hard to tell how long they'd been on the island but it was clear that it was taking its toll on them. By the time I finished my cheeseburger they were both gone and I was left without any distractions. I drank another beer and watched the trembling bodies huddled across the street, as they attempted to stay dry.

I paid my bill and left the bar, stomping my feet as I waded through the puddles of muddy water that formed in the potholes on the dirt road. It didn't take long for my shirt to soak through and I took it off to keep me cool. It felt good to have the heavy drops pounding gently on my bare skin and soon enough I was covered in mud and water. Sam was reading a book when I came through the door. He looked up for a second before staring back down at the page. I took off my dirty shorts and hopped into bed. I flipped through a few pages of a book I'd lost interest in long ago, before my head rolled sideways and I drifted off to the sound of oversized beads of water clattering against our thatched bamboo roof.

Seven

Sam and I woke up early and went down to the pier to have a swim while the tide was still high. The bay on the West side of the island was already overcome with the smell of gasoline and sunscreen, as retired fishermen prepared to bring the days first batch of backpackers to the secluded beaches on the surrounding islands. I got out of the water and lay on the sand. A small rubber inflatable carrying a balding white man approached the only sailboat moored in the harbour. He pulled alongside the boat and loaded a few dozen crates over the side, before jumping on board and stowing them down below. A thick plume of smoke followed quickly afterwards, spewing from the small exhaust that hung just above the water line. He tied his inflatable raft to the mooring ball, pulled up the anchor and motored slowly over to a barge that was tied up to the pier.

We made our way down to the dock just before the boat was set to leave. The ship was nearly full but there was no sign of the boys. All of a sudden Kile came running down the street. He was panting and he could barely talk by the time reached us.

"Jesus, what the hell happened to you?" asked Sam.

"Where's James?" I asked.

"We...." he huffed as he tried to catch his breath. "We didn't know where you were."

He propped himself up by resting the palms of his hands on his knees. He was still gasping for air. "We were waiting down here. We didn't know where you were, so we went looking for you?"

"I can't believe you ran all the way up those stairs?" I said.

He wiped his brow and cracked a smile, "Neither can I."

"What about James?"

Kile was now standing up straight, "We split up to cover more ground, hopefully he'll be here soon."

Just then the Captain motioned at us. "It's time to push off. Move it or lose it!" His voice had the sunken authority of a washed up merchant who'd seen one too many crossings. We tried to argue with him but he turned away and grumbled under his voice. He paced up and down the deck briefly before giving us an ultimatum.

"You can either come and leave your friend or you can all stay behind," he grumbled.

"But we've already paid a deposit."

He shrugged, "I don't care about your money. You can get it back if you come by the booth later this afternoon. I can't wait any longer. I've got a schedule to keep and a business to run."

We were about to give up on the cruise until we saw James' head poke out from behind an old man's back. He was flying down the pier straddling the back wheel of a bike. He came skidding in and handed the cyclist a bill without a looking at it before sprinting toward the boat.

"Glad you could make it," said Sam.

James shook his head and smiled as he finished catching his breath, "Me too."

We piled onto the boat and the Captain started barking orders to a local in cut off jeans. "Phu! Pull the dock lines and put the fenders down below. We gotta make up for lost time."

We weaved through anchor lines and the buzz of fishing boats that were ferrying tourists back and forth between the nearest islands. Once we passed the convoys the Captain threw the boat head to wind to and yelled at Phu to put up the sails. He introduced himself as Captain Bob and he spoke loudly above the ragging canvas as it was hoisted, explaining the itinerary for the day before making sure that everyone knew where to find booze on the ship. We hugged the shoreline as the Captain pointed out local wildlife, which consisted of nothing more than a few monkeys dragging their knuckles on the white sandy beaches at the foot of the escarpment. Despite having compiled years of unnecessary frustration, it was clear that Captain Bob was just as pleased as we were to be off dry land.

As we got closer to the tower of gnarled rock in the distance, the water flattened out and the breeze died to a whisper. We pulled behind the steep rock face, and Captain Bob threw the boat head to wind as he ordered Phu to take down the sails. He was no more than 5'4 and he clambered frantically around the boat, trying to get the halyards untied. Once the sails were down Captain Bob pointed the boat directly at the island. It looked like we were going to smash against the rocks, then at the last second the island parted gracefully into a thin slit that was no wider than a four-lane highway. The rocks pinched inward for about 30 feet before receding and opening up into a semicircular basin with a crescent shaped strip of sand at the end of the cove. Thick layers of vegetation covered the limestone cliffs, which rose like fleshy skyscrapers around us. Their reflection pitched into the pool of water below, where it was dissected by dozens of boats will with hundreds of sun-worshipers competing for space. The Captain sent Phu up to the bow to prepare the anchor as he addressed the crew.

"Over here, we have the main attraction. The reason you're all here: the infamous beach." He allowed a dramatic pause before continuing on, "We'll be anchored here for a few hours. You can use the kayaks and the snorkelling equipment, and you can drink as much as you want. If you need anything just ask me or Phu. Feel free to swim up to the beach and jump off those cliffs over there but be careful. I'm not rushing back to take anyone to the hospital," he said with a smile.

"I don't care what you do, or how much you drink just make sure you're back here by 5 o'clock," he added before sinking back down in the cockpit.

A stubbly Brit nudged me in the arm as I finished off my beer. "I'm reading the book right now," he said, hoping for a reply. When I failed to answer, he asked me if I had read it too. I shook my head. He turned away and fixed his eyes on the crowded beach and smiled, "I can't believe I'm actually here right now."

I stared at the diesel-powered antique boats that were pulled into the bay. "It's pretty surreal alright."

I put down my empty bottle and jumped overboard. Bob held court from the back of the boat, explaining the history of the bay and occasionally shouting to his first mate to get more drinks. "We can't let these people go thirsty now can we?" he bellowed, loud enough for everyone to hear.

Sam swam past me and started heading for the shore. I asked the happy couple if they wanted to join us but they were content enough treading water by the boat. We swam through the mobs of strapless bikinis with their faces buried in the salty cove. We cut as close as possible to try and get their attention but they remained focussed, skimming along the surface with their cheeks pointed purposefully towards the sky, alongside their plastic blowholes. We kept heading toward shore and climbed onto some dried-out coral on the far end of the beach.

The island had become protected as a national park back in the 1980s; right when the Vacant Universe was starting to turn the country into a household name for rootless middle class vagabonds. It was technically protected by law but there were so many people coming here everyday that any concept of preservation was reserved for well-intentioned ministers living in lavish suburban palaces in the capital. If you wanted you could even pay a small fee to sleep in a prefabricated campsite to experience the majesty of the wild island like the trailblazing adventurers that had pioneered the lifestyle over two decades ago.

We strolled along the sand doing our best to stay clear of the perfectly bronzed models that were posing for picture perfect moments they could upload to the rest of the world as soon as they were back on the mainland. Every bug-eyed graduate in the Western Hemisphere wanted to the chance to show off a little piece of their very own private paradise. These days it was more likely for someone to forget their passport than their camera. The thought of them being deprived of their digital zooms, memory cards and telescopic lenses and reinforced protective cases seemed as foreign as a swat team kicking down a door without guns in their hands. Their strategy was simple: shoot first and ask questions later. If you were lucky enough you'd end up with a few pictures that looked authentic enough to pawn off to the hordes of friends and family waiting impatiently for your safe return home.

I glimpsed a frisbee flying towards my head out of the corner of my eye and ducked ducked just in time. It bounced off Sam's shoulder and landed at his feet. He picked it up and threw it back to a group of eager looking bikinis. The disc wobbled in the air and landed in the sand before reaching its intended target. A rippled specimen with a thick head of sun-kissed hair and a wispy blonde moustache jumped in front of the girls and grabbed it. He tossed the Frisbee with a quick flick of his fingers, sending it sailing in a perfect arc towards the girls.

"Not going to pick any ladies up with a toss like that mate," he said as he walked up to us. He was wearing bright neon shorts and he had a healthy crop of hair dusted across his chest. "You two look lost."

"No. We're just here for the afternoon, like everyone else," I said trying to sound enthusiastic.

"We came in on the sailboat," Sam added. "The captain was just telling us about this cliff we could jump off on the other side of the island. We thought we'd go and check it out."

"Ya, that's where all the tourists go." He puffed his chest out as he spoke, "It's just down there. It's a decent little spot but there's better ones," he said without finishing his thought.

"So have you done the cruise already?" Sam asked.

He shook his head, "No, I'm staying here illegally, so I try and keep a low profile."

Sam looked over at me in embarrassment.

"So do you work at one of the dive shops or something?" I asked.

He scoffed at my suggestion "Mate, do I look like a dive instructor to you?"

He did – he was the spitting image of a chain smoking womaniser but I kept my mouth shut and let him continue on, "Not a chance. I came here 6 months ago and became addicted to the locals and their vibe. My visa expired but I couldn't face the thought of going home. Then, I thought to myself, what the hell am I doing with my life? I realised I was wasting my time travelling around, getting pissed and acting like a dickhead. So I decided to stay behind after my visa expired; you know, to do something to help pay the locals back for their kindness. It may look like all is fine and well for people like us but a lot of them live in wretched poverty. That's when came up with the idea to set up a charity. And now I'm helping all these people build homes."

"And how's that going so far?" Sam asked in an attempt to humour him.

"It's great. I'm actually kind of a big deal around here. But don't tell anyone, I don't want to get deported," he said.

"And you're doing this all for charity?" I asked.

"That's why I have this moustache. I'm growing it out for the month and taking donations and giving all the money to the village."

"Don't people normally do that to raise money for prostate cancer?"

"Sure, but you tell me who's going to benefit more from that money? A bunch of doctors working for some faceless pharmaceutical company, or a villager who's struggling to put rice on the table for his family."

I looked over at the bikini-clad floozies posing on the sand. I didn't want to have to talk to him anymore but I couldn't resist asking him how much he had raised.

"Well so far I've made about $230. It's not much but every penny counts. It may not seem like a lot of money to you and me, but an amount like that can go a long way in a country like this."

There was no need to tell me. Hell, I'd only been in the country for just over a week, and I'd spent twice that much just to keep myself drunk enough to get through the day.

"Well," I said. "Sounds like you're doing a great job."

"I'm just doing my part. Helping people one day at a time."

"I guess someone's got to do it." I said resignedly.

"It's just like Ghandi said, you got to be the change you want to see in the world," he replied with a self-satisfied smirk.

"Well good luck with that," I said before turning to Sam. "Our ride's leaving soon, so we should probably get going." I turned back to the benevolent Aussie, "Good luck with the houses."

"Don't need luck mate, just a bit of hard work and a big heart."

I wanted to grab a Frisbee and bludgeon the side of his face until his moustache turned red. The country was in shambles! All it needed was more people who were armed to the teeth with good intentions. It was a matter of sacrifice: doing whatever necessary to serve your fellow man. It's a dirty job but someone had to do it, no matter how full of shit they are. And who better to carry the banner for the greater good than a brain dead stoner in the midst of a fucking existential crisis!

We swam back to the boat as the sun crossed over the rocks at the end of the bay. Back on board, Captain Bob was doing his best to make sure that all the bottles he had stored down below earlier in the morning were going back empty. He had even started drinking himself. As a result he was now noticeably less high strung than he had been earlier on. He ordered Phu to pull up the anchor and to hand out drinks to anyone who was still thirsty. After doing a head count, he addressed the rest of the crew. "I'm sorry we couldn't stay for the sunset but we have to get out of here. It may be calm in here but it looks like the seas have been picking up all day. It's going to be rough so drink up and find yourselves a little space and hold on."

I leaned on the lifeline on the quarter stern and looked back at the beach as we sailed between the rocks. The smaller waves that had been ticking quietly against hull had been replaced by large rolling hills of water that smashed heavily against the side of the boat. With each dip of the bow the waves got bigger, as the boat bounced back and forth, pitched by the weight of 15 well-fed westerners. The Captain yelled at Phu to get the sail up but he seemed to be having trouble. I could tell that he was getting impatient.

"Is he ok up there?" I asked.

He shrugged his shoulders, "Oh, he's new, I just hired him two weeks ago. Still learning the ropes."

I offered to go up and help.

"You know anything about sailing?"

"I know my way around a boat."

The Captain furrowed his brow and took a swig of beer. "Ok, go up there and tie a bowline and reef the sail to two thirds."

"Two thirds?"

"Look around you son," he barked back. "Half these kids want off as it is."

I was drunk and feeling brave but I knew better than to ask any more questions. I staggered up to the mast. I tied the halyard off, put the reefs in, and started pulling on the line until the sail was up. I took out the slack on a winch and closed the latch to hold it in place. I looked at Phu, who smiled at me before patting me on the back. I couldn't tell whether he was thankful for my help or resentful for having undermined him. Then he went down below and brought me a beer. It wasn't a peace offering. It was just his job.

Bob killed the engine and pointed the bow at the island. The boat lifted up on the side of a wave and the boom rattled in the wind. The violence of the wind and the waves was a welcome relief from the shelter of the bay. Sam and the happy couple were leaning over the windward rail, smiling as the salty water splashed off the side of the hull and onto their bare legs. I went back to the cockpit where the only girl on the trip was huddled under her boyfriend's arm, trying to stay out of harm's way. Bob was certainly more content now that he was putting fear into the crew's hearts. The kind of sick pleasure that sailors who deal in landlubbers was the same one Bob got from dealing in disposable clients. Putting starry-eyed, adventure seekers back in their place was probably one of the only things that kept him going.

I didn't want to interrupt. But I had to know how a crazed balding man in his forties had become stuck trawling tourists back and forth between semi-deserted islands.

"I left Vancouver with my woman ten years ago," he said. "Took two years to sail down. I've been here ever since."

"You sure took you time," I said.

"Sure. There wasn't any rush to get down here. Hell, when I left I didn't even know where I'd end up. Just knew I had to get the hell out of Canada."

He definitely looked like the kind of person who had something to run away from. He was smiling now that he was drunk but you could tell that there was more to him than a mid-life crisis and a love for sailing. I figured it was best to leave it at that.

"You still with her?" I asked.

He glared at me through a haze of booze and faded memories.

"Which one?"

I hadn't really considered the possibility that there would be more than one, "The one you sailed down with?"

He kept one hand on the wheel and took a sip of his beer. "Well I dropped one off in New Zealand and picked another up in Singapore. Thirty feet of fiberglass and lead and nothing but water as far as the eye can see isn't exactly a lot of space for a man, nevermind a man *and* a woman. I've seen a few more come and go since I got here but right now I'm free. That's the great thing about life down here. You don't really need a woman to keep you warm at night."

Before I could make a joke about having a man to keep him warm, a brawny Welshman in a black tank top slipped on the deck and fell back into the cockpit. Captain Bob didn't even flinch. He had seen this happen thousands of times. He knew all he had to do was prod him to make sure he was alive and laugh it off until he knew he was ok. The Welshman pulled himself up and Bob handed him a beer as we kept crashing through the waves.

"Eight years?" I said focussing my attention back on the Captain. "You must really love this place."

He took a swig of his beer and looked back at the fading horizon.

"You see that island we just came from? I've been a lot of places in this world but I think that's maybe the most special place I've ever seen. Every time I pull into that little cove, I see something new, something that catches my eye – something that makes me think I have to come back tomorrow in case I've missed something before. I don't know how much longer I'll stay here. Those sorts of things aren't really up for me to decide. I guess I'll stick around until the day comes when I sail into that sheltered little bay and feel like I've seen it all before."

If I had heard it from anyone else I would have called them a lying piece of shit to their face. But when I heard him say those words they sounded almost reasonable. Maybe there was something that reminded him of that one place he could never go back to, or maybe he had just become stuck in a tropical daze. It may not have been paradise but whatever it was he saw in these islands, it was better than whatever was looking for him back home.

The sun had long disappeared when we reached shore. The small inflatable boat that Bob had used to load his precious cargo came alongside and ferried us back to the pier. As we climbed off the raft Captain Bob invited us to meet him at the Banana Bar to celebrate another safe passage later that night.

By the time we made it back to the stagnant pool I was too drunk to stand. I had to lean on the railing to get up the stairs, and as soon as we got in the door I collapsed face first on the bed. When I woke up again Sam was gone. I fumbled around the room looking for a drink or a note but found nothing. I staggered out to the porch. It was still dark, and the only thing I could hear above the hum of the crickets gathered around the stagnant pool was the muddled thunder of recycled electronic music rising from the beach. Sleep seemed like the only reasonable option, but I was too drunk and too dehydrated to go back to lie down. I knew that I would only go crazy sitting in bed waiting for the morning to come so I headed down to the beach.

It didn't take long for me to spot the happy couple. They were dancing manically on the sand. James turned around and caught my eye. He looked surprised to see me.

"Wow, you look like shit!"

"Thanks. You guys don't look too bad either."

"What happened to you?"

"I don't know. I guess I passed out. That Captain Bob really fucked me up."

I was dazed and they didn't seem as drunk as they had earlier on.

"What did I miss?"

"Not much, we went to the bar to meet the Captain and drank a bunch of cocktails," said James.

Before I could ask where Sam was he showed up with three large beers.

"Here you go sleeping beauty," said Sam before charging off into the crowd. I kept drinking until the noise pumped out of the speakers was reduced to nothing more than the sound of an aging monkey being dragged across a cheese grater. Before I knew it I was sober and my legs drooped in unison with my eyelids. All I wanted was a cold shower and my bed but the happy couple were all over each other and Sam wasn't going to leave his post until the night done. When the music finally stopped it was about five in the morning.

"That's it?" Kile moaned in dismay. "I was just getting started."

Sam shrugged. He wasn't willing to let the night and on such a sour note, "If you want a drink, you can come back to our room, we've got loads of booze."

I wanted to go to bed but I wasn't about to have a perfectly good night spoiled on my account. We walked back up the bungalow and Sam started pouring drinks. The gin was warm and we didn't have any ice. I slammed back the tumbler and lay down on one the beds. I tried to keep my eyes pried open. I could hear faint shouts in the distance as I drifted off.

"Austin! ..... austin... austin ... austin ... austin..."

But it was too late. I was gone.

...

Sam was reading in bed when I came to. "Sleep well?" he asked sternly.

I fell back onto my pillow and grunted. "What the hell happened last night?"

I paused before trying to answer my own question.

"Sure was," interrupted Sam

I went to the bathroom to take a piss. "Holy Christ, what a night," I sighed through the open door.

"You can say that again," Sam said. I could tell by the tone in his voice that he was holding something back.

"What time did the boys leave?" I asked

"When they had finished trying to fuck me!" chuckled Sam.

I walked out of the bathroom and looked at him. He wasn't laughing anymore.

"Ya, I saw that one coming," I laughed.

Sam shook his head to try and motion that he wasn't joking.

"You're full of shit!" I roared.

He smiled and started to laugh again.

I smiled back at him, "I don't fucking believe you!"

"Well start believing."

After going back and forth for a while Sam started to explain what had happened. "After you fell asleep there was a bit of an awkward silence. I didn't really know what to do, and then all of a sudden James starts to proposition me. It wasn't like they tried to rape me! They just tried to make me an offer I couldn't refuse."

"Fuck off..." I replied.

He continued on, explaining the details of what had happened until I believed him.

"Let's just say he has a way with words," said Sam. He smiled as he thought about it. "He was drunk out of his mind but he sobered up pretty quick when I turned him down. He was more embarrassed than I was. I just told them as long as it didn't bother them then the matter was settled."

I laughed. "Well you can't say you didn't see it coming. I'm glad they picked you over me though."

Sam flashed me a game-show host smile. "Can you blame them?" he laughed to himself. "You should just consider yourself lucky I didn't let them have their way with you after you passed out."

When we got down to the beach it was clear that whatever happened the night before had been forgotten, and were left trying to convince the happy couple that they should stay on the island for a few more days. They wanted to stick around but they had to make it across the border in the next 24 hours.

"If we don't renew our visas we'll be stuck on one of these islands for more than just a few days," said James.

"Fuck the visas. What's the worst thing that can happen?"

"I wish we could," said Kile.

James shook his head, "We could always risk it, but if we get caught we'll end up locked away in some medieval prison like a couple of prom queens. We've already stayed longer than we were supposed to as it is. It's just not worth it for the sake of a couple bucks and a quick bus ride across the border."

I laid back on the sand and closed my eyes, "You figure they'd want to keep you chained up here for as long as possible rather than risk having you run off to blow your hard-earned savings in another country."

The tide was coming in and the beach was slowly filling up with the remnants of last night's extravagances. We waited until the sun was directly overhead of us then made our way into the water, leaving a pile of books and t-shirts behind in the sand. Before the water was up to my knees I jumped in headfirst. I dove down for thirty seconds at a time, holding my breath and conserving it by taking long slow strokes through the water, then gliding with my feet side be side and my fingertips stretched out in front of my head. I drifted until my hair started to slip forward over my forehead, before pulling through the water again with my fingers pressed together like thinly sliced pieces of bread.

The happy couple and Sam were still standing in water up their wastes near shore when I came up for air. I went back under and swam back towards them. When I came up again I found myself staring at two small-breasted girls with damp hair standing up to their waists in water. They were hitting a tennis ball back and forth and everyone around them was straining their necks to get a look as the perfectly bronzed blonde and brunette traded forehands and backhands. They could barely go three volleys before having the ball drop in the water but that didn't seem to deter the crowds.

"I don't know how we would have missed a pair like that," said Sam as he watched the ball fly through the air. "They must be fresh off the boat."

James was staring keenly with his arm around Kile. "You guys should go and talk to them."

"Maybe later," mumbled Sam unenthusiastically as he waded back to the beach.

I stayed in the water until my fingers started to shrivel into wrinkled stubs. We saw the girls their towels on our way to the cabin. As we went by the brunette in the dark green bikini lifted her glasses to leer at Sam while the blonde in the baby blue string top turned and held her face close to her hands to disguise her laughter.

"What the hell are you waiting for?" James urged as he punched Sam in the shoulder.

"Don't worry, just give it some time," Sam said.

James looked at him in disgust, "You can take all the time in the world my friend. But if you don't try and fuck them I will," he said with a laugh, as Kile cracked up in solidarity.

We went for dinner with the boys later that evening. By now we were all sick of the Vacant Universe's number one hidden secret so we ended up stopping at a restaurant where the evening's menu was advertised in wooden troughs filled with ice on the side of the road. I took my time fidgeting about, examining the squid, the bright grey prawns, the fillets of ray and swordfish steaks. While I was trying to make up my mind, a man in beige canvas trousers and a salty red polo shirt came in cradling an enormous fish. It must have weighed nearly 30 pounds and it shimmered in the silver and blue light as he raised it over his head like a trophy. The waiters quickly ushered him in and started to talk with him. They exchanged frantic words. Soon the chef ran out and pointed to the kitchen. It was hard to tell whether they were arguing or agreeing with one another. After a few minutes in the kitchen, the man in the salty polo shirt left with empty hands and a big smile on his face. The waitress, who had been growing impatient with us, came up to take our order for the third time.

"We'll have that," said James, pointing toward the kitchen and we all nodded in agreement.

As we waited for our food I managed to convince myself that the kitchen, the waiter and the fisherman had actually planned the whole thing as a publicity stunt. But by the time I was done I was too full and satisfied to even care. Even if they had all been in on it together, it was still a nice change from our steady diet of curry, fried eggs and pizza.

After dinner we went to the bar where Sam and the happy couple had gone to meet with the Captain the night before. There was no sign of the Captain but one of his crew from England was handing out flyers in the street. He came up to the bar to get more flyers and recognised us from the day before.

"So you guys are back for more?"

Sam smiled. "We're not very fussy. Show us a tasty cocktail and a quiet bar and we're good to go."

I was still trying to figure out the connection between the bar and the Captain.

"So what's the deal with Bob? Do you guys work together?"

"No, no. He just brings people here after his cruises sometimes. We promote his cruise and he brings people here now and again. He also lets us go on the boat any time we want, as long as we drag some tourists along with us."

"Sounds like a pretty good deal to me," I said.

"He must make a killing," added James.

"He's just a good businessman. He knows we all love to get shit-faced and he knows that spoiled white kids have big mouths. The more drunk people are the more they'll be convinced they had a good time. And the more fun they think they had, the more they'll try and convince their friends how much fun they had."

With that the Englishman disappeared back into the street to wrangle more loners. I couldn't argue with his logic. I had personally told a few passers-by about the cruise without even think about it; partly out of drunkenness, partly out of sympathy for Captain Bob, and partly because I wanted to shove my self-satisfaction down strangers' throats for no reason at all. It all made for an extraordinarily lethal advertising campaign.

The bar had brightly lit pale yellow walls covered in novelty Mexican artifacts. The bartender's limbs were dark and stringy and his hair wound upwards into a lofty spiral of dreadlocks that would have been down to his calves if they had not been bunched into a sophisticated knot on top of his head. We ordered a round of strawberry margaritas based on his recommendation. After a few large swigs, I asked the bartender if he could top my drink up with more tequila. He stared through me as if he didn't understand the question before slipping away to converse with a scrawny man who stood as tall as the tip of his locks. The man grinned and threw a slanted glance at us before patting him on the back and sending him back to the bar. The bartender returned and topped up all our drinks with an apology. "Sorry, just had to check with the boss."

We perched on the bar ordering margaritas until the confessions started to kick in. His name was Abel. He was from Jamaica but he had grown up in Washington D.C. Like most people that seemed to end up getting stuck here, he had come here on vacation two and a half years ago and never got around to leaving. We polished off round after round without flinching, until we were scraping the last bits of tequila-soaked ice from our martini glasses. As we made our way out the Englishman stopped us. "Where are you guys going?"

"To the beach," I said.

The Englishman shook his head, "It's Friday..."

We all looked at him as if that was supposed to mean something. The Englishman sighed and continued shaking his head, "On Fridays we give out free drinks to girls who take their tits out. Just go up those stairs, there's a couple up there right now. American girls; definitely worth checking out."

I had no intention of making the trip down to Cancun to see a pair of American tits any time soon so why not just get it all over with in one go.

"It would be rude not to at least pay a visit," I said.

We made our way up of the rickety spiral staircase. Sure enough, there were two unexpectedly tanned pairs of breasts topped off with penny-sized nipples ready to greet us at the top. They were proportioned and shaped as you'd expect any well-packaged American product to be, and they were surrounded by a sad mob of sweaty men, all desperately trying their hardest to conceal their intentions.

We walked passed them and climbed a ladder to a platform filled with hammocks and large satin cushions. The moon was out and the tide was at it its highest point. Down on the beach small waves lapped gently on the shore as it prepared to retreat, curling and recoiling in a single colourless motion. I could hear faint shouts of joy climbing above the cacophony in the distance as the beach quivered with suppressed excitement. The party was just getting underway and the mobs of warm bodies were gathering at the water's edge as they prepared to dig their toes into the dry sand.

A group of well-groomed Swedes sat cross-legged on the floor across from us. James insisted that we buy them a round of drinks, so we introduced ourselves and did our best to make polite conversation. It wasn't long until we resorted to inviting them down to the beach to dance. On the way down Sam spotted the tennis enthusiasts. I turned my head to stare at them. I thought about doubling back for a moment but I kept following the trail of blonde hair in front of us. By the time we got to the next bar Sam had failed to catch up but James and Kile were still in there, doing their best to entertain the girls. The dirty blonde who been talking to Sam gripped her beer tightly, and picked away at the label with her clear coated fingernails. She tossed her head around impatiently anticipating his arrival but he wasn't coming back. I wanted to stay but I couldn't leave Sam to fend for himself, and I excused myself as sheepishly as possible.

I found Sam in his usual spot, dancing away with the two girls. Sam grabbed me by the arm and shoved me between them and an emaciated boy with a chiselled jaw. "Austin, this is Jasmine.." he said as he pointed to the Brazilian, "and this is Lana."

I extended my hand to greet them. "Girls this is Austin. But you can call him Tintin," said Sam.

I shook my head at Sam, and the blonde responded by doing a strange half-curtsy.

Jasmine, it turned out, was not Brazilian but German and so was Lana. After they'd finished school they both spent 9 months slaving away to earn their freedom. Jasmine had worked in a designer boutique while Lana did her time stocking shelves and scanning barcodes in a national supermarket chain. Once they had enough money the escaped to Australia with their boyfriends. They bought a car and drove around the country, drifting from one job to the next. Their car eventually broke down somewhere on the coast and they couldn't afford to fix it. They ended up bartering with a greasy mechanic and they sold it for parts before booking the first outbound flight they could find.

"Oh and this is Phillip," said Jasmine "I'm so sorry, I'm just so bad with these introductions…" she giggled to herself. "He's a friend from back home. We used to work together at the Abercrombie and Fitch in Frankfurt. I couldn't believe it. I didn't even know he was here. Then this morning I was finishing my breakfast and I caught him walking down the street looking like a lost boy."

He definitely looked the part. He was threateningly good looking and he had the numbing vacant stare to go along with it. It was the kind of glazed indifference that sells better than sex. He looked almost scared. It was clear that he wasn't used to having an endless supply of freedom at his fingertips but it wouldn't take too long until he got sucked in like the rest of us.

"Isn't it such a small world…" said Jasmine with a pitiful smile.

"It sure is," said Sam.

We wandered through the crowds together and started to dance. Sam kept his eyes on Jasmine. She had was thin with emerald green eyes, and when she wasn't hiding behind a sensual pout, she was flashing her teeth through a tight-lipped smile that was deceptively inviting. Luckily for Sam her boyfriend had left her for another woman and their relationship had ended in disaster. Unfortunately Lana had her own chiseled specimen waiting for her back in Australia. I tried not to think about it, as I watched her swerve back and forth in short bursts of excitement. She looked so innocent and full of life with a kind of childish smile that made you forget where you are. It didn't help that she had a sensual habit of pulling a cigarette out of a soft pack of Lucky Strikes and purposefully smoking it like a Parisian prostitute. The way she pursed her lips as she exhaled was almost elegant, and the ease with which she automatically pushed and pulled the fag from her lips, with it pressed between her fingers, made her look younger than she actually was. After a while the happy couple rejoined us.

"What happened?" I asked James.

"Well, we couldn't fuck all seven of them," he said with a touch of melancholy pride in his voice. "One of them is still trying to hunt you down," he added nodding at Sam. "You might want to watch out."

I went to the bar to get a drink. I needed my fix. After a few days of wasting away in the sun, it was the only thing that would make me feel human enough to get through the night. The girls stood in front of us, kicking up sand into the night sky. They moved around us like moths dancing around a flame. Their skin glowed from the soak of the amphetamines and too many hours in the sun. It would all forgotten by the time the sun came up.

The music continued to shake through the air. It was nothing but a loudness – a cold empty loudness. This was debauchery at is most diluted and inane. The all night frenzies were loosening their grip and the charming cacophony was starting to fade along with it. But I was a glutton for punishment and I knew that somehow I would manage to stumble home at the end of the night, breathless, exhausted and begging for more.

The stars hung ominously over the bay as the night came to an end. We lost the girls in the crowd and we were left alone with the happy couple. We said our goodbyes and Sam promised them that we would wake up early to see them off. All they could do was shake their heads and smile as they walked down the beach with their arms around each other.

I woke up with the fan already struggling to beat away the heat that engulfed our shack. I put on some boxers and gave Sam a shake but he didn't budge. I went to the door to get some fresh air and noticed a piece of paper folded under on the ground. I grabbed it and held it up to the light:

> Well guys, it's certainly been a creepy few days. You seemed so peaceful lying there in bed we decided not to wake you.
>
> Just wanted to say how much we loved hanging out with you. We know how this meeting people travelling shit normally works but we hope that doesn't happen with you guys even though it probably will.
>
> Now that all that emo shit is out of the way, we hope the rest of your trip goes great. If you happen to be around at the end of the summer then we'd love to have you be the maids of honour at our wedding.
>
> Travel safe and party hard,

James and Kile

I lay back down in my bed and read the note over a couple times. The room was warm and it was hard to think. I smiled and folded the note up. I went over to Sam's bed and tucked the piece of paper under his pillow, then put on a bathing suit and went down to the beach to swim off the gin.

Eight

By the time Sam came down to the beach the ocean had disappeared. The tide had left behind a few dozen fishing boats that were slowly sinking into the sand. Swarms of colourful bikinis and hairless chests took advantage of the new territory, wandering amongst the boats as if they were part of a daring post-modern exhibition.

"You check your emails?" he asked.

I nodded.

"And..."

I shook my head the other way, "Nothing..."

"I guess no news is good news," he said cheerfully.

I shrugged, "I guess so..."

I was feeling anxious. It didn't help that I had been lying on a beach for seven days straight. I needed to do something to get the angst out of my system. With the tide out, the mile long sand bar had been transformed into an impromptu football pitch. I decided to join in one of the games while Sam stayed on the beach and watched on like an anxious housewife. By now he had perfected a concoction of painkillers and anti-depressants to get him through the day. He would start of with a Tramodol and a Valium. Once those had kicked in he would add a Paracetamol to the mix. And if things got really bad, he would top it all off a Robaxacet just for good measure. Washed down with enough beer, it was enough to make sure he would make it through the afternoon, so long as the sun went down before it all wore off.

Considering the usual state of the island during the day, the game was surprisingly full of life. There were players from all over and everyone yelled at one another in whatever language they could, deferring to English whenever a controversy arose. It felt good to let loose for a few hours but even with half the players already wasted, my body just couldn't keep up. It wasn't long until I was bent over on the sidelines covered in sand, panting so hard it made me want to be sick.

"Are you ok?" One of the chiseled Dutchmen asked.

"I'm fine," I said in between breaths. A few more desperate gasps. I took another deep breath. "This is great! But I think I'm dying..."

He let out a surly laugh and patted me on the back "Of course you are," he said as he ran back into the play. "We all are!"

I forced myself to play for another few minutes, running around like a madman with something to prove. I jumped in front of an errant shot and slid through the sand. It felt good to be recklessly sliding through the mud. I rolled my ankle going in for a ball and I was reduced to limping around out of a sad sense of pride. Luckily for me, the game came to an end just before I was about to quit.

Sam was gazing blissfully into oblivion when I came back. "Want a beer?" I asked, as I wiped wet clumps of sand off my back.

"Suuuure..." he moaned, unconcerned about how the words dribbled out of his mouth.

On my way back from the bar I spotted the girls hiding beneath pairs of thick-rimmed sunglasses. I went back and relayed the message to Sam, and he immediately snapped out his stupor.

"Well, what are we waiting for?"

We cut down towards the water before walking across the beach so that we could see their reactions as we approached. They were spread out on their towels with Phillip and his waxy stare.

"Hallo, we are happy to find you here," said Lana with a half-sarcastic grin.

"It sure looks like you were trying pretty hard," I joked.

Jasmine smiled, "It's true. This life is hard work... Lying in the sun all day and partying all night. I think maybe we need a vacation after we are finished here!"

Jasmine laughed, "If anyone deserves it, it's us."

"Well it's good to see that you are taking your work seriously," chuckled Sam.

"We are German," said Lana with a stern look, before she burst out laughing. "Nothing is too serious for us."

We spent the afternoon getting drunk on the sand with Sam sandwiched comfortably between Jasmine and Phillip. The poor boy was harmless, oblivious to what was going on around him. Sam didn't seem to care that he was even there. But despite his usual good humour, it was clear that he wanted him out of the picture sooner rather than later.

I turned over and looked at Lana. Her legs folded into two sets of pale peaks that rose pointlessly towards the sky. I tried not to stare but her skin looked so warm and inviting in the afternoon haze. Her breasts were small but firm and even in the scorching heat I could make out the outline of her nipples underneath her bikini. Her skin was pulled so tight against her bones that if her top somehow managed to fall off, the rounded crest of her apple-shaped breasts probably wouldn't flinch. I was in a trance when a soothing motherly voice interrupted.

"I'm sorry to bother you, but would I be able to borrow your lighter?"

She must have been sucked in by Lana's passive aggressive chain-smoking. I told her I didn't have one, while Lana fumbled through the sand, before handing her a yellow plastic lighter.

"Thanks," replied the voice which stalled unnecessarily on every vowel. I could just about make out her thin legs and blonde hair through the orange glare of the sun.

"I'm trying to quit but..." Of course; there's always a but, usually followed by a pointless life story. She was a middle-class zen-warrior – an au-pair from Sweden, travelling on a budget with more charm and goodwill than she knew what do with. She'd come here for a 'full cleanse' and now she was rewarding her hard work by letting her hair down for a few days. An old woman with tattered sandals came down to the beach, carrying a cooler full of beers. Sam flagged her down and counted out the heads.

"You want one?" he asked as he pulled more money out of his pocket.

"No thanks! I'm trying not to spend too much," she said coyly. "This island is so expensive compared to the rest of the country. It's crazy what people are willing to pay for a beer!"

Sam stared at her for a moment. "Don't worry. It's on me," he insisted.

She tried to politely decline but Sam wasn't going to give her the pleasure. He gave the woman a few bills and handed the girl a beer.

"Thank you. You're too kind," she blushed.

Sam turned his head towards her, "Don't thank me, thank Buddha or something like that…"

She rambled on until she was bored by the sound of her own voice and with the sun sinking behind the mountains in the distance, she wandered off to frolic on the dry sand.

Later that night we skipped the trip to the restaurant and went straight to the bar. We sat in the same seats that we had the night before. The waist high owner was behind the bar. He recognised us from the night before, "You are back," he smiled, "and you brought friends."

Sam smiled back and threw his arms up in the air, "What can I say we're hooked," Sam said smiling back at him.

"Well, you have come to the right place. Ook makes the best cocktails in town," he said.

"Who's Ook?" I asked.

"Who do you think?" he said, before grinning and waving both his hands at us. "Now, how many you like?"

I held up my fingers, "Four please."

The bartender turned away and Sam looked anxiously around the room, "Where's Phillip?"

Jasmine didn't even seem to notice that he was gone. "Oh," she said, "he's leaving fist thing in the morning. He went to pack but maybe he'll meet us later on."

Sam kept a blank look on his face and nodded.

"What about you?" he asked.

"We a few more weeks left still," Lana said. "A few days here, then back to the capital for a couple of nights." She paused as she tried to map it all out in her mind, "Then back to Australia."

She flashed a smile. She was thinking about what kind of trouble he was getting up to, praying that she had nothing to worry about. She turned to Jasmine looking for reassurance before looking down at the bar. "Only a few more weeks."

Ook dumped the mix from the blender into four cocktail glasses rimmed with salt. He stared at the girls with a furrowed brow.

"You have girlfriend now?" he grinned and nodded his head in approval. "Girlfriend is much better than boyfriend."

Sam and I looked at each other and laughed. "You'll have to ask them about that," I said.

The girls were still laughing, "As long as the drinks keep coming," joked Lana as she reached for one of the pink cocktails.

Jasmine barked at her in German and they started to squabble back and forth. When they were done Lana laughed and turned to us to apologise.

"Sorry," said Lana. "We were just talking about how much fun we had last night."

"No we weren't," Jasmine snapped.

Sam put his hands between them, but the girls ignored him. They finally stopped for a moment. Jasmine put her hand on Lana's shoulder and smiled. Sam handed them each a drink and they started to laugh again.

"What's so funny?" Sam asked.

"Oh nothing," sighed Lana.

Jasmine shoved Lana's shoulder. "Don't be such a drama queen! You know you miss Freiderich…" Jasmine shook her head before turning to me and Sam. "Don't mind her, it's just been a while since she's been laid."

"Was Sheisse machst du!" screamed Lana. Her cheeks went flush as she chirped at Jasmine, "You're one to talk!"

They started screaming at each other again until their cheeks started to glow. Sam slid his hands between them and tried to interrupt.

"Ladies, please. We're really not worth fighting over," said Sam in attempt to diffuse the situation. "If anything Ook is the man for the job. Look at those fucking cheekbones."

Ook stared at the girls and lifted his shirt up to expose his hairless chest. He rubbed his nipples and blew each of them a kiss and they burst out laughing. He continued to rub his stomach as he filled our glasses. We finished the first round and ordered another right away.

Every time I put my glass down, Ook was leaning over the bar with the bottle in his hand. I told him that we'd had enough, but every time I looked away he would fill our glasses with bright pink tequila. Eventually Ook started drinking with us and by the end of the night he was naked, except for a pair of oversized basketball shorts and a pair of shot glasses in each hand.

We stumbled out of the bar sometime after midnight. It wasn't long before we bumped into Patrick. His hands were full of flimsy black and white flyers which he waved around like miniature flags. The collar of his dust-covered tank top drooped down like a cheap pearl necklace, so that his hairless chest was completely exposed. He rocked back and forth at the entrance to the beach and his face sunk into a tanned shade of burnt cream that made him look like the ghost of Christmases yet to come.

"Hey guys, you're still here!" he said with a faint sound of hope in his voice.

"And now you have reinforcements." Patrick grabbed us both by the arms and whispered to us, "I don't know how you two pulled that off."

"Neither do we."

Patrick ran his fingers through his hair. "So where are you off to next?"

"We were thinking of heading South. We hear it's pretty peaceful down there."

"It's not a bad place to be. Just don't go too far or you'll end up in hostile territory." "Really?" asked Jasmine.

"Ya, they've just got some pretty nasty shit happening near the border. Muslims want to separate and set up their own fucking country. It's a fucking mess really. You know, same same but... Well, as long as you stay in the touristy areas you should be alright."

"I'm sure we can figure it out. We don't really want any trouble."

"So when are you leaving?"

"We're supposed to leave tomorrow, but..." I looked at Sam. "Well, you know how it is."

"I guess people just tend to lose track of time down here," said Patrick.

"It's the sun, it rots the brain right out of your head," I said.

Patrick smiled and shuffled quietly to the side, "So have you guys been able to find everything you were looking?"

Patrick may have been a mediocre car salesman but he was harmless. "What do you have to offer?"

He smiled at us without flinching.

"We have been looking to get a hold of some mushrooms," hinted Sam.

Patrick shook his head and flipped the hair out of his eyes. "You need to head East for that kind of shit." Before I could ask him where exactly he meant he offered an alternative proposition. "I've got some pills if you guys want."

"Really?"

"It's just some stuff I brought over with me on the plane."

"Are you out of your fucking mind?" I said. "They'll cut your goddamn hands off for that kind of shit!"

He grinned, exposing a row of perfectly polished teeth. "Give me some credit. They're just some prescription pills I have leftover from my travels. But if you mix them with some Red Bull and enough booze it'll keep you going all night long."

I had no desire to keep going all night long but what else were we supposed to do. I couldn't abandon Sam and now we had the girls to entertain. I was stuck on this island whether I liked it or not. The choice had been made for me the second I got off the plane. I would just have to suck it up and get on with it.

"I guess we could maybe we can take a couple off your hands," I told him.

Patrick pushed his hips out and rolled onto his toes. "I don't have them on me right now but I can bring you some tomorrow if that works for you..."

Sam shrugged his shoulders. "Well, we know where to find you."

Patrick rocked back on to his heels and wished us a goodnight before turning his attention to a brunette in a black bra. Part of me wanted to feel bad for him. The only way he could get through his days as a semi-coherent reprobate was by staying hopped up on some over the counter prescription garbage imported from Canada. But his charm didn't last and I was finding it harder and harder to have sympathy for someone who had given up a perfect life for this.

And for what? He had everything anyone could ever ask for waiting for him back home: free health care, a caring girlfriend, a successful career as a lawyer. Perhaps I was giving him too much credit. At the end of the day, he was just a piece of shit, and when he went back home he would force his shitty life on his shitty friends, and his shitty spineless girlfriend, and he would make a big name for himself in a shitty judicial system that rewards the kinds of shitty crooks that bend the rules to help crooks that are even bigger pieces of shit than they are, so that get away with all kinds of unfathomable horrible shit. And one day he would have shitty little kids that were raised to be just as shitty as he was; and so on and so forth until the end of time.

Nine

I was woken up by the sound of flip-flops clapping against the soles of calloused feet just outside the window. The clapping mixed in with the chorus of street vendors grumbling vigorously in an attempt to pawn off worthless trinkets to wannabe alcoholics. My body was wrapped in sweat-drenched sheets and my thighs rubbed against one another in the damp heat. I looked around the room. It seemed unfamiliar. There was no fan, and the single prison-sized window was barely ajar. I fumbled around under the sheets. I wasn't alone. I turned around and pressed myself against her. Her back was covered with cool beads of sweat. I peered over her shoulder to make sure it wasn't Lana. I saw the short brown hair and pint-sized nostrils and breathed a sigh of relief.

    I thought about getting up and sneaking out of the room. If I was lucky I might never see her again, but the chances of that happening grew slimmer the longer we stayed on the island. I put my arm around her and tried to think of something filthy to say but I drew a blank. She slid her hand over her hips with her eyes still closed, and gripped the back of my thigh. She pulled me closer towards her. Her skin was covered in a thin film of salt. Her cheeks wrapped firmly around me as the sweat rolled down my chest and onto her back. I thought of Lana. I wondered what she would think if she could see me now. She'd probably just laugh and roll her eyes. I thrust into her back and felt the damp rush between our bodies. She held me in place for a moment. Our bodies remained pressed firmly against one another. I pulled away and she pulled me back. The small puddle between us grew bigger as we slid back and forth. Then, in the dying the seconds I let go and slumped onto my back and the sheets grew cold and damp.

We spent the rest of the afternoon in bed, sweating and drowning out the sounds in the street with pathetic innuendos. By the time I went to have a shower, the sun was already going down again. I got dressed and let myself out. I walked down the road and the next thing I new I was on the beach. Sam was waiting for me in our usual spot with Lana and Jasmine on either side of him. He grinned at me and clapped his hands sarcastically as I walked towards them. "See girls, I told you he'd show up."

"Where the hell were you?" scowled Jasmine.

"Why? Were you worried?" I said in embarrassment.

Sam smiled, "Why would I be worried?"

"He was looking everywhere for you," interrupted Jasmine.

I glanced at her then turned to Sam.

"I was in some room just around the corner. Not really sure how that happened."

Sam laughed and looked over at Lana, "You were all over *her* until you found out she had a boyfriend."

I was dizzy and dehydrated and I felt like I was still drunk.

"I'm just glad you turned up," said Sam.

Jasmine crossed her arms and pouted at me, "He just got back from the hospital. And then he went to the prison."

Sam laughed, "I figured of all the places you might have ended up those were the best bets. Then I realized that you probably would have given them your real name so I started asking around for Tintin. They looked at me like I was fucking insane."

I laughed, "Really?"

He nodded, and the girls smiled approvingly.

"I was going to check the morgue next but I don't think they have one of those here."

"Well, hopefully we don't stick around long enough to find out."

Sam looked over at Jasmine and cleared his throat, "Speaking of which," he turned to me and smiled, "I took care of the room."

"What do you mean?"

"I went down and had a nice chat with the Northerner. We're

booked in for two more nights."

I smiled, "You sneaky bastard."

I was sad to see the happy couple go but Sam was right. The girls were good company and they were willing to put up with our shit without much of a fuss. Things weren't really going to get much better than this and they would probably give us exactly what we were looking for all along: just a short break from reality before we could finally get on with our lives.

...

Ook was noticeably drunk when we showed up to the Banana Bar. We took our places at the bar and he proceeded to line up tumblers of tequila on the rail, before mixing a round of strawberry margaritas. He filled our glasses as quickly as we could empty them, and he took turns serving and swallowing drinks from the other side the bar. It wasn't long until his shirt was off and he started putting on a show for the girls. They laughed at the sight of him gyrating with two hands on his miniscule potbelly, much to the delight of Sam and I. The routine continued on for a few hours until we were all happily slumped over the bar clinking glasses and pounding the top of the bar with our open palms.

An Englishman with a blonde coif and Bermuda shorts appeared from behind the girls while Ook was in the midst of his routine. He asked what we were drinking then ordered himself a double gin and tonic. He latched onto Sam's basterdised accent, which had been polished from too many years of living abroad. He asked him what he was doing here. Before Sam even had the chance to open his mouth the Brit had already started reminiscing about the first time he came here. By his count this was has third visit and he wasn't even thirty yet.

His first trip happened the year he finished school. "Of course, that was long before anyone was shooting movies and getting book deals," he pronounced boastfully. He came back once more during his summer vacation with some friends he had met at university. On their second visit they knew all the tricks of the trade. They discovered new places and revisited old ones and by the end, they went back with another pocketful of unforgettable memories. When it was all said and done, he was offered a job with one of the big four accounting firms in London, where he made a lot money on the boom and bust of the late Millennium. Now he was back for his self-titled 'victory lap'.

His rosy cheeks inflated into pink balloons every time he spoke. They would grow bigger and bigger, and it looked like they were going to burst until finally he drew a breath with a gasping exclamation. Occasionally, I would catch out a few emphatic phrases through his boisterous lisp. "Sure it takes a bit of luck mate. But at the end of the day some people have it and some don't."

I took a sip of my drink as he continued to ramble on about his worthless mountain of accomplishments. "But mate, I never forget that I would never be where I am today if it hadn't been for this place."

I turned away and focused on Lana. She seemed to laugh at everything he said. The more I noticed it, the more impossible it became to judge whether her laughter was genuine or just a sweet attempt to fill the silence.

The Brit interjected and offered to buy a round of drinks. I declined. He replied that he had enough money to fund the rest of all our trips combined, including the girls' return to Australia. I got the impression that he was telling the truth and that if we questioned him enough we could probably get him to do it just to spite himself. I shrugged him off and he soon disappeared and to a table of girls next to us. As soon as he left, Ook lined up a round on the house and I continued to drink myself into a stupor.

By the time we bumped into Patrick he was already a mess. His hair was damp and he had his arm slung around some dark-haired stranger who looked young enough to need a babysitter. He was excited – almost too excited.

"Hey! You're late!" We all looked at one another in confusion. "I'm just kidding, there's no such thing."

I hated to admit it but he was right. Time was worthless down here. The only really commodities were people. Time wasn't worth shit unless there were bodies to fill the hotels, and the brothels and the beaches.

"Sorry if we kept you waiting. We were just having a few margaritas with Ook," said Sam.

"Sounds fancy," he shrugged without an ounce of facetiousness in his voice. He lived on the beach and he worked on the beach and he played on the beach, and the thought of breaking his habit must have been growing more terrifying by the day.

"I've got something for you," he said, before turning to his concubine. "You'll have to excuse me for just one second." He reached into his pocket and dropped a small ball of tinfoil in Sam's hand. Sam handed him a purple bill and we left him with his girl on the side of the road. Once we were out of view, Sam pulled out the pills and handed me one. He stared at them in his hand as I swallowed one. "Wait a second…"

"What?" I asked as I took a sip of beer.

He shook his head, "This is just Focussin."

"So..."

"My brother used to take have to this shit for his ADD."

I laughed. "No wonder Patrick's always bouncing off the walls. He should probably stop selling his meds."

I didn't realize how wasted I was until we got down to the beach. The air was filled with the thick stench of teen spirit, and the beach overflowed with the painted limbs of overly sexualised corpses. I swam through the packs of warm bodies, alert and unassuming. In a matter of seconds I was surrounded by tribes of naked bodies drenched in sweat. They writhed violently between the waves of music as it rattled through the trees towards the ocean. There was no stopping them. Every night we gathered in front of the tiny hamlet in the middle of the jungle, expecting something to change, hoping for something magical. But the real magic was in the constant pounding and sweating that drove us all to the brink without ever pushing us over the edge. It didn't matter how many of them fled for the mainland in the morning. There was always another regiment of morally defunct hedonists waiting at the dock by the time the sun came up.

Sam and Lana danced together while Jasmine stood off to the side making subtle movements towards him. Sam played along. His eyes were wild. They were dissecting every inch of her body, and once Jasmine noticed, she let her usual deadpan smile give way to a more convincing gaze.

I closed my eyes for a moment and pretended I was somewhere else. I could have been anywhere, Berlin, Cancun, Miami. I could have been dancing the night away with strangers on any beach in the world but when I opened my eyes I was still there, with Sam and thousands of other savages thrashing recklessly into the night. My pupils began to dilate and the skin between my fingers turned clammy. My eyes struggled to process the perverted thoughts that were running through my head. I worried that I might look out of place. But I was just being indulgent. No one even noticed I was there. I opened my mouth to scream but nothing came out. I stood there dancing with my mouth wide open, grimacing and squinting in the dark, and shaking like a madman in an attempt to shake the nervous feeling from my bones. I felt hopeless. I was cracking up.

I turned to Sam, "Give me another one of those things."

"Are you sure?" he asked with a slur. "I don't really think they're doing anything."

"I don't care," I said excitedly. "Just give them to me."

He handed me a pill and I tossed it into my gaping jaw. Lana stared at me with her awkward blue eyes across the sand as I took a deep breath. As soon as she came close to me I latched on for dear life. Her hands rested effortlessly on my shoulders and we danced together for a while without saying a word. I slid my hand down the small of her back. I could feel the damp soak of sweat bleeding through her cheap cotton shirt. I let my hand slide further down, over the tattered hem of her cut off shorts that were wedged firmly between the well-rounded folds of skin between her legs. I closed my eyes and hoped she couldn't feel me throbbing against the inside of her thigh. She kept pulling me closer. The salty stench of her skin filled my nostrils and I felt a sharp pang at the bottom of my gut. It felt like I was stuck in a terrible dream. I tried to stop focussing on the moistened curves of her body but I couldn't take my eyes off her. I was helpless. I wanted to strip her down and throttle her in front of thousands of strangers like a wild boar.

I couldn't let this drag on. I had to break free. I pulled away and started to walk down the beach.

"Where are you going?" she asked.

I shook my head and kept stumbling away from her, "I just need to get some fresh air."

She grabbed my hand and stared at me with her blurry eyes. "But we're already outside," she laughed.

"I know…" I said, "I know, I just…" I pulled my fingers across the small of her back and turned towards the mountains.

I kept walking until the noise of the crowds faded. When I got to the far end of the beach I turned back and stared at the swarms of flesh flickering in the cheap fluorescent lights. The mob filled the entire beach. There wasn't a single bare patch of sand visible in front of the ramshackle discos that thundered on monotonously under the dull glint of the stars.

I staggered up to a decrepit mud hut to get a drink. There was a small stage with a dozen grown men singing karaoke in bras and frizzy wigs, with mismatched mini skirts covered in silver and purple glitter. Sweaty locals mingled with hairy-chested fratboys on stage, urging them on for their own amusement. I felt like I was going to be sick. I ordered another drink but the anti-social thoughts kept creeping into my head like bad memories of crimes I'd already committed. I kept drinking hoping to numb my senses. Just try not to think about it.

I'm so horny – but that's ok my will is good...

I tried to blink but my eyes wouldn't focus. My eyelids were peeled back and pinned in place by a week's worth a legal speed and booze and an overdose of knockoff prescription pills meant for brain dead delinquents and social rejects. I started to panic. In any other part of the world they would have laughed at me. To them I was nothing more than a degenerate, a pervert, a hopeless romantic. But on this island I was just another would-be king, manically fumbling through the crowd with purposeful sense of entitlement. Another beer; and another. Eventually I began to feel normal again. I had never felt so alive in my life and it felt fucking horrible.

Jasmine was draped over Sam when I came back down the beach. I looked everywhere for Lana, before prying myself between Sam and Jasmine's sweaty faces. I asked him where she had gone and Sam whispered in my ear that she left because she thought I had run away. I pushed him away and started up at the top of the hill. I had to get away from the beach. I stumbled up the main road and stopped to get a slice of pizza from one of the plywood shacks. I grabbed a bottle of chilly and doused the soggy crust with blotches of red paste, and rammed the whole thing into my mouth at once. As I was swallowing I inhaled a cloud of spice up into the back of my nose. It stung like hell and I started convulsing – sneezing and tearing up and rubbing my eyes and nose – which only made matters worse.

"Give me a can of coke!" I growled at the old man behind the counter.

I cracked it open and started to walk home with tears in my eyes. I passed the massage parlours and did my best to ignore their taunts.

"Massage... You want massage... Big boy, big boy, come here... Make you happy!...

I kept walking, trying to block them out. The bungalow was only a few hundred yards away. If I could just make it there in time I could lock myself in the bathroom and beat myself to death like a trigger-happy teenager.

Ten

I woke up feeling strung out and anxious. It was still early in the morning and for once the room felt cool. Sam still wasn't in. He was probably loving it up with Jasmine: having the fucking time of his life.

I tied to go back to sleep but I was restless. I'd failed to take care of my raging erection when I got home and now I was seething. I went to the bathroom and tried to squeeze one out. I tried to think of something, anything, Lana, Jasmine, the Swedish mermaid but nothing stuck. I tried tightening my grip; switching hands; faster, slower; but my imagination was shooting blanks. There was only one answer: I was going to have to put matters into someone else's hands.

I put on a pair of shorts and some dark rimmed sunglasses. I pulled a baseball cap down over my eyes and rushed down hill. The sun was already starting to creep out above the mountains and a few restaurants were already opening up for breakfast. I walked passed the yellow-toothed local whore and the thick curtain of cloth that covered the rolls of fat underneath. She had been taunting me for days now but I wasn't going to give her the satisfaction of making her think that her relentless prodding had finally worn me down. There were dozens of massage parlours on the main road. They all looked like so clean and clinical, like hospital operating rooms. Each one had large floor to ceiling windows and long tubular lights that hung over beds with paper-thin curtains for privacy. None of them were going to do.

I turned down a back alley and paced up and down in front of a small parlour with dark crimson drapes. There was a woman outside smoking a cigarette in a nightgown beside a wooden sign with prices painted in big purple letters. On my third pass she finally propositioned me.

"Massage?"

I still felt drunk, and the words came flying out of my mouth without even thinking, "Happy ending?" I muttered sheepishly while avoiding eye contact.

"Of course," she grinned without hesitation. "We give you happy ending. I give you good price; massage and happy ending."

I watched her lips as she mouthed the words. I couldn't stand the thought of lying there while she stroked my back, waiting impatiently for her to flip me over. I needed my release and I needed it now. "No massage, just happy ending."

"No massage?"

I shook my head.

She thought I was trying to be cheap. "Same price…"

"Sure, same price," I said without hesitation.

She smiled and stubbed her cigarette out on the wall. I followed her in and she directed me behind a dark red curtain. I stripped down naked and lay on my back with the muscles in my thighs clenched tight. The room smelled of cheap oil and scented candles. I panted with my hands across my chest as I waited for the inevitable. She came in and whispered something to me under her voice. She feigned a smile as she leaned over me. As soon as she grabbed me I fell back on the bed in shock. I stared at the ceiling fan as it sputtered over top of the cracked plaster ceiling. She had a firm grip and thick calluses between the palms of her hands and her fingers. The dead skin felt rigid as it slid up and down in an efficient monotonous rhythm. Every time she squeezed I recoiled in delight. She started talking and I closed my eyes. I tried to pretend I was somewhere else but I couldn't stop focussing on her weathered grip as she slid her hand up and down. She wasn't a girl – she was a woman, with a husband, three kids and dinner to put on the table at the end of the day. I wanted her to stop but I was frozen stiff. She sensed the tension building through the dead skin on her fingers. She squeezed back methodically as she started to stroke harder and faster.

I tried to stop thinking about her family. I tried to stop thinking about what she was going to cook them for dinner. I tried to stop thinking about why the hell I was here in the first place! I tried to stop thinking… Stop thinking! Stop thinking! Stop! Stop! Stop!

Stop…………..

It was too late.

She tossed a wet napkin on top of me and wiped me down like she was changing a diaper. I felt empty as I went to reach for my pants. She smiled at me with vague indifference and let out a patronising laugh. "All better…" I smiled back at her and rushed back to the room with my tail between my legs.

Sam was waiting for me on his bed. "You go for a swim?"

I shook my head and lay down on the bead. "No."

"Emails?"

"No." He was running out of guesses.

"I caved," I whispered sheepishly.

He looked at me without flinching. I told him what had happened, trying my best to sound embarrassed. When I was done he let out a big laugh, "Did you go to that crazy whore with the yellow teeth?"

"Give me some credit."

"Well then what's the big deal?"

I tried to think of something to say but nothing came out. Sam tried to offer me some kind of consolation.

"Don't worry about it. If things with Jasmine keep going the way they are, I'll be next."

I took a cold shower and we went to meet the girls on the beach. For some reason Lana kept smiling at me and I did my best not to look her in the eye. As soon as we sat down the girls started to complain that they were bored. They said they were sick of sitting around on the beach. They wanted something to do; something different. We suggested taking them on Captain Bob's magical extravaganza but it was late in the afternoon and the ship had already left.

"Well what do you want to do then?" I asked.

They threw out a few uninspired suggestions. It was starting to look like we were going to spend another day lazing around in our usual spot. I lay back in the sand and watched the swimmers enjoying what was left of the tide. Then Jasmine spoke up, "Maybe we should rent one of those boats or somesing."

We talked it over for a moment. With a bit of water still left in the bay we decided to make a run for it. We bartered for a few plastic kayaks and we filled them up with 6 bags of ice and as many bottles of beer as we could carry. As we rolled the boats down the sand the owner rolled his eyes at us and pointed at his clunky wristwatch.

"Two hour! You come back," he said pointing up at the sky. "Storm coming!"

I could just about make out a patch of grey on the horizon, "Don't worry, we come back," I reassured him.

We dragged the kayaks past the wooden long-tails that were pitched on their side in the low tide. When the water was deep enough, we hopped on and paddled towards the bright blue gap where the fleshy mountains pinched off the entrance to the island. Beyond the gap the water opened up towards the horizon punctuated with deserted islands. We drifted with the tide until we got to a white sand beach carved into the outer face of the rock. We paddled towards it until we were carried on the crests of the small waves that crashed gently against the shore.

The beach was inhabited by a few dozen tourists who were eagerly feeding a family of monkeys out of the palms of their hands. We pulled our floating bar up onto the beach. The girls rushed up to a local man in a white shirt who was selling bananas to feed to the apes. They got in line behind the other tourists and waited their turn to feed them. Sam and I sat drinking in the sand as the same scene repeated itself over and over again: a small troupe of monkeys approached the zookeepers feigning curiosity until they were within reach. Then another few would circle behind them and snatch at the fruit before scurrying away amidst a roaring cackle. The girls were not amused by the game and they soon walked back to the boat as the monkeys all laughed in unison.

"I don't think I like them," said Jasmine. "They belong in a zoo."

A grey blanket of clouds crept over us as we lay with our feet in the waves. The sun was fighting to outrun the singular silky cloud, but by the time we left the sun had yet to close the gap. On the way back, we were greeted by a pounding rhythm rising from the beach. It wasn't the usual late night grind that was served up to us night after night. It was a loud and monotonous rhythm without any of the usual prefabricated harmonies copy and pasted on top. It almost sounded like the bay was filling with the roar of thunder, but there was no sign of lightning. The bass echoed down the bay as we neared the beach. It was still early for the party to be starting up, even by the island's standards. If there was one thing that always on time it was the bars. But this was different. There was nothing but a beat, played at just the right tempo, at exactly the right pitch, pounding monotonously over and over again. Just one beat banging on monotonously without interruption with the occasional slur of a high hat just for good measure.

    We pulled our kayaks onto the sand and followed the sound of the beat to the far end of the beach. The shoreline was still dotted with devoted sun worshipers, sprawled out in the customary position on their towels, praying for the death of the single cloud that was slowly starting to engulf the skyline. There was no one dancing, and no one was paying attention to the short man with a moustache and a military haircut, who was concentrating on the music through a pair of headphones and a series of computers. We made our way onto the rubber slabs that were laid out over the sand to serve as an impromptu dance floor. We started to jump up and down in a circle. The beat kept driving on as the sky continued to fade into a warm shade of grey. The tempo didn't change, and the man with the moustache controlling the music was doing his best to make sure that it stayed that way. Then, without missing a beat, the sky opened up. The rain came down hard and fast. Thick globs of water fell like stones, pelting the few hundred people that were still on the beach. They began to scramble, trying to keep their cell-phones and designer towels from getting wet. Within minutes the beach was empty and we were left to dance alone in the rain.

    The music mixed in with the sound of the rain as it clattered against rooftops, skin, and sand, producing a cold metallic orchestra and my nostils filled with the smell of damp skin and sand. I could see Lana laughing from behind the beads of water that flung themselves from the tips of her hair as she shook her head back and forth. Tiny puddles formed in the divots on the plastic and the water rose around the edges of our feet and we kicked water up at one another and stomped in the puddles to the rhythm of the beat. After 45 minutes the rain let up and the graying clouds passed out of sight. The girls were soaking wet and we threw our arms around them and let out a wild shout. It felt good to be wet and cold, and without a goddamn care in the world. The beat pounded on and the beach was empty. Even with the music still thundering along in the background the air was quiet. For the first time all trip, the island felt peaceful.

Eleven

I had a long cold shower before heading to the bar. On our way there, I stopped in front of one of the restaurants that was showing its nightly back-catalogue of classic American films. It was a gruesome war movie that I recognized from when I was a child. I stopped to watch it as Sam walked ahead. It was the scene where Martin Sheen, war correspondent and future president of the United States, is travelling up the river in a gunboat, on a mission to assassinate a well-fed Marlon Brando, who has gone insane and raised his own private militia to defend an abandoned trading post in the jungle against the American's imperial invasion.

"What's up chief?" he asks.

The dark-skinned boat captain speaks up in an authoritative Midwestern accent. "Junk boat captain… We're going to take a routine check…"

"Well let's forget routine now, n' let em' go," Sheen insists.

"These boats are running supplies through this delta captain… I'm a gonna take a look."

"Chief my mission has priority here! Hell, you wouldn't even be in this part of the river if it wasn't for me."

"Until we reach our destination captain, you're just on for the ride."

The boat approaches and the soldiers start barking orders in English to a group of local fisherman. No one on the boat understands what's going on. A man in a wide-brimmed hat tries frantically to diffuse the situation. All of sudden one of the soldiers snaps.

Shots fired! Shots fired. Bullets riddle through bags of rice and bodies. "Everyone's fucking dead."

One of the peasants tries to get up, she's screaming and crying. She has a look of pity on her face.

"She's still breathing, she's alive!" yells one of the men.

The captain wipes the sweat from his face. "Well go on then… Help her on to the boat."

An anxious Martin Sheen takes a deep breath and pulls a pistol from his hip. *Bang! Executive decision – fucking bullet right in the head:* "I told you not to stop. Now let's go."

Ook and Abel were both waiting for us behind the bar. We were the only ones there and they served us round after round until we were cross-eyed. Ook tried to keep us amused by telling us the same jokes that he had been telling us every night since we had first wandered into the bar. We smiled and went along with the routine as he continued to pry us full of booze. When we finally couldn't take anymore, we stumbled down to the beach, drunk out of our minds.

By now the thought of having to stumble along with the rest of the crowd had become unbearable. There were no longer any breathtaking moments of pure ecstasy, or climactic eruptions of joy and the music had been reduced to a nagging rumble that slipped through the gaps in the trees like the sound of a streetcar grinding to a halt on frozen winter tracks. Occasionally there would be the hyena shriek of a drunken American girl that was getting ready to remove her top to the delight of the lucky few that were already rubbing up against her, and barely a night passed by without the grunt of a proud rugby player trying to muscle a school of floozies into the water as they pretended to put up a fight. But eventually those too slipped into the manufactured subway soundscape of the beach.

If it hadn't been for the girls we would have already lost our grip on reality. Sam was certainly in better shape than I was. He had managed to trick himself into thinking that he was falling in love, and Jasmine was happy to let him go on bashing his brains against the same futile pair of perfectly formed breasts. Lana had only continued to grow restless as the days dragged on, and she was dragging me down with her.

As the bars were closing down for the night, I found myself at a table with two dirty blondes wearing dresses made out of light woven fabrics, with symmetrically shaped earrings that dangled from intricate gold chains. They looked out of place, and the more I thought about it, the more I realised that it was probably what had attracted me to them in the first place. I tried to convince myself that I was talking to them to cure my homesickness, and for a moment it almost worked. But they were dry and tedious and their twisted sense of self worth made me remember why I left London all those years ago.

After a while, Sam stumbled onto the wooden terrace. "Tintin, there you are, I've been looking everywhere for you"

"I've just been talking to these two lovely ladies."

He looked them up and down and nodded in approval. "You want a drink?"

I didn't want one – I needed one. But before I could answer one of the girls raised her voice. "Who are you?" she said in a familiar condescending tone that made my skin crawl. I should have just gotten up and left with Sam. Instead I decided to make desperate a desperate attempt to smooth things over, "Don't mind him he's in love with a German."

Sam ignored my comments and set his sights on the girl. "Who the fuck are *you*?"

Shit, this wasn't good. I didn't want things to get out of hand. But all he really did was say what I should have said when I tried to cozy up to them in the first place: *'Who the fuck are you?'* So succinct; so effective. But I had managed to let my imagination get the best of me.

"Who is this is asshole? Do you know him?"

I tried to stay as calm as possible, "He's my friend, the one I was telling you about. He's harmless."

But Sam wasn't going to let it slip, "Ya, I'm his friend, and I wanted to know if he needed a beer. Is that a problem?"

It shouldn't have been. But girls weren't going to be talked to like that. One of them turned to me and chirped at me in her charming accent, "Do you *know* him?"

I didn't have long to think. In the end Sam rescued me from my dilemma, "Look, I just want to buy my friend a fucking drink. Do you have a fucking problem with that?"

"You need to leave *now*," shrieked one of the dirty blondes.

"I'm not going anywhere until I get a drink for me and my friend,"

Sam barked back.

As soon as the words flew out of Sam's mouth, the other girl snapped her fingers and yelped something over her shoulder. All of a sudden, a pair of shirtless tattooed thugs stepped out from behind the bar. I looked down at one of their hands and saw his fingers twitching. They had been looking forward to this moment all night. The taller one with long hair looked back and a pack of angry figures started to emerge from the shadows behind him.

Sam hadn't noticed the gathering troops. I got up from my seat and grabbed him by the shoulder and mumbled some half-assed apology as I backed away into the thinning crowd. I didn't bother looking back to see if they were following us. Sam put his arm around me as we walked away.

"What the hell happened back there? Can't a man buy his friend a drink in this town?"

"I don't think they liked the look of you."

He grinned and squinted his eyes "Of course they didn't! What a bunch of backwards whores. Bunch of fucking whores…" he said as he looked back at them. I tugged him towards the path and walked a little faster.

"Where are the girls anyways?" I asked.

"They went to bed a while ago."

"Why didn't you go with them?"

"It wasn't up to me. Besides, I couldn't leave you behind to get shanked by those crazy whores all on your own."

I let out a quick burst of laughter. "I don't know what I'd do without you."

As we walked down the path away from the beach, we bumped into Abel.

"Hey guys, what's up?"

"Nothing much, just had a run with a few locals."

"I hope you guys weren't looking for trouble, because if you look hard enough you'll find it."

"No, just talking to some girls. But their boyfriends didn't take to kindly to that."

"Local girls?"

"No some holier-than-thou debutantes, who seem to think they're a pretty big deal," said Sam.

"Ya, we get a lot of that down here. They're just fetishists looking for a cheap thrill. Stuck up bitches who got everything they ever wanted in life except for daddy's love."

I laughed and brushed the hair out of my eyes, "Seems, pretty fucking ironic to me."

"Well they can only go so far. It's not like some chick who's been used to credit lines and foie gras is going to give it all up to go live with a village of cannibalistic tribesmen in the mountains," he shrugged and let out a baritone chuckle at the same time. "You just have to be careful. It doesn't take too long on an island this small before you end up finding trouble. All the drinking and sun with nothing to do all day can take its toll on a man. It's inevitable. Just imagine how it affects someone who's been here their whole life and will probably never leave. Especially when he sees a bunch of punks pissing and shitting all over his home like it's a Mexican brothel."

He was right, except the island might as well have been a Mexican brothel.

I shook my head, "I don't know how you do it…"

He let out a slightly more pronounced chuckle, "Don't get me wrong, I don't want to spend the rest of my life here but as far as I'm concerned I don't really have a home. There's no way I can go back to Washington, and there' no fucking way I'm going back to Jamaica. I guess I don't really have anywhere to go." He paused for a second. "Sure, I've had a gun pulled on me once or twice and I've had a 12 year old kung-fu junky try and shank me with a rusty blade, but for the most part I just keep to myself and take it as it comes."

"I guess you're just lucky."

He shrugged his shoulders and his dreads bobbed up then fell back down again. "Maybe." He thought for a moment, "But I'm not the first, and I certainly hope I'm not the last."

He seemed content to leave it at that and changed the subject, "You want to come down to the beach and smoke a joint?"

I raised my hand, "No thanks, I think we'll cut our losses for the night. But we'll see you tomorrow."

"Suit yourselves," he sighed, as he put the wrist-sized spliff into his mouth and strolled away in the opposite direction.

When we got home I lay in bed, staring at the fan, thinking about Abel. He could have ended up on any one of these god-forsaken islands scattered across the equator, but for some reason he had ended up here. I'm sure it all made sense to him and deep down inside I knew he was right, but I still couldn't figure it out. Thoughts started creeping into my head. I found it hard to concentrate. I clearly wasn't going to solve this problem right now. Even if I wanted to I would have to decide what the problem was in the first place.

Rule number 1: Don't ask questions you don't already know the answers to.

I turned my face over onto my pillow and squeezed it tight. The curtains were being pulled into the room by whimpering gusts of the fan as it rotated back and forth along the wall. I tried to drown out the voices by repeating the motto in my head. It was nagging – a constant nagging – and I couldn't make it go away. My thoughts were growing louder. Constant nagging thoughts. My thoughts were so loud I couldn't hear my mouth. The noise kept building inside until finally my brain took mercy on me and shut itself down, and I drifted off without a care.

Twelve

The fan was combing over my bare feet with varied intensity at 25-second intervals, teasing me with the promise of comfort, before turning its back on me again. When the flow of air peeked, it was just about enough to keep me from feeling dizzy. The rest of the time, I might as well have been sleeping under a heat lamp in a ditch. I went out to the porch to have a thought. Sam was sitting in the wicker chair reading his book. Beads of sweat were already clinging to his chest, which was gradually turning to an indigenous shade of umber. The air was the thickest it had been since we landed and I had to take a big gulp to get my first hit of oxygen for the day.

"Couldn't sleep," he said without turning around, "I had a dream that I was drowning. Then I woke up and realised that I was just choking on this infernal air."

He wiped the sweat from his forehead with the back of his forearm.

"Maybe it's a sign," I said.

Sam looked up from his book and stared at the horizon before quickly turning his attention back to his book. "Maybe."

Little was said over breakfast. Lana's cheeks were now permanently flush from the sun, and there was no evidence that she had spent a handful of debauched staying up all night, raving away like a madwoman. Jasmine looked just as healthy as she hid behind her usual early morning smile. She spent the meal looking back and forth between Sam and her feet, while Lana pushed her eggs around the plate with her fork. I worried we might have done something that could have soured the mood the night before. I tried to spool together the reels of tape inside my head. Nothing. It may have been our last day together but it would be a shame to leave things and such an empty note.

The silence continued, interrupted by occasional bouts of nervous laughter, until our waiter was clearing our table. Lana uncrossed her legs and spoke up as the last plate was pulled away.

"We were supposed to be leaving tomorrow," she said. "Our flight leaves next week. And we need to get to the capital before then…"

"Don't do it. It's a fucking zoo." I interrupted. I stopped my train of thought for a moment. "Well, this place is a zoo… the capital is more of an industrial 3rd world safari. Either way you're fucked."

Lana tried to continue. "I know…"

"You might as well have stayed in Germany," Sam barged in. He tried to sound light-hearted but it was clear he meant what he said.

Jasmine continued where Lana had left off. "But we have been having a great time with you. It seems a shame to end the trip this early." She stalled and looked at Sam.

"We were going to go the capital, but…" She looked at Lana before looking back at both of us, "We wanted to know if we could join you for a while."

Sam started to go red before she finished her sentence. We'd put on a good show so far and the girls seemed to buy it, but I was worried about how much longer we could keep up the charade. Sam took a big gulp and tried to wipe the anxious look from his face.

"What about the capital?" he asked. "What happened to shopping and temples?"

They both giggled, "We can leave if you like. But we're just having so much fun and we thought it would be nice to spend a few more days with you. That is, if we're not intruding."

"Of course not," Sam protested quickly. If they hadn't brought it up, we probably would have just ended up stuck on this island waiting for someone else to rescue us. "It sounds like a great idea. Right Tintin?"

I nodded and smiled reluctantly. "I guess we might as well end things on a high note."

"It's settled then," said Jasmine as she put her hand on Sam's thigh. "Besides, we can always go shopping when we get home."

We spent the rest of the afternoon down by the water, planning out where we would go next. There wasn't a cloud in the sky, and now that the storm had passed, the beach was full of life again. A flock of seagulls glided carelessly in the blue space between the escarpments at the end of the bay. Lana lay in the sand, patiently smoking a cigarette and watching the birds as they came in to peck away at the scraps soggy pizza crusts that had been left behind the night after a night of mediocre debauchery. As soon as they left she lit another cigarette. She smoked it slowly, enjoying each drag more than the next.

I kept watching her tiny dancer's lips as they spewed out thick clouds of smoke. I looked for a twitch or a sigh but the only sign of life were the small dimples buried in the corners of her mouth. She was happy – happy to be here – happy to be anywhere. Anything was better than the tedious repetition of scanning barcodes and stocking shelves in a dimly lit warehouse. I was half passed out when I heard her hovering at my feet. "I'm going to get some ice-cream. Anybody want to come?"

Jasmine jumped off her towel and walked off with her. I turned to Sam once they left, "What the hell are we going to do with these girls?"

"What do you mean? They want to follow us…"

I fingered through the salty residue on my scalp with the tips of my fingers, "I know they do. What are we going to do about it?"

"What can we do? We're here anyways, we might as well enjoy this while it lasts. When's the last time you had two German girls wanting to follow you half way around the world? Just think about that for a second. Look at where we are right now!"

I shrugged my shoulders, "I just figured it would be nice to have a bit of a break. Maybe spend a few days away from all this madness."

"What better way to get away from all this than to have two German ladies distracting us in a tropical island paradise."

It wasn't exactly the answer to our problems, but I couldn't really argue with his logic. The girls were a welcome distraction and they were doing a good job of keeping up morale. More importantly, they made it easier to forget about the happy couple. They may not have been as entertaining but they didn't have to be. As long as they were laughing or pouting, or at least within arm's reach, they made it easier to get through the day, and that was good enough for now.

Just then, the girls came back with ice cream dripping down their wrists and a fistful of beers. "Were you just talking about us?"

Sam smiled at Jasmine, "Of course not. We were just planning on where we were going to take you."

The sun dipped behind the edge of the island and Sam and I trekked back up to our bungalow. It had been almost ten days since we'd moved in. The room was littered with the empty glass bottles, plastic jugs of water and sweat stained clothes piled up around our beds. The stagnant pool across the way had been replenished by all the rain in the last few days and in the darkness it seemed like it was about to overflow. I could hear the swarms of mosquitoes' buzzing in approval and it wouldn't be long until the crickets joined in.

The heat rose into the night sky, sucking the stuffiness out of the room and replacing it with a humid breeze. The mosquitoes swarmed as I collapsed onto the mattress. The sand crumbled off my feet and onto the sheets. They hadn't been changed since we arrived and the mix of dirt and sunscreen had left them stained in a murky shade of brown. I used my big toe to scratch the scabs on one foot then switched to the other. No matter how well we hid, they always managed to get our feet. I closed my eyes and pulled my head under the blood stained sheets, pretending that the prick of the mosquito was just a figment of my imagination.

…

We woke up a few hours later and headed down to the Banana Bar. Ook greeted us with a grin and a pair of margaritas. It was still early but the bar still seemed more hollow than usual. I felt like a leather-skinned pensioner who was busy getting over his mid-life crisis in the Keys. I was starting to see why someone like Bob settled into a place like this. If you played it right, you could live a quiet enough life keeping mostly to yourself, occasionally poaching a few lonely bottom feeders for company and extra income.

It wasn't long before the girls showed up in matching pairs of tattered jean shorts. Lana seemed less boyish than she had before. Her cheeks were full and her tiny breasts punched emphatically out of her loose fitting tank-top. Ook kept pouring us cocktails, which became gradually more lethal as the night dragged on. After six rounds, it became harder and harder to keep my eyes off her, as she stirred her drink with a yellow straw. My hands reached for the edge of the bar, looking for something to hold on to. Sam was still standing tall on the edge of his seat. I locked my eyes on him and waited for him to stare back. He had a magical glint in his eye. He cocked his head back and forth between the girls, then back at Ook. They all seemed to be smiling and laughing amongst themselves, but I couldn't make out what they were saying above all the noise in my head. I slumped on the bar and glared at them. The girls were supposed to fix everything but they were only delaying the inevitable. And what the hell were we going to do once they left? Another island, another beach, another pair of perfectly tanned tits to keep us from losing our minds...

My head filled with violent thoughts. I was wasted and I had the strange urge to smash everything in sight. My fingernails dug into the palms of my hands as my fingers clenched themselves into angry balled up fists. The next thing I knew, I was staring at Sam with a smile on my face. He turned his head and caught my glance and smiled back. He turned away then looked back at me. We stayed focused with our eyes locked, without flinching, in silence. The orange light cut through the glaze that covered his eyes. The veil retreated further with every blink. I tried to look away but I was fixated on him. My heart pounded reluctantly faster and faster, and I could feel my stomach suck up against my spine.

I had spent the last 10 days trying to keep myself subdued with a violent lust but now that it had faded I felt empty and deranged. I had the strange urge to hit him. I wanted to smack him and wipe that shit-eating grin of his face. And I wanted him to hit me back. I wanted to fight!

Sam ordered another round. After a week of mixing pre-packaged amphetamines with gin and cheap beer, a drink just wasn't going to cut it.

"I don't think I can stomach another one," I pleaded.

Ook looked stared at us waiting for an answer.

"Ook!" Sam raised four fingers in the air and pointed to each of us, without looking away, "Four more please!"

Ook scurried over from the far side of the bar, his bare chest glistening with booze under the orange light. He filled our glasses and we emptied them before he could turn around again. The shredded ice burned my throat on its way down and I sobered up almost immediately.

The room went quiet. Beads of sweat seeped impatiently out of my brow. Sam stopped blinking for a moment. My muscles tensed up and my nerves trembled all the way through to my clenched teeth. Something had to be done. Sam's bloodshot eyes kept urging me on. I started to smile. The more deranged my thoughts became the more I started to grin, until I was almost laughing out loud. It had only been a few weeks but we'd already sunken into the same routine of boredom and narcissistic debauchery that we had been running from in the first place. I wanted a big screen TV, and a 16 ounce steak, and an Elvis record, a wooden baseball bat and a small soundproof room with four walls and a stereo where I could be left alone to do as I please.

Sam's eyes were still staring, unblinking. Something had to give.

"Let's go back to that bar we went to on the first night," I said, trying to cut him off.

Sam laughed at me, "What the fuck for?"

"To beat the living shit out of each other," I laughed.

"Who the fuck do you think you are? Tyler Durden?"

"No I'm Edward Norton! And you can be Anthony Burgess," I snapped back.

He grinned and stared at me cock-eyed, "What the fuck are you talking about?"

My smile grew wider, "Ok fine, you can be Patrick Bateman… And I'll be… Raul Duke!"

"How fucking drunk are you?" he asked with an abrupt laugh.

I laughed back, "Pretty fucking drunk! What the fuck do you expect? I've been drunk all day, I've been drunk ever since I got on the plane, I've been drinking everyday since we got to this god-forsaken island, and I'll drink whenever I goddamn please!"

I downed the last of my drink and wiped my mouth with the back of my hand, "I'm fucking shit-faced but I'm dead serious."

"Is that so?" he said with a grin.

"Why not? We said we'd go back and we're leaving tomorrow aren't we?" I said.

I felt brave and alive as more bullshit spewed out of my mouth. "Or did you book us in for a few more nights?"

"Austin! What is wrong with you?" Jasmine protested, "You two are friends, you shouldn't be fighting."

"Why not? I'd rather get the shit beat out of me by him than a by stranger." I looked over at Sam. "Come on, what's the worse thing that can happen?"

Sam shook his head, "Do I really need to answer that?"

Jasmine continued to sit unemotionally with her chin cradled in the palms of her hands, while Ook attempted to talk us out of it as we paid for our last round. "You are crazy! Friends should not fight like this."

"Don't worry, we'll be back before you know it." I shook his hand and made him a promise to win the fight for him, and we left for the ring.

The bell rang as we walked in. The two fighters returned to their corners. One of them was a skinny South American built like a racehorse. The man in the other corner was an Eastern European bull, whose muscles were so big that every time he clenched or flexed them he could hardly move. I stared at the balding European as he stomped around the ring. He looked vaguely familiar.

"Hey Sam," I pointed up to the ring. "Isn't that the guy who wanted to fight you the first night we were here?"

"Jesus! That's him," he said. He was clearly relieved he wasn't up there about to get pummelled by the hulking Slav.

A waitress came over to our table fanned out a set of menus in front of us, "You want to order?"

I pushed the menus away, "No," I said. "We want to fight."

The waitress snatched the menus back in a huff. "Too late. Only one more tonight," she said curtly before storming away in disgust.

"Come on let's get out of here," Sam said with a noticeable tone of disappointment in his voice.

I shook my head and gestured towards the ring, "We might as well watch this guy beat the living daylights out of that poor Spic before we go."

We sat back down and waited for the next round to start. The two of them began to size one another up as they moved slowly towards the middle of the ring. The little racehorse looked eager to get a few punches in. He was quick and moved around the Slav with ease. He threw some quick jabs and the Pole took them proudly on the chin. He threw a few more before the Pole had the chance to digest the first few blows. He was struggling. He hadn't expected things to go this way. As soon as he got the chance he clutched onto his head and squeezed it like a ripe grapefruit. The referee came in to break them up but after half a dozen more punches to the face, the Pole latched on again. This time he held on long enough to bring the sturdy racehorse to the ground. He'd been reduced to wrestling on the floor to avoid taking punches from someone half his size. The referee tried to intervene but the Pole refused to let go. The crowd stared to boo as the referee tried to pull them apart. After one last attempt to pry the Pole of his victim, the referee had no choice but to blow his whistle and call the fight. He grabbed the Southern stallion from underneath the pole and raised him up by his right hand. The crowd let out a bellowing chorus of unimpressed boos and faint cheers. The champion was embarrassed to have won on a disqualification and he pulled his arm back down in disgust.

We got up from our table and headed toward the door. As we walked past the ring I heard a shout from behind. "Hey!" I turned around. There was saw a local man with thinning patches of hair on the sides of his head and a sweat stained tank top waving his hands at us. "You want to fight?" Sam and I started to walk back. "You want to fight?" he repeated as we approached.

"We do."

"Which one want to fight?" He wagged his finger back and forth between us. "Both?"

"Me and him," I repeated his gesture. "Two!"

"You know how to fight?"

We looked at one another and shrugged our shoulders. "How hard can it be?"

The skinny Buddha rubbed his bald patch in response.

"Eastern style boxing." He pointed towards the ring where next fight was going on, "Very simple…" He paused so that his two main attractions could do a comedic demonstration before elaborating, "Punching, kicking; no biting, no wrestling… Tree rounds, tree minutes, last one standing wins."

We nodded to show that we understood.

He took his hand off his head "Ok, you go…" He pointed to a teenager with a shaved head and mumbled some unenthusiastic gibberish to him.

They brought us to a changing room behind the ring. Chips of dark red paint crumbled off the concrete walls. Two scrawny boys ran up to us with a pair of shorts that were still fresh from the last fight. I stripped down and slipped the soaking wet trunks on. The cheap polyester cloth stuck to my thighs like wet toilet paper. Once we were dressed we headed back to the table to sit with the girls. Their complimentary drinks sat untouched in front of them. "Not thirsty?" They shook their heads. I sat down beside them. Jasmine put her arm around Sam and rubbed his back.

"Don't worry girls it'll be alright," I said, hoping to convince myself that everything was under control.

"We're not worried," Lana grinned, "We just think you're both idiots." At this point it was the closest thing to consolation that I was going to get.

"Stop it. Just stop this nonsense," Jasmine blurted out. "You two are being so childish. Do you think you are going to impress us by fighting each other?"

I'd forgotten about the girls. I hadn't even considered that they thought this was somehow all about them.

"Relax, we're just having fun!" I smiled and looked over at Sam. "It's not like we're going to try and hurt each other."

Neither of them responded and we all sat in silence. My knee was jittering up and down, as it slammed my heel up and down against the pavement. "I just need to use take a piss," I announced nervously. I got up from the table and ran past the rows of bloodthirsty sunburn victims and locked myself in a stall. I took deep breaths and held them in each time, hoping that the extra oxygen would settle my stomach. It was pounding in sharp spasms.

When I was done I went to the thick sheet of aluminium that was serving as a mirror and splashed some water on my face and chest. My reflection danced across the polished surface on the wall. I could feel the booze pumping through my veins, trying to throw me off balance. Every time my heart beat it filled my head with a rush of adrenaline. I gnawed on my bottom lip, splashed a bit more water on my face and made my way back to the ring.

I tried to think of the last time I had been in a fight to settle my nerves. I had been drunk – that was at least something. It was that time outside the bar in the middle of winter... But that wasn't really much of a fight. I started to panic. Had I even ever been in a fight before? If I was, I liked to think that I had won.

The greasy Buddha was waiting for me when I got back, "Two minutes…" One last chance to bow out and run away. But Sam already had his gloves on. I tried to wash away the parched taste in my mouth with some water. The ice rattled in my glass as I tried to put it down without dropping it. I pressed my tongue hard against the back of my teeth and bit down hard. My bowels rumbled and I considered going to the bathroom one more time, if only to avoid pissing myself when I got punched in the stomach. I realised my mistake right away and quickly tried to wipe the thought of being punched from my mind. I picked my gloves off the table. They were soaking wet with a day's worth of mindless violence, and I had to crawl my fists up into the spongy padding with my fingers to get them on. Once they were inside the moist interior, my hands began to relax. I looked over to the man who was getting ready to do the punching. He seemed calm on the inside and even calmer on the outside. I tried to fake a smile but he caught me in the act.

"You know we don't have to do this," Sam said.

"I know." But we both knew it wasn't true. We were only offering each other the necessary hollow comforts that are required at a time like this.

The little Buddha came over to our table. "Ok," he pointed to the ring, "Time to fight."

I staggered up the rickety steps to my corner and looked out at the crowd. I felt like I was the main event in a dilapidated meatpacking factory. Lana stood on the canvas on the other side of the ropes smiling at me. This was all a big joke to her. She knew her boyfriend was safe somewhere on the other side of the world, even if he was fucking some big breasted surfer girl. But that didn't matter right now. She was getting ready to watch two desperate drunks punch the shit out of each other, in the hopes of trying to feel alive. Jasmine placed the palm of her hands on Sam's shoulder. His arms looked massive underneath her palms and I started to wonder whether I'd made a mistake. It was too late for that kind of thinking though. There must have been at least 100 people there, waiting for us to beat the living hell out of each other and we couldn't let them down. The music came down. I turned back to look at Lana. She leaned over the ropes to give me a kiss on the cheek. I felt a shot of adrenaline shoot through my arms and into my fingers. All of a sudden my head felt clear.

I walked out to the middle of the ring to meet Sam. His head was squeezed in between two pieces of blue foam padding. Beads of sweat were dripping down his chest in a mix of booze and nerves. At that point, I realised he wasn't so much worried about what might happen to him, as he was about what he might do to me. The referee grabbed both of our wrists just below the gloves. "No hitting behloh the behlt," he pointed to our sweaty groins and looked at both of us to make sure we understood. "Ok." He made the motion of his knuckles pounding together before bowing his head and taking a step back. Sam stood three feet away with his hands down by his sides. I moved toward him. He went to wrap his arms around me and I reciprocated. I closed my eyes so I wouldn't have to see Jasmine smiling in the far corner. I heard Sam's muffled voice through my padding but I couldn't make out what he was saying. By the time I was done listening I had let go and Sam was standing 6 feet away from me with his hands in front of his face. The fight had started. I backed away from Sam. I didn't want to be the one to throw the first punch but I didn't want to get hit either. I could hear manic voices rambling through my head: the birds and the bees, and bumblebees and butterflies, and ballet dancers stinging like gonorrhea or something like that…The room was spinning and I was starting to lose my balance. I tried keep on my toes and moved around as much as possible but the room kept spinning faster and faster. I tired to stay focussed but then all of a sudden… Wham!

"What th…"

Wham! Whack! Wham! I tried to put my hands up to protect my face, then… Thud! Crack! Right to the stomach, then the ribs. *At least you didn't piss yourself.*

I hadn't even thrown a punch but I was already out of breath. *Too much drinking, too much idleness.* I back-pedalled and tried to slow the onslaught. I moved my shoulders and my head back and forth, trying not to fall over my feet. It was impossible to get my bearing while I was getting punched in the head.

The more I moved the faster the room spun around. Everything seemed brighter now. If only my arms didn't feel so heavy…

I made a charge at Sam with my head down. Whack! Thud! He grazed my cheek before I leaned in and let my fists fly. I hit something hard with my left, then something soft with my right. The next fist felt no resistance, and my face followed the next one through the air and right into the waiting glove. Ugghh! Thud! Thud! Whack. It all happened so quickly but I managed to I keep track of each one as they landed in a row; one, two, three; corner of the eye, upper abdomen, top of the head.

I startled back and tried to take another run, every third punch felt like it hit something, but with my eyes closed it was hard to tell. It felt like I was in an excruciating dream. Every so often I would get a brutal reminder that this was in fact happening. *Thud! Thud! Thud!*

Ding!

I was awake now. All of a sudden I could see again. There were lights going off all around but there not a camera in sight. I could feel a laughter rise in side of me and I grinned as I made my way back to the corner. I smiled at Lana and she smiled back. It couldn't be going that badly if she was smiling at me. And I certainly didn't feel too bad. I kept smiling as my veins throbbed heavily around my muscles, constricting and contracting faster and faster. My legs felt light but my head way heavy. Maybe this wasn't such a bad idea after all.

The music stopped and we made our way back to the middle of the ring. I was determined to turn things around. As soon as our gloves touched I slid my hand up and tried to get a quick punch in. I watched as my fist connected with the side of his head, then got ready to throw another one but then…

Thud! Right on the nose! My face started to sting and I could feel the blood rush into the back of my eyes. I blinked to rinse the tears out of my eyes and stood back up. I stumbled and felt my leg reach out to take a swipe. My shin connected and cracked. *No kicking!* But I had been hit enough times to allow myself to forget.

It hurt like hell but at least Sam had backed off. I tried another one, aiming higher this time but I missed. The tequila wasn't helping but I was growing desperate. Sam tried a kick of his own and I could feel his bone compress against my shin. *Crack*! Another rolling barrage of fists. *Bam! Bam! Whack!* I tried to reach through his arms to land a punch but I couldn't find anything to hit. I managed a glancing blow and I got ready up to take a jab but I was met by two… four… five… blows that sent me flailing backwards into the ropes.

It felt like my hands were tied up and dangled on a string in front of my face. I could see them there, bouncing awkwardly in and out and side to side, but I couldn't seem to get them to do what I wanted them to. By the time I had composed myself enough to launch another attack it was too late.

Crack! My jaw seized up against me skull. Thud! Crack! Thud! They were getting heavier and I was having trouble breathing! Thud! Thud!...

Thud   Thud

Thud   Whack   Thud
                                        Thud

Ding!

A whimpering cheer rose from the crowd behind and I spun around to see what was happening. One more shot to the head and I would have been out cold! I got back to my corner and took my first breath in over a minute. My jaw was seized shut and I was reduced to using my nostrils to gather air. At least Lana was still there, still smiling. She handed me a bottle of water, which I poured over my head before trying to spill some into the side of my mouth.

"How am I doing?" I asked, hoping that talking would somehow make me feel better.

"Not bad." She was telling just the kind of lies that I wanted to hear. I could tell part of her wanted to urge me to quit but she was getting too much of a kick out of the blood letting, even if she was too embarrassed to admit it. "You're hanging in there."

I was nauseous, and the thought of having to step back in the ring to take another beating made my knees buckle. The only thing that made me feel sicker than the thought of taking another punch was the idea of giving up. I may not have had much to gain but I had everything to lose. I tried to force a laugh from the bottom of my stomach and somehow was able to eek out a deranged smile that filled me with excitement.

I looked over at Sam. He could hardly believe I was still standing. The music came down and he made his way out to the middle of the ring. I held on to the rope for a few seconds, trying to suck in as much oxygen as possible through my twisted jaw before going to meet my fate in the middle of the ring.

The lights were flashing brightly but still not a single camera in sight. We had managed to drawn a bit of a crowd. They all moved closer to the ring to watch the final pummeling. The bell went. Our gloves grazed one another and that was the end of it. I tried to find something to grab onto. I clutched frantically at his face with my sweaty fists. But every time I tried to reach for the surface I was dragged back under. Thud!... Thud!

Shhhhh... Just white noise and darkness. I threw a leg up in the air, aiming for his face but it missed. Thud! Thud! I pedaled backwards and stumbled onto the ropes.

This wasn't a fight. It was a massacre. Every time I came up for air, another wave would crash down on me. Thud! Thud! I could feel my brain starting to swell from the lack of oxygen. Each time I squirmed to the top for a breath there was another wave waiting for me. Crash! Thud! I was slowly being swept out to sea. They kept pounding down, holding me under for minutes at a time. With every second that went past, I sunk deeper and deeper. I was drowning. I felt a calm rush come over me the longer I was held under. Every now and then a flash of light would break through – the undertow was finally spitting me out, I was saved.

Thud! Thud! Thud!... False hope and insecurity.

Panic started to set in. I was in danger of going down for good. The room was spinning. My veins were pried open in an attempt to maintain the flow of oxygen to my brain. I could feel every ounce of air left in my lungs fill the inside of my cheeks. My nostrils flared as the air passed through them. Then with the only ounce of strength I had left, I kicked up and let my fist fly through the darkness, hoping to connect. I latched on to something hard and firm.

Thud!

I crashed back against the tide. I looked up through the water and saw Sam's padding spun sideways. He couldn't see a thing. He was vulnerable. *Finish him!* I cocked my fist and took a run towards his chin.

Ding!

It was all over. I collapsed on the canvas. I was panting like a dog. A chorus of faint cheers rattled through my head. It was all over. I propped myself up on my hands and knees and stood up. Sam adjusted the padding on his face. I had never been so happy to see another human being in my life. I didn't know whether I wanted to hit him one more time or just fall down on my knees and laugh. He walked towards me. As soon as he was close enough I threw my arms around him and held on for dear life. I could hear him laughing through the padding. "Jesus Christ! I thought you had me there."

His shoulders shook against my chest as we laughed. The crowd clapped and whistled as we patted each other on the back, then the referee came out and grabbed both our arms on either side of him. He raised Sam's tired fist in the air and the crowd let out another loud cheer. I had just got the shit kicked out of me but I couldn't stop laughing. I had survived and I was just happy to be alive.

Lana was waiting for me in the corner with a bottle of water and an elated smile. She gave me a kiss on the cheek and I shuffled back to the change room like a wounded mule. It had only lasted 5 minutes but it felt as if we had just gone twelve rounds. I took deep breaths. The more air I sucked in, the more tequila and sweat poured out of my skin. My jeans stuck to my legs as I pulled them back on and waded back to the table.

The girls were smitten with a sick sense of pride, and I was proud to be standing in front of them, beaten to shit and temporarily sane. There were two buckets of booze waiting for us – a token of appreciation for providing 15 minutes of dangerously average entertainment to the tired crowd. I retched at the thought of having to take a sip. They announced the final fight of the night. We watched on as two semi-professional fighters in religious dress and no padding flipped limberly over the ropes. After running around the ring, trying to get the crowd involved, the bell rung and they proceeded to acrobatically kick the shit out each other in a carefully choreographed fight, replete with back flips and flying windmill kicks. It was nothing more than an elaborate wrestling match starring second-rate martial arts experts but the crowd was on it's feet cheering on every clinically executed blow.

The first round came to an end and we left our drinks at the table before heading down to the beach. We stopped by to check in on Ook on our way there but when we got to the bar he was nowhere to be seen. Abel was clearing a table by the door. He took one look at us and shook his head. "What the hell happened to you two?" I had forgotten that I still hadn't put my shirt on and I was still sweating uncontrollably. We told him that we came to say goodbye and he informed us that Ook's wife had come to visit and dragged him home because he was too drunk.

"I didn't know he had a wife," I said.

Abel laughed, "Ya, he's got two kids too. Why do you think he spends so much time at the bar?"

I was sad that we didn't get to say goodbye to Ook, and I was even more upset that we couldn't tell him about how Sam beat the living hell out of me. He would have liked that. We tried to force ourselves to have one last cocktail at the bar but I couldn't stomach it. Now that it was all over I didn't know what to do with myself. We said our final goodbyes to Abel headed to down to the beach for some fresh air. The heat outside was unbearable and the primal noises rattled up from the water as we wandered down the path. I was getting ready to avoid Patrick but when we passed his usual spot he wasn't there.

The party on the beach was still going as strong as it was on the day we arrived. I looked around at the madness. I thought I make out the two pudgy Brits mauling our Scandinavian neighbours amongst the crowd. Even the girls seemed disappointed at the sight.

"What's wrong?" I asked, looking at both of them. "Don't you guys want to party?"

They shook their heads. I wasn't in the mood to try and figure out whether they were being sincere. The noise of the morning-after ravers filled my head like a constant nagging tinnitus. I could feel my brain swell against the inside of my skull. Whatever had happened in that ring had rattled me pretty good. I couldn't remember the last time it felt so good just to breath. We made our way past the brightly painted silhouettes. They had the usual crazed looks in their eyes, like they were ready to cut someone's head off and roll the remains down a hill as part of a routine sacrifice. I couldn't bear the thought of having to look at this god-forsaken beach any longer.

I was still sweating uncontrollably as we walked down the beach. Once we were passed the crowds, I stripped down naked and threw my pants in a bush, before running into the ocean. Sam came running in behind me. I held my head under the pitch-black for as long as I could, until finally I didn't feel the need to throw up anymore. I threw my head back and gasped. I took a few deep breath and stared back at the demented sexual wonderland had finally taken its toll. After a while I began to shiver and I waded back up the beach with my hands over my pale groin. I threw my pants back on and fell back on the sand with my eyes closed.

"Are you sure you don't want to dance for a bit?" asked Sam half-heartedly as he walked out of the water.

But the girls just stood there in silence as the noise echoed up the beach. Jasmine leaned in and kissed Sam as he put his shorts back on. He glanced down at me and waved me on as they spun around and started to walk up the beach. "Well what are you waiting for?" Lana asked as she repeated Sam's gesture before walking ahead. I rubbed my eyes and jumped off the sand and shuffled after her. Sam and Jasmine were waiting for us at the end of the road. "I guess I'll see you tomorrow," I asked.

"I guess so," Sam smiled, "Take care of yourself."

"You too," I said as Sam trekked up the hill with Jasmine at his side.

I limped along beside Lana, my fingers still twitching with adrenaline and booze. The bones in my shins felt like well-chewed toothpicks that splintered with every step I took. When we got back to Lana's hostel I dropped straight onto Jasmine's bed. Lana went to the other side of the room and I pretended not to watch as she stripped down to her bra and panties, but I could see enough through my fingers to notice that they didn't match. She sighed as she crawled under the sheets on the other side of the room. I lay there thinking about crawling in next to her but I couldn't bring myself to do it. I just lay on my side, breathing heavily. I could barely wiggle my toes, and my head was throbbing uncontrollably. I tossed and turned back and forth, hoping to get her attention.

"Are you ok?" she whispered.

"I'm fine," I said as I rolled my head away from the soothing sound of her voice. I squeezed my eyes closed as tight as I could and tried to block out the obnoxious thoughts that popped into my head. It wasn't long until the rustling in the bed next to me was snuffed out, leaving me alone with my thoughts and bruises. I had never felt so drunk and tired and exhausted in my life, and I lay there half awake until the sun started to come up.

Thirteen

Sam was staring at the fan as it passed back and forth over his bare chest when I walked into the room the next morning.

"Where's Jasmine?"

He sighed, "She left a while ago".

"That's strange, I didn't see her on the way up."

Sam stared at me with a tired look on his face. He walked over to the desk and swept loose pages and dirty clothes out of the way until he found the bottle. He popped off the cap and shovelled a handful of pills into his mouth. He was certainly less beat up than I was, but he moved back to bed with a bit of a limp. I didn't bother asking what had happened the night before.

"You ready to go?" Sam grabbed his bags off the two beds.

"Ya, let's get the hell out of here."

We packed the rest of our clothes, left the keys in the door, and made our way past the mosquito-infested pool one-last time. The girls were waiting for us on the dusty road outside on their room. As soon as we passed the last stretch of hostels and pizza shops we were hit with the smell of fish warming up under the sun at the local market. The women standing behind the counters of the plywood stalls did their best to swat the hungry flies away, while keeping their eyes on their children as they played in the dirt. The girls stopped every so often, trying on 2-dollar pairs of brand-name sunglasses, and taking pictures of the filth-covered children hiding coyly behind their mother's legs.

The ship was waiting at the dock and the rich smell of diesel filled the air as the engine rumbled on. We joined in behind the faceless mob that was slowly being herded up the narrow gangway at the end of the pier. The stench of stale booze and shame was overpowering, which was only made worse by the thick plumes of black smoke that occasionally wafted up from the back of the boat. We managed to push through to the front to get a seat on the roof where we watched the next batch of pearly white Oopma Loompas make their way eagerly down the pier. The air was cooler than the day before, and the fishing boats were already busy dragging tourists away to the remote reefs on the outskirts of the island. A saleswoman with a thick binder approached us as we pulled out of the dock. She was recruiting bodies to fill the resorts and run down bungalows at our final destination. She leaned into the sunlight and held out the binder filled with sheets of laminated print-outs.

"You look..."

"No thank you," barked Jasmine without hesitation.

"Hold on," I grabbed the folder from her and flipped through it as she smiled from under her blue and yellow tilly-hat.

"What can you offer us?" I asked.

"You like to smoke?" She pinched her index finger against her thumb and held them up to her lips. I shook my head and held my hand up to stop her train of thought.

"Happy shake? You like to be happy?"

I'd had enough happy endings for one trip, but when she started making childish grimaces and waving her hands around her head like a lunatic, I knew exactly what she was talking about. Sam had promised me two things if I came on the trip with him: more overly tanned Scandinavians than I knew what to do with and even more hallucinogens. I was skeptical at first but then I remembered that Patrick said we needed to head East to get our fix. Things had certainly changed ever since the girls decided to tag along. But they didn't need to know that we had an ulterior motive, and if we somehow managed to end up on an island overgrown with magic mushrooms we could always put on a brave face and chalk it up to coincidence.

I smiled back at her then pointed at the girls. "We're on a honeymoon. We are all getting married – my friend and I are getting married to these two fine ladies." The girls started to giggle. "We need two of your best rooms right by the beach, facing the ocean," I said with a smile.

She bowed and acknowledged the strange arrangement. She pointed to a picture with white plaster bungalows lined up along the edge of a white sand beach. I nodded, and she pulled out a cell phone and started mashing the buttons. She blasted orders over the phone then pressed a button and shoved it in her pocket. She told us that a taxi had been arranged and that the rooms would be ready by the time we arrived.

"Happy?" she asked. Before any of us could answer she stuck her chin out and repeated herself with a big fake smile, "Happy?"

"Yes," I threw my arm mockingly around Lana. "Very happy."

"Shouldn't we look this place up in the book?" asked Jasmine

I looked over at her, "Don't worry about the book, it'll all work out in the end."

The boat continued to head toward an island in the distance until we pulled into a small inlet, passing impenetrable forests of mangroves, which spread up from the water's edge. On the one side there were decrepit docks with an assortment of brightly coloured trawlers and sailboats, with a few crumbling concrete buildings behind them. When the boat finally pulled into the dock, the woman waved us through the crowds and directed us onto the back of a truck before getting back on board to trawl for more business.

It was just after lunchtime when the truck pulled off a paved road and down a gravel path. Sure enough, the impish man at the front desk was expecting us. He took us straight to two white stucco cabins with little terraces overlooking the ocean. For the first time since we'd landed, I could taste the salt in the air.

"Not a bad place for a honeymoon," Sam said.

I smiled at him, "Not bad at all."

We dropped our bags off and walked out onto our beachfront property. The sand stretched on forever in a straight line on either side of us. We had the whole island to ourselves. I walked down to the beach and ran into the ocean. I dug my arms in one after another with my face pointing towards the bottom. Once I got all the way out, I dove back, skimming the bottom along the way. The gentle undertow pulled me back and forth, holding me down by the rushing water for a moment before releasing its grip and launching me headfirst towards the shoreline. I came up for air at the edge of the water and laboured up the beach. Jasmine was lying in a heap on Sam's chest. Her bony hips looked almost sensual beside Sam's bulging forearms. Jasmine looked over at him and made a clumsy effort to look serious while giggling to herself. Her mossy green eyes reflected the dark shades of the trees in the distance, and they were surrounded by dark eyelashes that made them seem longer than they actually were. Spread out at regular intervals, they made her eyes appear full and focussed every time she stared at Sam. But he was too focussed on her hips and her tiny feet to notice, and she didn't seem to care as long as her bony shoulders were wrapped firmly in his arms.

The sun climbed higher until it became too hot for us to bear, and we headed to the bamboo harem beside the hotel's reception for a drink. The words Free Times Café were painted in big green letters above a hand craved wooden weed leaf. We ordered a round of beers and sat down on the ocean of fake silk cushions that were scattered on top of embroidered crimsons rugs at the foot of a few wooden knee high tables. A group of locals lingered around the bar playing a game of pool. An English girl in oriental canvas trousers walked up to them and the pool sharks dropped their cues and rushed to greet her. She didn't look a day over 21 but she had been here long enough to learn enough simple phrases to make small talk. After they were done she came over to our table with a stack of menus. I could tell by the look on her face that she wanted nothing to do with us. It was a matter of weeks, maybe a month, until a place like this would be turning down reservations. Soon enough the madness from the surrounding islands would spill over and end up here, and she would be forced to deal with the inevitable runoff. Every hotel owner and drug dealer in town was waiting, quietly praying for the day to come, but thought of it was enough to make her want to runaway and start again somewhere new.

I scanned the menu and pointed to the elaborate cursive letters next to the Alice in Wonderland cartoon. I looked over at Sam. He nodded. "We'll have a couple of those." The English hippy rolled her eyes. "Unless you girls care to join…"

Lana looked confused, "I'm fine. But you should do as you please," she said with a smile.

The hippy went back to the pool table and handed down her

instructions and the sharks shrugged their shoulders in defiance. She continued to prod them until two of them disappeared reluctantly behind the bar. She came back a few minutes later with a bucket of frothy grey mush speckled with grainy black dots. I took a small sip. The sandy texture pasted itself on the back of my tongue as a bitter reminder of what the poison was capable of. I washed down the gruel with a swig of beer. I offered some to Jasmine and Lana before quickly talking them out of it. They had become enough of a liability as it was, and with no one else around I wasn't prepared to accept the consequences of what might happen if something went wrong.

We kept drinking as the sun fell towards the water. As time dragged I looked at the palm of my hand to see if it was working – nothing. I was growing impatient and searching desperately for signs only added to my frustrations. After an hour the hippy came back to check on us.

'Everything ok?'

I stared at Sam. "Everything's fine," I said. "I think we'd liked to order some more."

The hippy stared at both of us. "Are you sure?"

"We're sure."

She spun around and returned to the bar. I stared at the bluish white foam of the ocean as it dragged itself up and down the edges of the sand. A band of horses galloped toward us along the edge of water. They were carrying a group of blonde princesses in brightly coloured sarongs. The horses laboured heavily underneath them as they struggled to maintain a steady canter in the dying heat. They had large majestic frames but their ribs stuck out from underneath the thick layers of padding that were stuffed under the saddles to ease the bumpy ride. The girls were oblivious to their suffering and their heads bobbled merrily back and forth as the beasts dug their bony hooves deep into the sand and soldiered on.

"Hey Tintin." Sam looked over at me. "You feel anything?"

"Nothing more than a few beers and a bit too much sun."

It had been three hours since our first dose and the sun was still hanging stubbornly over the water. On the other side of the world, the days were continuing to get shorter, but being staring at the red hot sun get reluctantly pulled out of the sky made from the shores of the island made it seem like our lazy afternoons were just pointlessly dragging on.

"Just get some more," Lana said with a smile.

Sam smiled at her then looked over at me. He flagged down the hippy and ordered another round. "We've either wasted all our money, or we're about to make a huge mistake," he said laughing to himself. The waitress came back with two more muddy buckets and four bottles of beer. We grabbed the sludge and shot the cool sandy poison down our throats all at once before the waitress made it back behind the bar. As soon as I swallowed the last mouthful, my stomach began to feel warm and weightless. I could feel the warmth accelerate as it pumped downwards into the pit of my stomach, back up through my veins and into the tips of my fingers. I locked gazes with Sam. I could see the flow of blood beginning to pool in his cheeks and around his eyes. It wasn't the gin's fault; we hadn't had any gin for days.

I felt my lips twitch into a smile, "Shit Sam! I think we've done it!"

I flipped over my hands and watched my palms go to work before making a fist and hiding them under the table. Lana started to laugh for no reason and I felt my guts buckle. My stomach churned in rapid spasms and my heart struggled to pound fast enough to pump enough oxygen to my brain. The next thing I knew we were both on the floor melting uncontrollably with joy, until we were reduced to hysterical childish sobbing. "Jesus!" Sam giggled as he buried his face in his hands in an attempt conceal his lack of control. He was about to go off the edge and I was close behind. "This is going to be a long night."

My insides were being tickled into violent spasms of laughter and colour, and my eyes bulged and reeled as they tried to take it all in. But it was too much. I was panting hard and fast. With every move the colours came harder and faster. I tried to shut my eyes but that only made things worse. The girls' faces flashed in bursts of orange and green. I tried to avert my eyes but I couldn't stop myself from awkwardly dazing at Lana with a mechanical grin holding my face in place. Then all of a sudden a vital organ burst. I blinked and blinked again. The sun was still hung lazilly over the horizon, refusing to go down, and its blazing fire reflected coolly on both of their faces. I could smell the oversized leaves of the palm trees melting under its weight. "How do you feel?" Jasmine asked sincerely. *No time for questions!* This was definitley not the time for questions.

Sam recoiled and I fell back to the floor. I had to close my eyes to stop them from playing tricks on me, but nothing could stop the warm merry-go-rounds and explosions of stars that were dripping down the backs of my eyelids, in neatly tessellated patterns. The drip-drop food colouring stained the concave surface of my eyes. I lost my focus. My heart beat faster. I started to panic. I tried to scream but my teeth remained firmly clenched between the tired muscles of my jaw. *Just lay back and let the poison take hold. You're not in charge here anymore. Madness and insanity have arrived!* I opened my eyes. The sun still hung there, teasing me, as it quietly burned a hole in the sky. Then, without warning, it dipped itself into the water and set the ocean on fire. The horizon recoiled and gave way to a bright pink mushroom cloud which crawled sluggishly towards the sky, climbing higher and higher, until it blew a hole clear through the ozone layer. The sky bled slowly into the ocean until every last inch of blue had been drained from the bloody shroud. Soon global warming would be nothing but a distant memory. The splattered ink continued to hang in the sky, immune to the advances of Mother Nature until gravity took over and dragged the sun out of sight.

 I was overcome with shock and awe. Never in the history of the world had there been something so terrifyingly inspiring! I tried to keep myself together, smiling diligently and nodding at the faces around the table, trying to make the noises coming out of my mouth sound like words. But it was no use. The fucking sky was on fire and I was drowning in it! I felt my eyelashes flutter and my pupils rolled back into my skull twitching faster than the speed of R.E.M. *It's the end of the world as I know it! And I feel...*

Shots fired! Shots fired!

Bang!

Bang!

Bang!

Nothing...

Clear!

Right into the veins. Redirected from the depths of the belly recycled through the heart, processed by the brain, compressed, repackaged and diluted before being sent back to your lifeless extremities. After the quick hit, my body became numb. I was subdued now, nothing to worry about, just let the medicine go to work. My veins constricted as the flow of poison slowed. *Relax: it's all natural!* Natural poison – unfettered, unfiltered natural poison. No chemicals, no preservatives, no hormones. Just what the doctor ordered! I drifted in and out of consciousness without the slightest idea of what was happening. "What the fuck is going on?" he said from a considerable distance. *How the fuck was I supposed to know?* Where was he? He could be miles away by now! *It could take weeks even months to deliver the message.*

Lana and Jasmine were... *"not my lovers...* draped in an angelic glow that made it look like their hearts were melting on their skin. I stared as their candlelit faces flickered in the darkness, leaving streaks of blueberry chalk that swerved from their cheeks and under their eyes all the way down through their breasts and thighs. A mad fucking orgy of chaos and pure bliss. It was only the first day of the honeymoon but it could have been our last and I wouldn't have cared less.

I was already breathing heavily when the second batch kicked in. *Another shot fired...* I tried to slow the contractions in my stomach. I'd lost all control. I knew that if I tried to interfere it would only lead to disaster. Once the poison burrows itself in your veins the only thing that you can do is hope. With the fire of the sun faded behind the stars we became trapped in an aquarium surrounded by whales and jellyfish swimming peacefully between the nets on the walls. We were stuck underwater but no once seemed to panic – everything was quiet and calm – and the bottles remained stubbornly fixed to the tables as the bloated faces floated around them in serene passes. I snatched one of them quickly and started to drink from before it floated to the top. I watched the hippy waitress come over to our table out of the corner of my eye. She towered over us with her hands on her hips. "I just wanted to see if you needed anything else." At least I think that's what she said. For all I know it could have been, *"You frat boy cock-suckers are all the same. You just can't seem to quit while you're ahead."* I tried to interrupt but by the time the word's came to my lips she was gone. The next thing I knew she had come back with another round of beers and she was gone before I had the chance to explain myself.

Where the hell is Sam! Where the hell are we! I squinted confusedly at Jasmine. "Where's Sam?"

"He just went to the bathroom." She reassured behind the glow of her alien skin.

Sam came back looking like a ghost. He sat down at the table and stared me straight in the eye. "Whatever you do." He said straining his jaw with every ounce of seriousness. "Don't go in there." He fell into Jasmine's lap and started to laugh manically.

Jasmine put her hand on his head as he disappeared between her thighs. I could hear Michael Jackson's ghost whispering sweet nothings in my ear: *"They say I am the one."* My heart started to pound harder until I couldn't control myself anymore. "Fuck Sam, we've really done it this time." I roared out loud. Sam turned over and lay there with his mouth open looking towards the thatched roof. He bellowed like a king before disappearing back into her lap.

I watched Lana grab the flame in middle the table. She drew it towards her face and her skin burst into a fiery orange ember. She lit a cigarette and stared at me with a Pocahontas smile. She proceeded to smoke it with the cool efficiency of a 15-year-old Parisienne. Her voice sounded muddled underwater but it was soothing. When I closed my eyes I was in an open meadow, overgrown with white laser-lit lilies. By the time the third dose kicked in the walls of the aquarium were breathing heavily. The giant squid that hung above us slithered across the walls, chasing the fish out of sight as we drowned slowly beneath it. My brain was trying to sleepwalk me through the mess but soon enough it gave up. We were in the belly of the whale and there was no way out. A group of snarling pirates in tailored suits and felt hats playing poker as mermaids looked over their shoulder hidden behind a rocky cove on the other side of the room. Their scripts were tired and the actors were going grey with long nose hairs and polished toenails! This was no time for stern faces and phony etiquette. *What the hell were we doing here anyways?*

"Do you see them?" I whispered, unsure of whether or not I was speaking out loud.

"Hmm?" Lana whispered.

I startled back at her and stammered on. "The mermaids... The fucking mermaids over there playing poker." *Shit I hope they didn't hear me.* I cocked my head back toward them and clenched my teeth.

"Don't worry Tintin," Sam's voice reassured me "They're not going to bother us."

His mouth kept moving but I lost track of the words somewhere between his lips and the edge of the table. I stared at him as he laughed hysterically, wondering what he was laughing about, before realising that I had already joined in. Lana's skin was breathing heavily. I felt a sharp pain in my chest. I grabbed one of her cigarettes and lit off the candle that was burning in the middle of the table and stared at Lana as she radiated the light. I felt like I was starting to sober up – a momentary lapse at best. It was only a matter of time until the next wave came and knocked my eyes into the back of my skull.

The sky was draped in a thick black cloth, with thousands of stars shooting throwing themsleves across the sky. I tried counting every single one but I gave up after I got to 156. The trawlers that had been fishing under the cover of darkness shot fireworks into the atmosphere in anger, trying in vain to bring down the heavens. Each time a ship sent a technicolor volley off into the sky, they were met by a flurry of enemy fire. Rockets with felt-tipped warheads flew back and forth exploding on impact and scorching everything in their path. The battle continued through the night until the darkness was so crowded with nuclear violence that I had to look away. The third wave was finally here.

"What is it?" asked Lana as she put her hand on my back.

"It's nothing it's just those goddamn fireworks," I stared back at the sky and twitched with excitement. I let out a demented chuckle, "Can't you see the fucking sky is falling!

Lana shook her head in frustrated disbelief, "You don't actually see fireworks do you?"

I turned around so that she could see the twisted look of amazement on my face. "Sure..." I said as I point up to the sky "Look, the whole fucking sky is on fire!"

She stared into the distance like a lost boy waiting impatiently for Peter Pan to appear. But it was futile. She was crushed, and the look on her face broke my heart for a second. Then I looked back at the sky and let myself drown in the violent spectacle. When I opened my eyes again, she was still there with the radiant tapestry draped over her face. "Where's Jasmine?" I asked.

"She went to bed about half an hour ago."

Sam didn't seem to have noticed. I stretched out my hand and grabbed the cigarette from Lana. "That's a shame." He looked at the palm of his hand and sighed. "To be honest it's probably for the best. I'm surprised she stuck around as long as she did in the first place."

"Tell me about it," I turned to Lana, "What the hell are you still doing here?"

She snatched her cigarette back and took a drag. "I was having fun." It must have been well after midnight. I checked the clock. It had been almost seven hours since we had first sat down. *"Billy Jean is not my Lover..."*

I couldn't take it anymore. "What the hell is going on?"

They both looked at me in confusion.

"If I hear that fucking song one more time... I thought Michael Jackson was dead. What the hell is wrong with these people?"

Lana shook her head and laughed. She was drunk and she slurred her words as she talked, "You've been saying that for the last few hours now."

I froze. I wasn't sure whether I was embarrassed or not. "Well then why doesn't somebody fucking do something about it?"

I looked around the aquarium. We were all alone except for the hippy waitress who was now on the other side of the bar smoking a well-earned joint.

"Should we settle our bill?"

"We already did," she said with the calming patience of a mother.

"Well," I lay back down and shut my eyes for a moment. "I'm not really sure what we should do then."

The candles were snuffing themselves out under the weight of the melting wax and the walls of the aquarium started to breath more slowly. There was little evidence of the schools of fish that had been swimming around just a few minutes earlier. The trawlers must have scooped them up once they finished shooting down the sky.

We retired to the plastic beach chairs around the pool. I lay there in a heap of sweat and fear, watching the sky shudder as the stars flickered in silence. They were no longer firing desperately at the boats and the fishermen were now going about their business, quietly hauling their catch back to distant ports. Lana looked content as she took humble drags from her cigarette. Even the ocean held its breath as it lapped sparingly against the dry sand. I felt like I could simply melt into the waves and disappear forever.

"I think I'm going to bed," Sam gasped.

"You going to woo her?" I snarled.

"Are you crazy! Look at me! I'm in no state to be around other human beings..."

"Well, at least you'll be in good company," I sighed.

Sam grunted and stumbled toward our room. Lana stayed with me and split another cigarette with me. Her face blossomed under the reflection of the sky as the illusions started to fade. I knew that nothing good come of this and I was relieved she was sleeping with Jasmine tonight. I watched the ember as it crawled towards her finger tips. I switched back and forth between squinting at the sky and watching the smoke pass through her lips. When the ember reached the bottom she lit another one. She put her lighter away and handed me the cigarette before heading to her room. I lay there for a while, idling in the breeze. The air was warm and the stars sputtered around in circles like whirligigs. It wasn't long until I lost interest in my visions. I stubbed out the cigarette that had long since burned down to the filter and went to join Sam in the honeymoon suite.

Fourteen

I woke up the next morning full of pain and doubt. The ecstasy of last night's adventure had all but worn off and the injuries from the fight were slowly creeping back. My neck was wrenched tight and I could hear the miniscule vertebrae in my spine grinding against one another every time I shifted in bed. I couldn't even roll onto my side without feeling something crack or pop out of place. I had faint visions and blasts of colours and warm candlelit angels to watch over us as we twitched in fits of uncontrollable joy and fear. What it a matter of Religion? Most definitely not. Spirituality? Not likely. Hedonism? Only in the most vulgar sense of the word. From that point on, all ties to reality had been cut.

I threw on a pair of shorts and went outside. Sam was hunched over a plate of fried eggs and fresh melon. "Where are the girls?"

Sam looked up from his book. "They went in to town. Lana needed to buy more cigarettes."

"I didn't know there was a town on this island."

"Probably not, but I saw a few gas stations on our way here."

"I guess I shouldn't have smoked all of them," I said quietly.

"Don't worry, they'll survive."

I went back into the room and had a long shower. It had been weeks since we'd had hot water and it felt good to have it scald my skin. When I was done I grabbed a book and lay in the hammock on our front porch. The ocean was calm. I tired to read but I couldn't help being distracted by the cruel monotony of the ocean lapping the shore like a tired dog.

I woke up to the familiar sound of shrill voices lapping over top of the calm of the ocean. I pulled the book off my face at the point where I had drifted off and rubbed in the small stain of saliva that had formed on the page. I pried my eyes open to a squint so I could see them. They were crowded giddily around Sam in their bikinis. I quickly closed my eyes again and forced myself back to sleep. I couldn't handle that – not right now.

I woke up as the sun was starting to set. I went over and joined the girls and Sam in the aquarium.

"How was town?" I grumbled.

"Not very exciting," said Jasmine. "But we got to ride a motorcycle."

Lana held up two packs of smokes and waved them in my face to show that the mission had been a success. We sat down and ordered some drinks. I was dead sober but the girls were still glowing. They fidgeted about under the table as they drank their beers. Lana smiled at me. I could tell what was about to come.

"We've decided we don't need to go to the capital," Jasmine said gleefully. "Our motorcycle driver said that there is a huge party in the jungle in two days. It's supposed to be even crazier than the one on the beach." It had taken us long enough to get away from the pedestrian madness of the last island but they were already dying to get back into action.

"This is the closest thing to paradise you'll ever find," I said hoping they would believe me.

Jasmine looked at me disapprovingly. "But we're bored. We want to party."

There was a delayed silence. Then Lana piped up sheepishly. "We were also thinking that we wanted to try mushrooms."

Jesus Christ, I thought. This could only end in disaster. Of course Sam and I had already made plans for it to end that way, but dragging two innocent girls down with us felt – well, it didn't really make me feel anything at all. But that was beside the point.

We tried to talk them out of it but Lana was insistent, "Why not? We want to see the fireworks too."

I wanted to tell them that it wasn't all pretty colours and fireworks. *You fucking hypocrite! Are you actually going to stand there and lie to these girls trough your teeth? Who the hell are you to tell them what to do?* Sam looked over at me. After what happened last night, it wasn't a question of if. It was matter of when.

I tried to shrug off her comments and suggested coming up with a plan to make it to the party in time. We sat down with the girl's German copy of the Vacant Universe and scoured over the maps and bus schedules.

"If we want to get there in two days time, we'll have to leave first thing in the morning then take an overnight boat to the island. It'll be tight but it can be done!"

"That sounds like it should work," Sam said as he leaned back in his chair. Jasmine and Lana nodded in approval.

"We also thought that now we're be married, we should all get tattoos," said Lana, before Jasmine jumped in, "Matching ones..."

I rolled my eyes. It was bad enough they wanted us to pry them full of drugs. Now they wanted us to tag ourselves with a permanent reminder of it all. The last thing I needed was some tribal stamp of approval to haunt me for the rest of my days. Then again we'd already made it this far.

"Sure why not," I tossed out.

"And what about mushrooms?" asked Lana.

I scratched my head for a second and looked at her. Nothing good was going to come of this but what was I supposed to say to her? Now that the cat was out of the bag there was no turning back. If they were going to insist on their fireworks, we were going to fucking give them fireworks.

"If you're going to start stuffing your face with mind-altering drugs, then I suppose this is the place to do it."

Their faces shifted back and forth looking for something to focus on. They hesitated for a second. Then they finally caved. "Ok... Let's do it."

I went up the bar and talked to the English girl in the canvas trousers. I tried to order a round but the she shook her head. "Sorry, but you cleaned us out yesterday."

"You mean you don't have anymore?" I asked skittishly.

"That's what I said." She grabbed some empty bottles off the bar and threw them into a plastic milk crate. "We're going to have to send someone to pick some more."

'*Bullishit,*' I thought to myself, '*it's not like they grow on trees.*"

'No, they actually grow in elephant shit. And every time we want some, we have to go and send someone to pick them. The fresher the better!"

I came back told them and relayed the message. "She says we drank them dry last night." Lana shrugged her shoulders in relief, before letting them slump back down, "There's always the next island."

We sat around as the sun melted into a thin veil of grey clouds. None of us moved until well after the heat of the day was completely snuffed out by the dark blanket of lights. My jaw and neck started to loosen up as the pressure in the air continued to drop. The water was dark and the stars refused to come out. I could hear the rumbling of the storm as it started to roll over the horizon. Then there was a tingling rap on the roof above us. It didn't take long for them to grow to full sized globs that smacked heavily into the narrow strip of sand below.

As the rain came down harder, I could make out a donkey in the distance, labouring across the sand. As it came closer I could see that it was one of the white ponies that had been strutting down the beach when we arrived. He was dragging a thick metal fence post behind him. It was attached to his neck with a length of chain and he hunched over as he pulled himself across the beach, dragging a collection of empty shells and clumps of garbage that were caught up in the chain behind him. I panicked for a second. I worried I might be having a relapse. But when I saw the girls' pitiful reaction I knew I wasn't hallucinating.

We spent the rest of the night drinking slowly, huddled under the thatched roof of the aquarium, surrounded by a thick wall of rain. The noise of the water falling all around us drowned out the soothing island jams coming from behind the bar. It was a nasty storm and the smacking and trickling of water on the outside made the aquarium seem safe in comparison to the moonlit beach. A few of the local sharks challenged the girls to a game of pool. Sam and I watched on as they smashed the balls with the felt-tipped cues. They knocked the balls around the best they could but in the end it only served to draw out the inevitable loss. When the sharks were done with the girls they challenged Sam and I to a game. By the time we had all taken turns trying to hustle them, we were all down a few beers and whatever small amount of pride we had left.

Lana licked her wounds and headed to bed, and Sam retired with Jasmine soon after. When I came into the room Lana was spread face down across the bed with her legs crossed in the air with one hand cradling her sunburnt face and the other holding open a book, which lay open on top of the sheets. She cocked her head up from the page as I walked in.

"I see you've found my books," I said, as I threw my shirt onto the floor.

"I was just looking at them," she said, as she flipped the pages back and forth haphazardly "I hope you don't mind."

"Not at all," I said.

"I especially like this one." She held the book up to her face, then flipped to the place where she had wedged her pale thumb between the faded pages. "Will you read it to me?" she asked as she patted the empty space on the bed beside her.

I looked at the spine. It was an old collection of Tom Gabel poems. I smiled and sat against the wall before grabbing the book from her:

... When you sleep,
You can't feel the hunger
When you sleep,
No one is lonely in a dream...
...When you sleep,
She's standing there with open arms,
And one night could last forever,
And if you asked her,
She'd never let go,
And you'd stay forever...
... And the sun's always rising
In the sky somewhere,
And if young hearts should explode
From all the lies they've been told...
To live through a night like this,
I would trade it for the silence.

Lana smiled at me with her pitiful blue eyes as I closed the book on the bed. She was calm but her face was filled with a heavy melancholy emptiness. She was desperate to see her boyfriend. She was madly in love with him and she knew he was probably busy barebacking around the Gold Coast with some bronze-nippled surfer girl. But that didn't matter. Her mind was set. And now she was willing to settle for anyone who was willing to pretend that they cared.

My brain seized up. I knew I was supposed to play along – tease it out of her, before filling her with superficial resentment and regret. But I just couldn't bring my self to do it. It was too sad, too depraved even for me.

I turned the light off and she crawled into my armpit. I wasn't sure what to do. I wanted so badly to just reach down to grab her inner thigh and wait for her to beg me to stop. But every time my knuckles twitched with excitement my stomach would respond by churning violently, before sinking back to the depths of my bowels – shame and paranoia and doubt all rolled into one. I put my hand around her back, out of harms way, and held on for as long as possible.

"Did you really see fireworks last night?" she whispered with her toes tucked between the heels of my feet and the sheets.

Her innocence sparked a sadness in me. One day she would make a model single mother, full of love for her three kids and a proud resentment for her deadbeat husband. But that was still a broken home and a few thousand miles away. I hung my limp fingers on the soft bones of her hips and clenched my eyes closed as tightly as possible, hoping that she would mistake my heavy breathing for a deep sleep.

Fifteen

We were picked up by a white mini-van just after sunrise. It was already full with shoddy backpacks and their loyal guardians when it pulled in, and I ended up getting stuck in the front seat beside the driver. He spoke broken English with a deranged stutter, which was exaggerated by a tendency to aggressively rub his runny nose between mumbling. He rode the clutch hard into the floor, shifting between gears without taking his foot off the pedal, so that every time we sped up the engine jerked me forward off the edge of my seat. Occasionally he would swerve as he reached for the breast pocket of his shirt. He would pull out a small glass vile and shove it into one of his nostrils and suck the nauseating vapour up into his sinuses, before rubbing the tears from his watering eyes.

We came to a flooded river and pulled onto a rust-covered ferry that would take us to the mainland. I stayed in the front seat with the driver as the van emptied out the brown steel of the decaying platform. When we got to the other side I checked in the rear view mirror to make sure that Sam and the girls had gotten back in. When I looked back I saw the pudgy hobbits sitting glibly with their hands crossed over their knees like schoolboys who had just been told off by their headmaster. They looked at least as bad as I felt and it appeared as if they had somehow managed to lose the Danes. It was only a matter of time until the same fate came to us but for the time being Sam and Jasmine were in love and Lana was content to be quietly homesick.

I sat in the front seat with no one to talk to. I hadn't spent this much time alone since I'd gotten off the plane. We didn't have many days left to go but that wasn't much of a consolation. What was I going back to? I had no job, no prospects, no income, no assets, no leverage, no stocks, no net value, no bonds, no credit, no debt and no mortgage. I had ambition, drive, and ideas. Shit! I had more ideas than you could shake a finger at. But it wasn't easy finding someone who was prepared to deal in something as fickle as ideas. I just needed to catch a break, a foot in the door, anything to get me started. I suppose I could always go back to London and convince someone that I had what it takes. Maybe I could get Harry's dad to take me on for a while, just until I could make a name for myself. It might take a lot of begging and convincing but there was no shame in that. Maybe I would get lucky and have some long lost relative pass away and leave me the kind of inheritance that would let me continue on this twisted adventure forever. If nothing else it would keep me motivated, haunted by the fear of my own mortality.

The driver kept reaching for his breast pocket and taking deep whiffs from his bottle as we swerved amongst the jagged green mountains. We drove on for hours, heading north along the width of a flimsy mass of land that split the ocean into pair of foreign coastlines. We passed through festering swamps and endless plains overgrown with blades of grass the size of scarecrows. I could make out temples balanced sensually on the overhanging monsters in the distance. The clusters of roadside bunkers that clung devoutly to the side of the road that were the only signs of civilization for miles at a time. We were driving past one of the concrete hamlets when a shot rang out. Bang!

Everyone in the van dropped their heads between their knees in anticipation of an attack. The van lurched forward and to the right where the rubber of the tire had finally given out. The van wobbled to a stop and the passengers went back to being unfazed by their surroundings. We cleared out of the vehicle and I sat on the gravel shoulder throwing small rocks at the chicken-wire fence in the sweltering heat on the side of the road while our driver changed the tire. After half and hour, he managed to muscle a spare tire onto the rusted axel. We all piled back in and assumed our positions as the freshly painted mountains continued to recede behind us, until they were nothing but a few green dimples shimmering on the horizon.

We had a few hours to kill when we got the next town. Sam and I were starving but the girls wanted to go exploring so we split up. We dodged around mopeds and speeding delivery trucks as we looked for somewhere to eat. We ended up finding a greasy burger joint at the bottom of a hill, which had a never-ending set of polished marble steps leading up to a brilliant white temple that was capped and crested in gold. We sat in silence eating our burgers and drinking coke in the shade of the monument.

"You going to tell Jasmine about the temple?" I asked Sam, as we headed back to the bus stop.

"It's probably best if we don't. We'll never hear the end of it."

I woke up as we pulled into the industrial port where the ferry was waiting for us. The edge of the water was lined with waterlogged cargo ships and algae covered sailboats moored underneath the watch of rusting mechanical cranes. It was dark out and we went over to an open-air market with food stalls to eat portions of rice and beef served in mismatched plastic bowls. The table next to us was full with a bunch of NGO workers that laughed indecipherably at each other's quirky insecurities. Then came the enthusiastic rendition of happy birthday, which they followed with a spirited round of applause as they all stood up and clapped on in self-congratulation.

We bought a bag of beers and boarded the boat. It was an old style Mississippi paddleboat that had been converted into a floating heroin den, with thin green mattresses spread out on the floor at regular intervals. We were getting ready to pull out when the voices of the happy birthday choir started to echo up the stair well. They walked past a dishevelled junky with the long fingernails and put their bags down on the flattened mattresses next to us.

"You sound like you're from the same place we are," one of them said with a bright white smile.

"Ya," Sam said, jumping at the chance to shut them up. "We're from the 51st state, eh!"

"Oh! Cool," she said indifferently. "How long have you been here for?"

"Too long," Sam said.

One of the girls that had her face buried in her backpack took offence to Sam's comments.

"That's too bad, you're missing out," said the girl in the middle, in the matter of fact tone of a bloated Telletubby. Sam didn't respond as she continued to lecture us. "We actually live here. We all do..." she exclaimed as she pointed to the other two girls who were busy organizing their rations of toothpaste and tampons into concealed fanny packs. "We teach English in the North of the country. The flooding got pretty bad in town so we figured we'd come and do a few touristy things for once," she said expecting to get a rise out of us.

"We actually don't know very many people."

"Great..." Sam mumbled in response to her first statement, completely oblivious to the fact that she had continued talking. "That's really great..." he repeated.

We were all tired and we just wanted to get on with it and be left alone in peace.

They returned to their huddle for a moment. "Do you like diving?" one of them asked hoping to spark our intrigue.

Sam kept on ignoring her. When she kept prying I blurted out something about us being part of a neo-conservative polygamous cult, and she went back to fidgeting with her refillable bottle of water. The engine shot great billowing plumes of smoke into the sky as we pulled out of the docks. The boat was old and it sat heavy in the water. I could hear the sound of the bilge pumping heavy and often above the rumble of the engine to keep it afloat. Jasmine nestled between Sam and her bags with Lana lying close beside. The window was open and the air moved in as the boat pushed slowly across the water. The heat filtered up from below but I felt refreshed and I couldn't get myself sleep. We pulled further away from land until we were surrounded by the colourless green of the ocean. I kept my head poked out the window to keep myself from choking on the fumes. I felt at ease once the boat started to move. Once we got into open water the stars grew brighter. They cast a murky halo in the dark wake of water that surrounded the boat as we ploughed noisily through the night. Every time I looked back at Sam and the girls they looked like they were in a peaceful dream.

By the time the boat pulled into the dock the darkness was slowly fading from the sky. A rundown purple truck was waiting to take us away at the end of the dock. The driver asked us where we wanted to go.

"The beach," I blurted out.

"Which one?" he asked stubbornly.

We were all too tired too deal with this shit. All we wanted was a place where we could rest until the sun came up. "Any one," I said in frustration. "We are going to the big party tomorrow."

He grumbled and put the keys in the ignition. The road was sheltered by thickets of spindly branches on either side as the island dipped and rolled into an endless maze of hills and valleys. Small slivers of sun began to creep through the thick black overgrowth that hung overhead and the grey bark began to glow as we took corners at high speeds. All of a sudden, the driver slammed the breaks on to avoid hitting a pack of fluorescent drunks that was stumbling across the street.

The driver mumbled something under his breath and shifted back into gear. We took another corner and almost hit another glow in the dark junkie as he tripped into a bush. I kept my eyes on the side of the road as we took off again. There were signs strung up on white vinyl banners over the road advertising tomorrow's big party. But something wasn't right. I kept watching the sings as they passed by "What day is it?" I asked.

Sam was half asleep. "How should I know?" he grumbled. When he saw that I was still waiting for an answer he ventured a guess. "Sunday?"

Same day as on the signs. As we got closer the streets began to fill with herds of neon sherpas. They were trekking down from the jungle back to their beach huts. I was too tired to care that we'd missed the party. I wanted to strap a cowcatcher onto the front of the truck and plough them all into the ocean.

We sped down the final hill as dusk pierced the hazy skin of its bloody orange sphere. The ocean faded to its natural shade of brilliant turquoise and the thin strip of sand in front of the fortified bungalows shimmered in a toxic shade of silver. The parasitic mob was instantly blinded, and the ravers on the road quickened their pace as they sprinted for the cover of darkness.

The truck came to a stop in front of a hotel at the bottom of the hill. I ran across the street to strike a deal with the concierge, who had his lips pressed against a steaming mug of coffee. We argued back and forth until he finally he agreed to give us two rooms for the price of one. We went across the street and checked into our rooms, which had a striking view of the flashing sign of the 24-hour convenience store across the way. Behind the shops, the pink flesh of the sky was slowly revealing itself. I turned down the thermostat and shut the blinds, before falling into a deep sleep in the comfort of air-conditioned bliss.

Sixteen

I was up against the ropes. I could hear him yelling in the distance: '*Hit him! Fucking hit him!*'. How did I get myself into this situation? I could hear the music rising in the background: Dada- duh, Dada da duh, Dada duh dada da dah. The triumphant march of Rocky Balboa was being trumpeted out over a megaphone like a broken record before a grinding voice chimed up: *"Come down tonight to the arena to watch the big fight! .... Drinks specials all night long. Bring your friends! And don't miss the chance to see..."*

The sun cut through the floor to ceiling blinds. I was craving far more than the 2 hours of sleep we'd had, but every 15 minutes another truck drove past and rattle our windows *"Come down and see for yourself..."* Sam rolled into the room with Jasmine as they announced the main event. "We're going to grab some food. You coming?" I rolled out of bed and threw on some pants. The streets were empty and the dusty rectangular buildings looked like disused painted cardboard cut-outs that had been used on the set of an ol' fashioned shootout in some distant Western studio.

"Hey, isn't that place that Phillip was telling us about?" Sam said, pointing to a large yellow sign at the end of the road.

"It looks like it," said Jasmine.

We followed the yellow glare to the entrance of the building. A bowing waiter handed us menus as we walked in the door. The walls were plastered with colourful pieces of construction paper marked up with sweeping cursive messages. They weren't written in English and they definitely weren't Asian or Russian. The emotional flow of the script and the abrupt gaps in between the words looked familiar but I couldn't place them. It was even on the menus, which were covered in English on one side and the cursive script on the other. I overheard the table next to us talking and all of a sudden it clicked. I'd seen that writing on TV, spray-painted onto the sides of bombed out shelters and scrawled across tattered god-fearing banners. Whatever it was, it wasn't any of our business.

I went back to focussing on my meal as we tried to figure out what we were going to do now that we had missed the big party.

"When are we going to get our tattoos?" chirped Lana with a smile.

I had already forgotten about our promise. I had hoped the idea would have faded as soon as we left the last island, just like everything else. But Lana was dead serious and so was Jasmine. All of sudden Sam's jumped in, feigning enthusiasm, "Why don't we get them after lunch."

At first I thought he was just trying to humour them but then he started debating the merits of one design over another, and I realised there was nothing funny about what was going on. Once we were finished eating we headed out into the street, looking for a tattoo parlour. There was hardly a lack of them but they were all either filthy or closed. We walked back to the hotel with our heads held low. Then, just as we were passing the exotic convenience store that flashed outside our window a man sweeping the front of his parlour greeted us, 'Hello. How are you?" he asked with the familiar enthusiasm of an old country gentleman. It was the oldest trick in the book. We walked past him and talked amongst ourselves, then doubled back. The old country gentleman introduced himself as Juan. Two artists huddled over an antiquated computer screen in the corner. They nodded at us before returning to the screen. "Don't mind them," Juan said. "They don't speak very good English."

They both garbled incoherently at him and he laughed. "See what I mean…"

He ushered us in and invited us to sit on the black pleather sofas. "So what can I do for you?"

"We need a souvenir, something so that we never forget this trip," said Lana.

"That can be arranged," he replied without hesitation.

The only problem is that we couldn't agree on a design. We argued back and forth for a bit until Juan ordered his inked-covered pointdexters to work. They sat there scribbling away on large pads of white paper. Every once in a while they would flip the pad around and show them to us and we would counter by trying to explain what we were looking for, using Juan as our translator. When that didn't work we started miming it out by grimacing and gesturing with our hands. But everything they came up with was pre-programmed and uninspired.

After watching them go at it for half an hour Sam grabbed the pad of paper and started to sketch something out. "I didn't know you could draw," said Jasmine.

"I can't." he said as he put his head down. Jasmine looked over at Lana and then at me with a worried expression on her face.

After a few minutes he held up his masterpiece. It was angular and distorted, and it looked like it had been drawn by an autistic child who'd spent the last 2,000 years locked up in a dungeon. We all burst out laughing and the demented figure on the white page laughed back. We'd finally found what we had been looking for.

Juan admitted he had never seen anything quite like it, but that wasn't going to stop him. He had been doing this long enough to have seen it all. He didn't really care what people wanted to plaster over their bodies. To him business was business, especially in low season.

"I have seen people wanting to get penises tattooed on their forehead."

"When they were sober?" Lana asked alarmingly.

"Maybe not so sober. But people can get angry, even violent, and then what I am supposed to do?"

"Do they ever ask for their money back?" Lana asked, worrying about what might happen if something went horribly wrong.

"All the time! They wake up, come down here screaming at me. Telling me that I ruined their lives. They are saying they don't remember anything... blah blah blah. I tell them if this has ruined your life, then you have bigger problems to deal with."

He paused as he twirled the needle between his fingers like a drumstick, "I am not a priest or a lawyer. I am just an artist. If you tell me to draw it, I will draw it."

Juan continued to prepare the ink and offered us beers from a magnet-covered mini-fridge. When we had finished them all, Sam went across the street to buy more from the 24-hour convenience store that was run by Juan's sister. We took turns sitting in the chair and he kept telling us tales as we got inked. When he heard that Sam was living in London the tone in his voice grew soft. "I've been to London one time," he said. "That is where I learned how to make tattoos."

It sounded like the usual elaborate hoax. Why would you go all the way to London to learn how to be a tattoo artist when you were surrounded by endless strips of parlours here?

"Really?" I asked.

"Yes. I used to live in a small flat in Camden. Right near the tube," he said as he exhaled heavily. "I had a girlfriend from Spain. Oh God, she's the most beautiful creature you have ever seen."

He pointed to the desk where the other two were sitting and told me to check the drawers. "In there, under all those magazines... Have a look."

I rifled through the piles of automotive and PG skin-mags until I got to the bottom of the drawer. Sure enough there was a matted photograph of him with his arms around an odd-looking mulatto girl with a jet-black fringe and a nose ring, taken in front of Nelson's Column in Trafalgar Square.

"That was five years ago..." he said resignedly. He lit a cigarette and stuck it between his lips as he continued to work away on Sam. "One day she will come here to visit me." He paused and looked out the front of the shop, then went back to his work. "Or maybe I will go back to London... or maybe Spain."

The fight truck chugged by with another grim reminder: *"Come see the Mighty Russian Bear take on the Chinese Tiger in a 5 round winner takes all..."* The girls took their turn in the chair and we kept drinking. There were two ladies standing outside the shop saying prayers with their faced caked in white chalk. "What are they doing?" Lana asked.

"They are in exile, from Burma," Juan said without looking up. "They use the paint to protect them from the sun. They are praying to Buddha for a safe journey home."

"You mean Myanmar?" asked Sam.

He looked and paused for a moment, "Right, Myanmar..." he groaned.

Jasmine groaned back as he dug the needle into her back. As Juan put on the finishing touches, I asked about what we could do on the island now that everyone had left. He gave us a few options. When we explained the real reason we had come here Juan's eyes lit up. He knew exactly what we were looking for. "You have to go to the mountain."

I asked him to elaborate but all he said was, "Go to the mountain and you will see. You will not be disappointed."

I'd read about the mountain in the Vacant Universe. They made it sound like a dilapidated Rastafarian heroin den for mindless degenerates, and like most things it was labeled as just another rundown tourist trap. Once it was dark we headed back down to the beach. The charcoal mountain poked out of the ocean at the tip of the island. It rose upward toward the sky until a thick concrete slab proppsed on top of thick cylindrical pillars drew an abrupt line across its face, cutting it off from the sky above. The industrial base-camp hung precariously in the dark, begging us to climb to the top.

When we got to the top of the stairs we were greeted by graffitied monkeys and dragons, which were painted on the walls. The concrete floors were covered with knock-off Persian rugs and polyester cushions thrown on the floor in a pathetic attempt to make the mountain seem warm and inviting. A group of obnoxious field trippers huddled around a pile of backpacks in the corner were awkwardly passing around a pre-rolled joint. They looked strange and out of place. All of a sudden a roar of excitement withered from the circle and two of them exchanged a high-five, before returning to their miniature high definition screen. "I can't believe you finally beat that level..."

We went to the bar and tried to order a round of mushroom cocktails, and the bartender directed us to the decrepit shack with a corrugated tin roof at the back of the mountain. They served us a thick grey sludge in small plastic cups. This was as good a time as any to give the girls a chance to run away.

"Are you sure you want do this?" I asked.

They both smiled eagerly, as if they were about to embark on some kind of magical adventure. "We're here aren't we..." Lana said stubbornly.

I raised my glass and squeezed the gruel into the back of my throat. We ordered some beers and sat on the cold hard concrete floor as we waited for the poison to kick. Lana smiled giddily at the view down below. She was caught in a profound daze, "It all looks so small."

I waited for her to finish her thought but it never came. We sat in a circle, staring at the trees swaying over the water, waiting for something to happen. I tried to block out the threatening thoughts. I wondered whether I could make a run for it. But it was completely out of my hands now and no amount of cocktails or prescriptions drugs, or warm-blooded company was going to change that. I should have stayed home and joined in the protests, if only to keep myself from feeling so fucking hopelessly guilty.

The familiar feeling started to creep back as a slow pounding rhythm rose from the speakers. My eyes began to water and I could feel the blood in my fingers being reduced to a fine pulp. The palm trees in the distance started to dance. It wasn't long until the girls joined in with gaping smiles smeared across their faces.

We climbed to the top of a fortified gazebo that hung over the bar perched on wooden stilts. We began waltzing around to the monotonous beat which was steadily growing louder. The girls spun around and around – ring around the rosy – spinning around on their tiptoes until they fell down on the floor, collapsing into an avalanche of rosy cheeks. My eyes twitched back and forth, faster and faster, until I couldn't keep track of their spinning limbs anymore. My brain shook into a frenzy of warm colours – orange and red and crimson and peach. Warm colours. Warm and safe inside my stomach, moving faster through my veins to the tips of my fingers.

Lana burst into a fit of hysterical laughter, her cheeks twitching uncontrollably until she was nothing more than an ethereal glow of skin and teeth. Her laughter mixed in with the pounding of the beat. The noise continued to rise to a violent crescendo, until all of a sudden, the bubble burst. Lana fell to the floor and her laugh slowed to a whimper. She lay still for a moment, before jumping up and running to the edge of the stairs. When she got there she buried her face in her hands until she disappeared out of sight. This was more than just an intermission – this was a fucking crisis!

I rushed over to the spiral staircase and tried to talk to her. I put my hand on her back, but she shuddered and buried her head deeper between her legs. For a moment I was sober again. But how was that supposed to help? Just a few hours ago, she had been the only thing keeping us sane and now she was crumbling right before my eyes. The sweet pastels in her face vanished in a flash and her skin become more and more alive with terrifying colours. *How did I descend into this hell! What did I do to deserve this! Who are these people? Where the hell is my boyfriend?* The colour continued to draw from her cheeks – blue, and red and pink – until she was almost her natural wintery shade of ivory. *I'm sure he's fucking some Australian whore right now.*

She gripped her hands tightly in front of her chest and rocked back and forth. I put my hand on her back. "Don't worry, it'll be ok. Just try and relax. Look around you, you're in paradise remember?" She looked up from her bare feet and stared me in the eye. Her eyes were filled with ripples of red waves and the veins underneath her skin were cold and blue. The pressure was building. It looked like her eyes were about to explode but they just stood there staring bleakly back at me. She blinked to try and keep herself from crying. *"There's no such thing as a paradise."*

I wanted to help but I couldn't allow myself to get sucked in by her misery. I charged back up the stairs. The thumping of the music rescued me just in time. Jasmine was smiling but her face was cold as steel. "How do you feel?" I asked.

She stared straight at me with her pursed lips. "I feel fine. I don't see what the fuss is?"

She was a proud little bitch. Even the world's finest concoction of narcotics wouldn't have put a dent in her conscience. She was in control – always in control; and she was terrifying.

"I'm glad to hear it but I don't think your friend is doing so well," I licked my lips. "I don't think there's anything I can do to help. You might want to have a look…"

She tried to keep a bold face but it was obvious that our antics were finally starting to wear on her. It was bad enough that I was keeping her from Sam and now we had submitted her friend to a state of self-imposed psychological warfare. Lana was in rough shape. It was a disaster! *And it's all your fault.* I turned to Sam for reassurance "What are we going to do now?"

He looked at me with a serious smile, "There's nothing we *can* do. She said she wanted to see fireworks and now she has to deal with the consequences."

I was worried that Jasmine's vacant smile had been rubbing off on Sam but he was right. There was nothing we could do. By the time I looked back over my shoulder to check on Lana she had disappeared. I rushed to the edge of the gazebo and looked over the railing. She was doing her best to concentrate on putting one foot in front of the other without falling down the stairs. It was only a matter of time until she realised the mistake she had made, but by then it would be too late. I would never find out the real reason she had come here. Maybe I was to blame for what had happened – this could have been *my* fucking mess! But no matter how much I wanted it to be true, I knew I couldn't be held responsible. She was going to go over the edge at some point. All I did was give her a little push.

The clouds that had been forming all afternoon started to open up. I looked down at the beach. I could make Jasmine and Lana's silhouettes huddling under a palm tree, hiding from the rain.

"Hey Sam..." I said as I pointed towards them.

He danced over with his arms flailing uncontrollably at his sides. He reached out and grabbed the waste-high wooden railing and looked down. "Don't worry, they'll be fine," he said, and he turned back to the middle of the pavilion, moving around in maddening spirals.

There was only one solution: more! We needed more hallucinogens! More psilocybins! More bass ... we certainly needed more bass! If it hadn't been for the guttural ticking of the bass we would have been doomed!

The music roared in a violent surge of thumping and pounding. The cancer was spreading fast; oozing through my veins. I was in bloom. My thoughts swelled into violent balls of pleasure. The bass and the drugs tugged away at my bowels. *What now?* Submit to unbridled barbarism, or risk choking on my own tongue. I ran to the bathroom, panting and sweating in a daze. I propped myself up against the sides of the concrete confessional. I clenched my teeth and crouched down. Wary faces began to dance out of the cracks on the cold plaster. They swirled around, pulling themselves out of the algae coloured filament until they peeled away and stood bowing over my head, grasping for my pupils. I stared them down without blinking and laughed out loud in an attempt to scare them off but the visions only grew worse. I felt noxious. My stomach dropped violently before sinking to its knees at the altar below. I was paralyzed. The cold plaster walls writhed in delight at the sight of me wincing. I closed my eyes, hoping to make them go away. Their faces were etched in fluorescent lines on the dark flesh inside my eyelids. They were hideous, gruesome creatures and they just stared at me, laughing manically. Then, as I clenched my teeth down on my bottom lip, I felt a self-satisfied grin crawl upwards into the corners of my mouth. I felt the wretched pulse beating through my cheeks and into the clotted arteries behind my eyes. I stared at the fading faces and laughed back at them and they collapsed into the darkness.

I pushed myself out of the stall and stumbled back towards Sam. Down on the dance floor, the organ grinder continued to turn its crank, maliciously churning the airwaves until my ears were filled a satisfied rage. It was bliss, pure heaven, nothing could rob me of this moment, and I wanted more. I replayed each and every scene over and over in my mind: Every skirmish, every fire fight. Burning flags and clouds of blue smoke choked up the crowds in the jungle. The monkeys down below squirmed robotically along the wall, laughing at us with meticulous precision. *Don't listen to them! They don't know what they're talking about...The bass, that's all the matters. That's all we care about. The rest is just noise.*

Sam was lurching back and forth. He turned to me with a yawning smile. I grinned awkwardly, "What kind of sick human being could make this kind of music?"

Sam pointed up at the dj booth, "_____ can," He growled at the stage and stomped his feet. I put my arm around Sam and stomped my feet along with him. I had no idea what the hell he was talking about. I just was relieved to have Sam by my side.

The throbbing grew deeper and my teeth shuddered. I could feel my insides rotting, being slowly eaten away by the poison. The tiny circuits between my ears and my jaw winced. It felt like I was chewing on a ball of aluminium foil. We danced and danced and danced and danced, until we couldn't dance any more.

Thump! Thump! Thump!

Thump...   Thump...
          Thump...

    Boom!   Boom!   Boom!

Boom... Boom... Boom...

My ears slurred the rhythms as I tried to keep up. *"More!"* I trawled for Sam. "Sam! *Where are you?"* He was just behind me; two arm lengths away; huddled over by the dancing monkeys and the dragons.

"There you are."

He stared at me waiting for me to say something. *Did he hear me?*

"There you are." His eyes were sunken into the back of his skull, burning slowly inside the back of his head.

He grinned at me with the bulging white of his eyes. "We need more!" The Bass! We had another round and I felt myself retch in a violent fit. The rain came down harder and small crowds of stragglers ran up the mountain, looking for cover. They huddled at the foot of the stairs occasionally coming through the pass to get a glimpse of the view. Every time this happened Sam would dip and bow greeting them with a threatening grin before retreating to his state of trance, moving around the floor, flailing his arms wildly in the air like a mad priest. He kept waving his arms in violent circles with a manic grin on his face he waved them on into the night.

Somewhere in the depths of hell, Christmas had come early, and it brought with it the comfort – the cold, quiet comfort of something bigger than any of us could have ever imagined.

The pounding dragged on as the rain came down harder, forming puddles on the concrete floor. I tried to move my arms and legs through the damp shower but they just dragged along like limp vines hanging off a dying tree. I looked to Sam for help. His face was contorted into a laughing ball of rage. He had no intentions of leaving.

"We can't stay up here forever," I pleaded.

Sam looked at me with an invincible smile, "Of course we can. Who's going to stop us?"

He ignored me and went back to dancing in circles with his shirt tied around his head like a mercenary.

By the time we abandoned the mountain the sky was beginning to grow faint. We climbed down the stairs and stumbled down the beach, with the waves washing up against our feet. We crawled through the door and I rushed straight to the bathroom. I stood in front of the bowl, straining pitifully as I tried to squeeze out the last of the poison with the lights off. When I came out Sam was staring at himself in the mirror, running his fingers over the strained muscles around his eyes. "What the fuck are you doing!" I shouted.

I rushed to the bathroom and snatched a fresh towel. "Jesus Christ," I caught a quick glimpse of the thick green veins under my eyes as I threw it over the mirror. I turned on the TV and looked for anything; anything except for reports from dark navy suits about bombs over Baghdad. I stopped on a channel that was showing runway models trolling up and down the catwalk in extravagantly useless concoctions: Milan – Paris – Tokyo – Cape Town – just what the doctor ordered. Sam popped two Robaxacet and turned off the light. He lay there for a moment breathing heavily in the dark. "If I stop breathing, make sure I wake up," he whispered pathetically.

I lay there with my eyes fixed on the TV, thinking about having to resuscitate Sam's lifeless corpse.

"What if I stop breathing too?" I asked impatiently.

He took a few more deep breaths then let out a heavy sigh, "Well… Then I guess we're both fucked."

Seventeen

The TV was off and the towel was still hanging over the mirror when I woke up. I grabbed the remote and turned it on. I looked over at Sam. I couldn't tell whether or not he was breathing. I threw a pillow at him. Nothing.

"Sam!" I yelled. "Sam! Wake the fuck up… It's not fucking funny!" I grabbed a book from my bedside table and threw it at his head. His foot flinched and I fell back onto the bed, and breathed a sigh of relief.

I flipped through the channels for a while. Then came the ominous knock. The girls walked in. Lana had a sheepish look on her face and Jasmine went straight to the bed where Sam was still lying peacefully. Once he was in a state to sit up, we went downstairs to get something to eat. Lana did her best to force a smile during breakfast. It was painful to watch. I ordered an egg sandwich and watched as Sam tried to cozy up to Jasmine to make up for last night.

Jasmine looked over at Lana, "We thought we would go and visit a temple today. Juan said there's a really famous one about and hour north of here. We thought we would rent some mopeds and drive up the coast." She looked over at Sam with her long eyelashes and her thin green eyes.

It was their last day on the island and they weren't going to leave the country without seeing a temple. Somehow the idea had managed to catch Sam off guard.

"Sure. That sounds like a great idea," he Sam.

"I think I'll just go back to the hotel," I said. "I don't think I should be driving around on a moped in this state."

"But it's already twelve o'clock," Lana protested.

"I know," I said.

After lunch I went to an internet café and Sam went with the girls to get a moped. I reluctantly checked my emails to see if there was any news before heading back to the room – nothing. I went up to the room. It was cold and I lay under the duvet switching back and forth between the BBC and CNN:

Socrates is dead! Brazilian soccer player and self-proclaimed philosopher famously said:" I've overdone my relationship with alcohol..."

"Arab League to vote on foreign watchdogs in Syria: hopeful for settlement"

"Australia sells Uranium to India: simply ran out of reasons not to give ally what they wanted"

I kept flipping through the channels. All of sudden the door opened and Sam appeared in front of me.

"What happened?" I asked

He flopped down on the bed beside me. "I don't know. I just figured it would be best to let them go alone."

I couldn't blame him. I probably would have done the same thing if I had been in his shoes. The girl's came into our room a few hours later, knocking on the door as they entered. "You survived!" Sam said as he sat up. "How was the temple?"

"It was O.K." said Lana unenthusiastically.

"It was beautiful," added Jasmine as she lay down on the bed beside him. "You really should have come." This was it. She knew she was leaving and it was her time to shine.

"You girls managed fine on the scooter?" Sam asked

"What? You don't think we could handle it?" snapped Jasmine.

"We almost made one crash but it was so much fun!" Lana elaborated.

"Well, we're just glad you made it back in one piece," said Sam.

Sam's move had paid off. Jasmine was smitten. She put her arm on his lap and put one leg up on the bed. Lana couldn't seem to wipe the look of disgust off her face. "I'm going to read. I'll see you in a bit." They clearly wanted to be alone and I couldn't sit there and watch the two of them any longer.

I grabbed my book, put on a shirt and left. I thought about going next door but I knew nothing good could come from idle hours spent with frustrated fingers, so I headed down to the pool instead. There were a couple of two thousand pound gorillas in the water playing with some local girls. They were hairy and they laughed eagerly as they splashed clumsily after their newfound prizes. The girls obliged their captors' advances by letting out shrill screams and trying to swim away. Girls like that didn't come cheap. They were usually reserved for big money family men who were willing to shell out enough dough to keep them around for at least a week. Once in a while they would be tricked to falling in love with them and they'd make a deal with their pimp to pay for their freedom. It was a queer quid pro quo but who was I to judge.

They swam up to the bar, which was blasting dull psytrance at 180 beats per minute. A portly elderly woman was standing there, drinking champagne and orange juice while keeping an eye on her granddaughter, who was crawling near the edge of the pool. She was arguing with the bartender about either the quality or the price of her drink. She grumbled out loud while she mimed her thoughts out in wild gestures. The bartender nodded mechanically to show that he understood, but she kept yelling at him for dramatic effect. When she was done giving him shit, she walked away with a glass in her hand and a kinky grin on her face in celebration of her small moral victory. When she was out of sight I went up to the bar. I asked if they had strawberry margaritas but the bartender shook his head apologetically. I settled for a beer. As the bartender turned around and reached for the fridge, a deep American voice rose over my shoulder.

"Looks like a storm's coming!"

I had been watching the clouds crawl over the sliver of sun that was left in the sky for the past hour. "Sure does," I replied coolly without turning around.

"Whereabouts you from?" he asked with genuine curiosity.

I was thinking about what Sam was doing to Jasmine right about now. "Jesus! Where do I start?"

He burst out laughing, "I hear you man!"

I was too tired to lie. "I'm from Canada," I muttered quickly to stop the conversation from spiralling out of control.

"Oh man! I love Canadians. What a great country. I bet you can guess what country I'm from," he said with a polished laugh.

I nodded, "I've watched enough TV in my time."

He let out another rolling barrage of laughter. His voice had the familiar soothing tone that kept Hollywood directors in business. It was almost enough to start cheering me up.

"Guilty as charged." Another warming laugh, "Northern California to be exact. How long you been here?" he asked.

I scratched my head. It had been so long since I'd had to think, nevermind talk to another human being.

"You to eh? Well, you must be having a great time," he said with a cheerful sigh. "I'm here with my girl, she's back up in the hotel, making love to her books." He shook his head and took a swig of his beer. "Don't get me wrong, I love her to death but when you spend 6 months on the road together you need to able to enjoy a bit of alone time."

"I know what you mean," I sighed.

Another charming laugh. "You got a girl too?"

"Something like that..." I gave him a vague rundown of how we'd ended up here, and he smiled intently as I talked. "If it wasn't for them we wouldn't be here right now. But they're leaving tomorrow. Then it's back to normal for us."

"Well, what the hell are you doing talking to me? You should be up there taking care of business!" he said with a warm chuckle.

"No she's already got a man in her life. My buddy's up there taking care of business with her friend right now. Who knows, maybe he's having his way with both of them as we speak."

"Well, someone has to do it," he laughed before taking a swig of his beer. "It's funny you know. I actually met this guy in a few months ago who had two German girls following him around. Sounds just like your story. Ha! Probably just another one of those déjà-vus."

"Maybe it's the mushrooms." *Did I just say that out loud?* I stared at him looking for a reaction but he didn't hear me.

"Smoke?" he asked, as he flipped a cigarette into his mouth.

"No thanks."

"Good for you! This shit'll kill you."

I smirked at him to acknowledge his wisdom as he thumbed away at the flint on his red plastic lighter. We went back to sitting around in silence. My beer was growing warm in my hands. The conversation had trailed off. He lit up another cigarette and looked over at me. "You got that girl on your mind don't you?"

He paused and pointed towards the sky with his smoke, "She might have a boyfriend. But she's come this far hasn't she. You got to go out there and find out what's going on. Or at least find out what she's doing to your head. Besides what's the worst thing that can happen in one night?"

He took a sip from his beer and stared at me with his big white smile. "You know, I've always said that women should be considered guilty until proven innocent."

I froze for a second and thought about what he said.

"Don't get me wrong," he added, "I love my girl but how was I supposed to know she was the one until I proved it for myself. That kind of shit takes time and a lot of fucking around. And if you start messing around with feelings and pretty little things without knowing what you're doing, you're going to get burned."

I was confused by his argument but I nodded to show that I agreed with him. "Shit man, at the end of the day it's all relative," he said as he took a satisfied drag from his cigarette, "But it sure sounds like she's guilty to me."

I watched myself smile in the mirror behind the bar as I nodded in agreement. "Ya, maybe you're right!" It was hard not to be charmed by his voice and his cool insight, even if he was wrong about Lana.

"Cheer up," he said. "These things always have a way or working themselves out." He flashed a set of bright Hollywood teeth from behind his dark lips. "Let me buy you a beer."

"You don't have to do that," I said. "I know I don't *have* to but I want to." He flagged down the bartender. "And I will."

He laughed and I joined in.

"Thanks," I said. The bartender placed two bottles in front of us and we raised them up in the air.

"Name's Sunny..." he said as the bottles chimed together.

"Austin," I said without hesitation. We locked hands in a firm handshake, "Pleased to meet you Sunny."

"It's actually short for Sundog," he continued on, "my dad was half native and my mom was a hippy."

I shrugged in disbelief but he was already reaching for his pocket. "Here look at my passport." He pulled it out and flipped through it backwards so that I could catch a glimpse of the black and blue ink of the rubber stamps before landing on the photo ID at the front.

"No shit!" I said. "They must give you a hell of a time at customs."

"You'd think so wouldn't you… But most of the time they're too busy laughing at the name and calling their buddies over to have a look."

"Well you're lucky. I've been stripped searched, detained – everything – you name it, the whole nine yards, and for sweet fuck all!"

"Ya, I hear ya. I travel a lot for work so I've seen it all before. The only time I ever got stopped was when I was carrying a bunch of coffee back from Honduras. I was packing it up last minute and just wrapped the it all in padding and duct tape so it wouldn't get all messed up on the plane. When I brought it through customs in Dallas they just lost it on me! Thought I was carrying a bomb or something. The name really didn't help that time, neither did the skin colour."

"Fucking cocksuckers!" I hadn't felt that knee-jerk of anger in a while, and it felt good to let off on a bunch of crooks whose only defence was that they were only doing their job.

"So are you in the coffee business?" I asked.

"Ha ha ha!" He burst out laughing and slapped the table with the palm of his hand. "Fuck no!" he kept laughing.

"So what do you do?"

He had a Cheshire grin on his face, "I'm from Northern California man! What the hell do you think I do?"

I only had two guesses but I didn't feel the need to find out which one was right. I just smiled and nodded. I started to relax. It felt good to talk to someone whose head wasn't screwed on right. He started spurting on about how he was raised in the back of VW van by his father, who was a doctor and his mother who was a social worker. They would drive around California, homeless and making a living wherever they could. I nodded along vaguely until he raised his bottle expecting me to do the same.

"That's where I learned how to hustle." He grinned at me and put on a rugged accent, "It don't matter what you do in this world. If you can't hustle, you're lost."

Sunny kept telling me half-made-up stories until he was finished his beer.

"Better go check on my girl," he said. "I'm sure we'll see you around."

"Good luck with that," I said.

He laughed. "There's no such thing. We all make our own luck. That's what I say." He let out another roaring laugh that echoed around the pool as he walked away.

By the time I got up from the bar the clouds had completely blocked out the sun. I still needed to go to the bathroom. I didn't want to go back to the room and I couldn't face seeing Lana. I walked down thee street looking for a restaurant. I saw Sam walking towards the pool in a pair of sweatpants.

"Hey," he said with a shit-eating grin on his face.

"You're done..." I said trying not to sound surprised, "I was just looking for somewhere to take a piss. How long have I been gone for?"

"A couple hours. It's almost seven..." he said as he looked up at the sky.

I sighed, "Jasmine must be pleased..."

"I'd like to think so."

We kept walking as we talked. The streets were empty except for a few mopeds zipping in front of us.

"I'm starving, want to grab a schnitzel?"

"Sure, I haven't eaten since breakfast. And I still need to take a piss."

We walked down the street. Sam had a cherubic smile that wouldn't go away as we laughed about where we'd gone wrong. We ate our food quickly and bought a large bottle of gin, a bottle of vodka and a bag of ice on the way back. We had missed the big night but the party truck had made enough rounds to brainwash us into going to go to a rave by a waterfall in the jungle. If we were lucky, no one would show up and we would have the waterfall to ourselves and we could dance and be happy together one last time.

We got back to the hotel and drank on the bed as we watched TV with the girls. Outside the clouds had settled over the night sky and the rain started to fall gently in the streets. I thought back to the afternoon we spent dancing half naked on the beach with the girls. I had the urge to run out into the street and I grew excited by the thought of reliving the moment. We kept drinking until we had finished half the other bottle. I looked out the window then turned to the girls.

"What are we waiting for?" I slurred.

Sam nodded and looked over at Jasmine, "Nothing."

She kept her arm around him as I rolled off the bed. Lana smiled at me but something wasn't right. She was ready to move on. I stood near the door and watched the TV. Sam took another look at Jasmine. He was happy now. He stared back at me and grimaced.

"Let's get out of here," he said as he pulled her off the bed.

The rain had picked up outside. The drops fell into thick puddles that pooled in the gaping potholes on the road. They were round and thick and they shot brown sparks of water into the air as they fell to the ground. There was no traffic in front of the hotel, so I left Sam with the girls and ran down to the nearest street corner to look for a taxi. I tried to stay dry by running under the awnings of shops but there were too much water for me to be able to hide. I found a bunch of mopeds waiting for business. I tried to haggle a decent price but no one was willing to budge. "Raining. You see?" They argued. "More dangerous now." He knew the hustle and had dealt with his fair share of belligerent middle class drunks. I was soaked through to the bone and didn't feel like arguing. In the end I shrugged my shoulders and agreed to pay up and I ran back to grab Sam.

He was waiting for me with his arm around Jasmine, who was shivering as he tried to keep her dry. Lana started walking towards me. I told them that I had found us a few mopeds that would be willing to take us to the party. I lied and told them I bargained for a decent price.

"Man, it's fucking pouring outside," muttered Sam.

I protested for a bit but there wasn't any point trying to argue. They had made up their minds. We went back up to the room and rung out our damp clothes. After a few minutes Sam and Jasmine went to the other room. When they left, Lana and I took one of the bottles of gin from the fridge. She was drunk out of her mind and she raised her glass up to make a toast. "To..." she giggled and she spilled a bit of gin onto the bed. She sat there glowing and thinking at the same time, not quite sure what to say.

"To..." she giggled again. "To nothing!" she bellowed triumphantly.

I clinked the rim of my glass off of hers and allowed a smile to creep onto my face. "To nothing..."

We polished off the bottle, then grabbed another mickey from the mini bar. We drank stiff gin and tonics as watched old American cartoons dubbed over in Chinese. Outside the rain was falling hard and I couldn't help but crack a smile. The wind picked up and clattered oversized drops of rain off the giant pane of glass at the front of the room. I looked over at Lana. Her cheeks were tickled pick with gin and she bounced restlessly up and down on the bed. I felt a sickening rush come over me.

Why don't you just man up and fuck her already! She's practically begging for it. It was certainly possible but I couldn't be sure. Besides what did I stand to gain from it? A few pumps and a thrust and it would all be over anyways. *Isn't that the whole point!* I might as well have just waited until morning and found a handjob-parlour to take care of my needs. Clean and efficient and a moist towelette to clean up the mess when I was done.

I shuddered. I felt her lips press against mine and I put my hand around the small of her back. It was cold from the rain and the air-conditioned breeze in the room. I closed my eyes and let my fingers take over as the grainy pastels of the cartoon projected onto her face.

Eighteen

"Austin, you going to come for breakfast?" Sam said through the bathroom door.

I pulled my head from under the duvet and looked out the window. Lana was gone and the sun had already slipped out of the ocean, past the edge of the windowsill. I sat in bed staring at the TV, trying to remember what happened. I could still feel the touch of her soft pink flesh pressed against mine. I felt ashamed.

"You coming or not?" Sam repeated, as he fidgeted through a pile of clothes.

"Ya." I got up and changed the channel. "I'm coming…"

I went to put on my pants but I was still wearing them. I was confused. Maybe it had all just been bad a dream. For once in my life, maybe I'd done the right thing. The girls were waiting outside our door. We went down to the schnitzel house and ordered a round of Cokes, three breakfast sandwiches, and a schnitzel. Jasmine laughed at me as I placed my order.

"You're going to have a schnitzel for breakfast? It's nine in the morning!" she protested.

I lowered the menu and cocked my head up just enough so that I wasn't looking at her, "I know it's 9 in the morning. But I've had 3 hours of sleep, my stomach is rotting, my head feels like it's going to explode, and I feel like having a fucking schnitzel!"

The food came and I devoured my sandwich in silence. I felt like telling Jasmine to fuck off back to whatever suburban cathedral fuck-hole she had crawled out of, but I just planted my elbows on the table and chewed meticulously on my schnitzel, occasionally stopping to sip Coke through a thin purple straw. Sam tried to lighten the mood with his routine self-deprecation. The girls responded with their standard gaping laughter. They each took turns solemnly reminiscing about our adventures, the way you do when you are preparing for a predictable ending. It had only been 7 days but it was for the best. They had to get off this island as badly as we did, and now their time had come. Soon enough Lana would be reunited with her boyfriend on some salty beach off the coast of some far off land with nothing to keep her going except for love and poverty. It was a horrible thought and I was glad it wasn't my problem anymore.

I didn't even know why I was getting so worked up about her in the first place. This was supposed to be a goddamn holiday! But here we were: tattooed and bruised, exchanging heartfelt goodbyes as if it were the end of the world.

People started to pile in for breakfast. The manager greeted them in Hebrew as he seated them. Jasmine was doing her best not to look at Sam. For the first time since we had met, her eyes seemed full of passion. I was relieved that all I had to worry about was whether I could finish my sandwich. We went back to the hotel, and I flipped through the channels while the girls packed their bags next door. When they were finally ready they rolled their suitcases into our room. We all tried to squeak out a few final laughs as they stood in the doorway.

"Let's just screw it all and move to a farm in the South of France, and start a vineyard…"

"Why don't we just book a ticket to South America and find a hut on a beach, and surf everyday and get married and have kids."

Anywhere with some sun. Anywhere where could keep ourselves busy enough to stop us from feeling trapped by each other's company. Anywhere but here…

We waved to the girls as we were sent they made their way down the stairs. Once they were out of sight, I crawled back into the room and fell back into the fumes of the manic dreams that were now the only reason worth getting out of bed in the first place. I woke up right where I started, lazing in front of a flashing screen, disgruntled and alone. We'd lost the happy couple and the girls had left. Now we were locked up in a cool hotel room waiting hopelessly for the big night to come. It was still 6 nights away and the town felt haunted with nothing but a few hustling scavengers and some stern-faced Israelis to keep us company.

We'd figured we could cut our losses and retreat to the mountain for the next six days, but with the town deserted and the girls thousands of miles away, it now seemed like a terrifying thought. We knew we would have to stay on the move. Otherwise it would only be matter of hours until we were back to beating the living hell out of each other in front of a disinterested crowd.

I flipped through the channels. Ever single one was showing footage of protestors dressed in white taking part in a massive demonstration in the capital. "What the hell is going on?" I mumbled to myself. I kept surfing the channels until I stumbled upon an English headline: *Nation celebrates the Kings' birthday!'* It was early December and the country was preparing to honour the anniversary of the longest serving head of state in the world. He'd put down coups and supported military regimes and now his loyal followers were jumping at the chance to kiss the blessed ground he walked on.

"So, what are going to do then?" asked Sam.

I scratched my head, "I don't know. Maybe we shouldn't have left the guide book behind."

"Bullshit!" he grunted, "I should have left you behind…"

I stared at him and laughed. "Hell, we should have never left home in the first place."

"Speak for yourself! I should have never asked you to come along. Or maybe I should have just run off to Australia with Jasmine."

"Don't be a fucking idiot. You wouldn't have lasted another ten minutes with that bitch."

Sam let out a sigh, "I guess we'll never know…" He put on a lonesome stare, and went back to thinking to himself.

"What about that beach that Juan was telling us about," I suggested. "The one just up the coast…"

Sam scratched his head, "Why not… Anything to get us out of here."

We headed down to the tattoo parlour later that afternoon. Juan was alone in the shop, sweeping the floors with a thinly bristled broom. He noticed that the girls weren't with us and asked where they had gone. We explained what had happened and he sighed as if it somehow meant something to him.

"Where is everyone?" I asked Juan.

"Oh," he sighed again. "It's the king's birthday, everyone is taking the day off."

"I didn't think they had holidays in this place."

"It's not a big deal here but in the capital everyone worships the king."

I shrugged my shoulders. Sam told Juan that we wanted to leave town. Juan gave us a strange look and I jumped in to reassure him, "Just for a couple of days. We just need to get away from here for a few days."

"The other day you said something about a secluded beach..."

"Ah yes..." he said with a wide eyed grin, "You should go north and stay with my friends Fiona and Tip. They have a small little place on the east coast of the island. It's paradise! You must go..."

"How do we get there?"

"You can take a truck or I have a cousin with a boat. He could take you there if you want."

We told him we'd rather go by water and he told us to come by the shop in the morning. We left Juan and walked around town for a bit. It was eerily quiet and we soon went back to the room to hide from the unbearable humidity. The first of the season's presidential showcases was on and I lay in bed, watching a bunch of bland looking senators in navy suits and crimson ties bowing and nodding to each other.

"This country is in a state of crisis! We've got no food, we've got no jobs... Our pets heads are falling off!"

The quadrennial circus sideshow was always good for a laugh so long as you could get over the fact that one of these shitheads might be me running the world into the ground in a matter of months. They babbled on repeating, reiterating and retracting in a series of miscalculated gaffes. It was a disaster of epic proportions but I couldn't take my eyes off the screen.

Sam looked up from his book, "Didn't you hear what happened to that prick?" he asked, pointing at the TV.

"What? That he's a bible bashing lunatic who can't even quote his own constitution?"

"No, some gay right's columnist got sick of listening to his rants, so he started this massive campaign to defame him. He made a webpage that said the dictionary definition of this prick's name was the mixture of shit and semen, which is found in man's ass after he has been fucked by another guy. Now whenever you type his name into any search engine it's the first thing that pops up!"

I watched him babble on behind the podium, imagining a thick bile of shit and semen dribbling down his chin as he spoke. I started to laugh to myself then held back. If only James and Kile had been here. They would have gotten a good kick out of that.

The debate dragged on and Sam started to get anxious. "Man, I can't watch any more of this trash." I agreed but I couldn't bring myself to turn it off. "Come on let's go out for a drink. The fresh air'll do you some good," he said.

"Just a few more minutes," I whimpered. But Sam wasn't having any of it.

"Let's go."

We went out looking for a bar. I was determined not to go to the mountain but everything in town was closed for the King's birthday.

"Do you believe this shit?" Sam said incredulously. "I know it's a holiday but this island is fucking ridiculous! At the rate this place is going, they can't afford to lose our business."

I shrugged my shoulders, "There's always one option…"

We struggled up the steps that led up to the mountain. I dropped down onto the concrete and Sam went to the bar. I looked down at the sliver of beach below. Last night's storm had brought the seas up and big black waves rolled upwards and crashed down on top of the bright lights along the water's edge. Sam came back from the bar with a girl in tow. She was hefty with big round cheeks that lacked colour, and a big mop of frizzy hair that bobbed up and down on her shoulders in the breeze. I grabbed Sam by the arm as she sat down. "What the hell are you doing?"

"Don't ask me," he snapped back. "She just started talking to me at the bar. What was I supposed to do?"

The last thing I wanted right now was to be surrounded by people, but she had already planted herself firmly on the cold concrete floor. There was no hope of getting her to move. As far as I was concerned Sam was to blame, so I left him to do the talking. She bored him with a relentless onslaught of her most recent adventures. I tried to tune her out but the shrill cackle in her voice was difficult to ignore.

"It's actually my second time here," she exclaimed with an expression of wonder.

I shook my head and wiped my brow. I didn't want to get involved but I couldn't help myself. I lashed back at her "Really? Why would you want to come back here?"

I should have known better. She already had her response prepared and she recited it with glee, "How could you not want to come back here." Her eyes were wide open. "It's so beautiful here. Don't you think so?"

"It's something..." said Sam.

"Just look at this view. It doesn't get any better than this."

She was right. It didn't get any better than this. This how things would be from now on. Just me and Sam and an overweight optimist to keep me from dashing my brains off the edge of the cliff.

"Don't you think it's beautiful?" she asked me.

I had to put a stop to this shit.

"I hate this place. I can't wait to go home."

She recoiled in shock, "How can you say that? Hate is such a strong word."

"I know," I answered sternly. "That's why I used it."

She tried to convince me that I had just gone to the wrong places. I just needed to open my heart – stop being so close-minded. I needed to travel more and meet more people.

"Isn't there anywhere you'd like to go?" she asked trying to inspire some hope.

I could think of a few but I didn't want this drag on any longer than it had to so I just threw out an uninspired thought. "South America?"

Her eyes lit up with joy. "Oh, you should go! It's beautiful there."

I looked over at Sam. Even he was starting to lose his patience. The fires down on the beach had begun to rage sometime after midnight as the nightclubs opened up to mark the conclusion of the King's special day. I told her that we were dying to check out the party in the hopes that would get rid of her, but she immediately invited herself to join. A group of dishevelled locals was spitting fire at a rabble of mesmerized fans as we approached one of the bars. Just next door another batch of drunks took turns trying jump rope over a leather whip that was doused in flames. We passed through the crowd a few times until our over-enthused acquaintance finally bumped into some friends she had accosted earlier in her travels and we left her behind to reminisce.

Sam and I made our way back to the room, but we bumped into Juan across the road from the hotel. He was drinking rum underneath the flashing neon lights of his sister's convenience store, while a hollow voice butchered Queen's *I Want to Break Free* over the radio. He insisted we have a drink and he handed us a couple of beers from a mini-fridge behind the counter. We sat on the ground while his sister and her friends played a game where the object was to guess whether the girl on the back of the drunken Caucasian's moped had a penis or not. The never-ending parade continued on into the early hours of the morning but there were never any winners, only conquests.

By the time I finally climbed in to bed, I felt more restless than tired. I turned on the TV for a bit but I didn't have the patience to deal with the news. I turned it off again but the sermons kept playing themselves over and over inside my head.

"*...It's high time we returned this country to the former glory of its slave owning, womanizing, founding fathers!*"

"*...Slash spending, hang the faggots, cut taxes, and then wait for it all to trickle down onto the faces of the snivelling masses...*"

"*...God bless all rape victims for bearing out God's will and god bless the shopping malls with their oversized parking lots, and God bless the lord for he is pure and righteous!*"

"*...and don't even fucking think about taking our guns or we'll find you and hunt you down like the liberal swine that you are! Praise the lord! Amen!*"

I nestled my face under my arm and took deep breaths, which quickly turned to panting. I thought I was having a panic attack. I stopped fidgeting with my toes and tried to calm myself down. I took a deep breath and held it in. I tried to count sheep, even though that never works. After a while I started to relax. My fingers stopped twitching, and I was no longer thinking about my breathing. I watched the sheep as they flew over the fence. I kept counting as they sailed through the sky: 17… 21… 57… 89… They were white and calm and weightless, and each time they jumped over the fence they bleated out the same soothing phrase: *'Long live the king!'*

Nineteen

We got up early next morning and went down to meet Juan. He was already in the shop, sweeping the floors when we walked in.

"So you are finally leaving." he said with a surprised tone in his voice.

"Just for a couple of days."

"I thought you would stay..." he said melancholically.

"Well we just need a few days to recover," I told him.

"Of course. The days can be long, especially now." He kept sweeping. I asked if his cousin could still take us in his boat.

"I say I get you a boat. So I will get you a boat."

He called his cousin and argued with him for a bit, then hung up and turned towards us. "I just spoke with him. He will meet you down on the pier in half an hour."

"Thanks Juan, we'll come see you when we get back."

"You may never leave. It is paradise there."

I rolled my eyes. "You'd be surprised."

"Make sure you say hello to Tip and Fiona for me."

"We will."

We walked down to the docks on the western side of the jetty. Juan's cousin was waiting for us on the beach in front of his boat. It was a sturdy long-tail made from thick planks that were painted red and blue with a thin white trim, which wrapped all the way around the boat from the stern up to the bow, ending in a thick knob of lumber that pointed toward the sky like a bull with a single sturdy horn.

He didn't have much to say and looked nothing like Juan. It was clear that they weren't related in any way. We paid him the agreed amount and piled into the boat, as he pushed us off the sand and pulled up the anchor. The oversized engine on the back of the boat had been scavenged from a truck. It was mounted clumsily on a pivoting turret at the back of the boat, with a 9-foot prop shaft welded onto its frame. It clicked unenthusiastically as Juan's cousin pulled the trigger. It turned over, then stalled, seizing a few times before finally kicking into gear. He dipped the corroded shaft delicately in and out of the water until the boat spun around and pointed toward the open ocean.

We passed the rugged escarpment that protected the southern tip of the beach before turning the corner and moving north along the coast. The waves had been building over the past few days. The boat bucked up in the air every time we cut through a wave, forcing the bow to point downwards. Each time we hit a wave Juan's cousin spun the engine on its turret, pulling it out of the water while easing the makeshift throttle that was nothing more than a piece of fishing line rigged up through a series of metal rings. Once the bow flattened out in the trough of the wave he would dip it gently back into the water and the heavy wooden frame would dig into the next set.

The island passed beside us in thick blotches of palm leaves and polished pink granite, which quivered under the weight of the sun. At times it felt like the boat was going to flip but our driver refused to flinch. He kept his eyes on the horizon as we ploughed through the waves at twenty miles an hour. After 45 minutes of being bounced against the painted hull, we pulled into a cove dotted with a few rickety bungalows on the edge of the jungle. Juan's cousin revved the engine and drove fast towards the shore, pulling the engine's rusted tail out of the water just in time as we slid up the pebble beach. We jumped off the bow and threw our bags on the rocks and Juan's cousin pushed back out to sea to return to the madness.

We followed a small river up from the beach, and into a large restaurant with a patio that was covered by a low-lying palm-thatched roof. There was no one in sight except for a tall man with a thinly groomed Confucian moustache and a closely shaved head. He was watering a planter full of wildflowers with a cigarette pursed between his lips. I walked up behind him hoping he would notice me, but he kept patiently attending to his plants as he exhaled a plume of smoke. I stood there in silence waiting for something to happen.

"Hello?" I whispered.

He kept his eyes in front of him as he moved the watering can over the flowers. The flow of water stopped and he pulled the cigarette out of his mouth as he spun his head around with a sigh. "Ahhh..." he looked me in the eye. "Hallo."

He had a deep voice that lingered on the last note of every syllable.

"We just arrived," I said. "We are looking for somewhere to stay for a few nights."

He continued to dissect without saying a word.

"We were sent here by Juan," I added. "He told us to come here and ask for Fiona and Tip"

"Hmm..." he put down his watering can. " You have come to the right place. I will go and find Fiona."

He disappeared behind the counter at the back of the restaurant. Five minutes later a frumpy woman with shoulder-length curly hair appeared. She was wearing a blue apron and she had bright green eyes.

"Hello, how may I help you?" She had an inviting Scottish accent that had been dulled by decades of ex-patriotism.

"We're looking for a room for a couple of nights," Sam said.

"We're not fussy, we'll take the cheapest thing you got," I added.

"Have you come to escape the madness?" she asked wryly.

"Does it show that badly?" I asked sheepishly. She didn't respond. She didn't have to. "Juan sent us here. He said he used to work for you," I said trying to change the topic.

"Who?"

"Juan?"

"Oh yes, Kwan." Her tired brow came to life for a second as she tried to remember. "He worked for us a while ago. Must have been three or four years now..."

Sam and I looked at one another in confusion.

"How is he doing these days anyway?" she asked.

"Fine... I think..." It must have been the same person, I thought to myself, "He opened his own tattoo parlour in town."

"Well good for him," she said.

"He said he learned how to cook here."

Her face slipped back into its regular pattern of monastic concentration, "That's funny. He never really cooked much. Just cleaned dishes and did laundry."

She made her way past Sam and I, "... but I'm glad to hear he's doing well."

She kept walking and waited for us to follow, "So you want somewhere cheap?"

"We're not fussy."

"Well, there's one room on the other side of the river with the bed already made up if you like."

She pointed to a set of waterlogged two-by-twelves sandwiched between large boulders, "Don't let the bridge turn you off."

She led us across a stream that was 20 feet wide. The wreckage of the elaborate suspension bridge that had been ripped apart by the recent floods was strewn underneath it. "It doesn't matter how many times we rebuild that damn thing, there's always a storm around the corner, waiting to tear it back down. 14 years I've been here and I've had to rebuild that damn thing 4 times. Hopefully we'll have a new one built by the time high season hits." She let out a deep sigh, "It's just a matter of time and money."

Our cabin perched on top of a large boulder. It had its own toilet, shower, a small queen-sized bed equipped with white cotton sheets and a mosquito net. It had a balcony with a hammock that was sandwiched between two pink rocks in front of the ocean.

We dropped off our bags and climbed the pink rocks in front of our cabin. When we got to the top we stripped down and draped ourselves over the pink granite. The stone was smooth, meticulously polished by centuries of tropical sun and relentless tidal storms. Even with the sluggish moisture that lingered in the air, the tired rock remained unscathed by the indecent build up of pubescent moss. I could smell my flesh cook as I lay face down, with my arms and legs spread blissfully across the rock.

"There they go," Sam mumbled to himself.

I peeled my face off the stone and looked out to the sea. There were four or five rust coloured tankers chugging toward the light blue sliver at the edge of the sky. I could make out the letters of Sam's company painted in white block letters on the bluish brown steel of one of the boats. He kept his eyes fixed on the tankers until they finally disappeared out of sight before letting out a disparaging groan, "Probably on their way to China with a fresh load of rubber."

As much as he hated to admit it, Sam was still hung up on everything he'd left behind, but there's nothing we could do about that now. I lay back down on the granite and let my skin bake until small pools of sweat began to form between my face and the rock. I closed my eyes and continued to melt away under the tropical sun.

Later that evening we sat around one of the tables on the patio, watching the ocean and drinking beer. The swell was coming in and small traces of foam crawled up the pebble beach every time a wave broke. Tip came to our table with some menus. He was unusually tall and his face looked serene as he leaned over us in the dim light.

He whispered in my ear as I thumbed through the pages, "You eat this." I nodded without looking at the menu and he disappeared with a bow. There were two girls at the table next to us. Other than a few other stragglers smoking on the cushions under the awning they were the only ones there. One of them had exotic pale brown skin and a matching smile. I thought about saying something to her. Then I noticed the modestly sized stone on her ring finger. My food came out and my eyes started to water up from the pungent fragrance of the spice. I had to polish of four bottles of beer to keep myself from crying through the entire meal. Tip smiled calmly every time he brought a fresh bottle back.

"Spice very good for you."

He saw me scoff and he cocked his head in a bowing motion, "Me..." he said with a pause, "I eat seven chillies every day, sometimes eight, sometimes nine," he added with a satisfied grin, before going over to build a large camp fire with the scraps of palm branches that were lying on the beach.

After dinner Sam went to bed. I stayed at the table and drank alone for a while. Tip caught me staring at the girls and came up to me, "You should not waste time." He had a drink in his hand and there was the faint smell of rum on the tip of his tongue. I told him I just wanted to be left alone but he insisted, and a couple of minutes later he had invited the girls over. They were both Dutch and I could tell they were slightly disgusted by my presence. The luscious one with the ring had just gotten engaged and her friend moaned on about how she was waiting for her boyfriend to propose. "It's only a matter of time really…"

It wasn't long until we started to bore each other, and they excused themselves on account of wanting to read before the power was shut off for the night. We said goodnight but we all knew that with no one else around, we'd be back the following night exchanging the exact same disinterested stares.

…

Fiona was on the beach to greet us for breakfast. Sam and I sat at a table and ate fresh fruit and eggs with our shirts off. Fiona and Tip's little daughters were down by the river, playing with large plastic building blocks and toy trucks. They were being watched over by a stubby local man with a good-sized gut and ratty dreadlocks, and every once in a while Fiona would go over to check on them.

She ran the place like her own Betty Ford boarding school. Breakfast was served from eight onwards, followed by tea, or beer and cocktails for those who were unable to go cold turkey. During the day borders kept themselves busy by reading, sleeping, swimming and smoking dried out bush weed. And if none of that was appealing, there was always the option of mediating on the inglorious indifference of your isolation. In the evening it was dinner and drinks, concluded by campfires and acoustic guitars on the pebble beach. At ten the solar-powered generator shut down and everyone was left to fend for themselves.

We spent the afternoon lazing around in hammocks. I woke up after a few hours and went for a swim off the rocks at the end of the bay, climbing across the sparse crevices and diving in head first from twenty feet up. I climbed back up the rock and lay in the sun. I looked back at Sam spread out across some cushions amongst the pebbles. He looked so composed on the beach with his book covering half his face. Still, he somehow managed to look out of place. I lay back and the scalding pink rocks and closed my eyes and dreamed I was somewhere warm.

Later that night we had dinner with the Dutch girls. Tip lurked around our table for the entire meal until he finally invited himself to join us.

"So you're from the Netherlands?" I tossed out half-assedly hoping to spark the conversation.

The desperate pasty girl nodded and then looked over at her exotic friend, "She's actually from Afghanistan."

I'd heard that word spoken so many times on the TV but I'd never heard it used in real life. I turned to her in disbelief, "But you've got such a thick accent…"

She shied away from the comment for a second before explaining, "I came over when I was five years old. I hardly even remember it." She reluctantly explained how her dad fled to France and his wife and kids followed behind a year later. Once he made it to Paris, she left with her mother and two brothers by foot. They spent a month making their way across the country by any means possible, hiding from authorities and keeping on the move. When they got to a village on the border they were smuggled into Uzbekistan in a shipping container, where they were held for 3 days without seeing daylight. After they finally got out they had to spend another year and a half living in a small Russian village before they were able to get fake passports and a one-way flight to Amsterdam. When she'd finished telling the story, my jaw dropped in disbelief.

"Oh my god!"

Tip was drunk and he quickly tried to correct me "You mean… Oh my Buddha!"

"What?" I snapped.

"You mean Buddha, not god," he grinned. "There is no god, only Buddha," he said with a chuckle. I looked into his eyes to see if he was trying to be funny but he was dead serious. I pushed him out of my mind and turned back to the Persian princess. After spending so many weeks wasting away, I struggled to think of something intelligent to say.

I thought about the mosque that had just been blown up. And there was that leak about the corruption between the Pakistani government and the American defense contractor. I remembered watching the two-hour TV special with the dull-eyed neo-fascist politician from the Netherlands who had called for the deportation of all Muslims in Europe. His name was on the tip of my tongue but it wouldn't come to me. I tried to get her to jog my memory but she didn't have a clue who I was talking about. I tried repeating his name but she was still drawing a blank.

"I don't know," she said. "I'm just finishing up at fashion school.

I'm not interested in politics."

I dropped the whole thing and went back to drinking my beer. Tip left and came back with a fresh glass of rum. He offered some to me. I held it up to my lips and gagged. He laughed, "Banana rum. It's good for you."

The moon shone with a damp yellow glow and the breeze carried the waves up the beach.

"Tomorrow will be a glorious sunrise," Tip said.

"Really? " The girls asked in unison.

"Yes, those clouds are a good sign. If you rise early you will see the most extravagant sunrise you have ever seen."

He smiled as he dragged his hand across the imaginary line where the sky met the ocean, "And tomorrow the men will catch many fish."

"Can we go fishing?" they asked Tip in excitement.

"Ha-ha-ha," he laughed as he stroked the greying hairs on his upper lip. I hadn't seen Fiona for a few hours but Tip hadn't even noticed she was gone. "You may go but they leave very early. Before the sun rises."

The girls looked at each other and chirped quickly back and forth. "What time?"

"Ah," he sighed, "You will have to be here by 6 a.m."

They smiled and nodded their heads. "No problem."

Everyone was now satisfied. The girls had an adventure booked and Tip had imparted his infinite wisdom. I watched the clouds drift across the moon in thick plumes of smoky angels. The moon cut through the gaps in the sky and singed the greying fringes of their wings as they floated by in the breeze. The wind carried the ocean upward and smashed dark walls of water up against the narrow opening of the beach, and the polished pebbles rumbled underneath as the water drew back out to sea. The generator rumbled one last time before shutting off, leaving the beach lit by nothing more than the smouldering embers of the fire and the occasional sliver of the moon. Everyone retired to the comfort of their beds, and I lay down on the pebbles, with my eyes fixed hopelessly on the sky.

Twenty

I woke up to the sound of Sam twisting back and forth next to me. I kept my eyes closed and tried to bury myself in my dreams but I was conscious now. He got up and opened the door to our twiggy balcony. I rolled over to his side of the bed and looked out the door.

"What the hell time is it?"

"Quarter past six."

I looked out at the ocean. A haze of grey clouds clung desperately to the edge of the world. "Another twenty minutes," Sam said with conviction. "If there's one thing that's never late in this country it's the sun."

I rolled over onto the far side of the bed and threw the knitted blanket over my head. I could make out the steady crash of the ocean throwing itself against the rocks above the hush of air pushing forcefully through my nostrils. I turned over and squeezed my eyes open. Sam was still squinting on the deck, waiting for the sun to come. But it never came. The dark cloud in the distance simply grew pale until it was possible to make out the line that separated the ocean from the sky. And then it simply stopped: no sunrise, no salvation.

Sam came back into the room and started to get dressed. He mumbled something about making the best of the day now that he was awake, and I rolled over and pretended to back to sleep. After he left, I rolled over again and repeated that old Tom Gabel poem in my head, as I dreamed about eight full hours of sleep.

Sam was lying on the rocks reading a book when I came down for lunch. I sat down in front of the cabana and waited for someone to come and serve me. Tip was nowhere in sight and Fiona was busy playing with her children. She saw me sit down and left them with their dreadlocked babysitter. Sam joined me as I was finishing up my eggs. We sat there, watching the ocean batter the pebble beach. The local fishermen were standing around a battered wooden outrigger. They were supposed to take the girls out fishing but the boat had sunk on the way out, and they were now arguing about the best way to patch it up.

Sam stared out at the ocean, looking for his ships, but they were long gone. "I kind of miss the girls," he muttered mournfully. I thought about saying something, but I saw that he was staring right through me at the horizon. I didn't need to finish his thought. It was time for us to leave.

Tip eventually stumbled out from behind the trees with cigarette between his lips. He looked like he was still drunk. He went straight over to the table with the girls without even looking at his kids. I couldn't figure out why Fiona had thrown her life away to come raise a family with a pseudo-philosophising drunk. It was bad enough that they had two kids together, but surely she could have left him behind. I tried to get his attention but he didn't turn around when I called his name. "Tip!" I shouted again but he was pretending to be deeply involved with something. I called him one more time and he finally stumbled over. "Tip, we need to get a boat to come and pick us up as soon as possible."

He let out a deep laugh, "No boats coming today... The ocean is angry, it's very dangerous."

"But we need to get back to the beach," I pleaded.

He calmly nodded his head back and forth, "There is a truck coming later on with some new guests, you can take it back if you like. When do you want to leave?"

"As soon as possible."

He bowed his head quickly then brought it back up, before disappearing behind the trees.

The truck pulled up a few hours later and the children ran up to us to say goodbye. We patted them on the head and they went back to playing with their plastic toys on the beach. Tip came up to me and I held out my hand. "Thanks for everything Tip. We'll see you around."

He kept a hold of my hand and smiled, "My name is not Tip."

I thought I might have heard him wrong. I waited, expecting another one of his bullshit zen slogans. But he just kept grinning without saying a word.

"What do you mean you're name's not Tip?"

"Tip is over there." I looked back at the aging dreadlocked stoner who was busy playing with the kids. It took me a second to figure it out.

"But I've been calling you Tip this whole time. How come you didn't say anything?"

He smiled and spread his hands wide as if he were giving a sermon. "You never asked," he exclaimed with a self-satisfied grin.

"So what's your real name?" I mumbled in frustration.

"Bob," he said with a grin.

At this point I didn't really care what his name was. All I knew was that if I had to spend another minute listening to his pseudo-philosophical bullshit I was going to lose it. He helped us throw our bags into the back of the truck and we waved goodbye to the kids as we drove up the hill. The truck wobbled over the potholes in the dirt and into the jungle. We shook back and forth, climbing higher and higher. The trees were sandwiched close together and the big fridge-sized leaves were clustered in dense overlapping patterns. The truck kept going until we could just about make out the shoreline through the tops of the trees, before we disappeared into the jungle for good.

We continued over the bombed-out road. All of a sudden the truck stopped. I didn't hear a tire go and the engine sounded like it was running just fine. The driver turned around in the cab and issued and order through the small sliding window. "Ok, get out."

"What?"

"Get out."

"What do you mean? We're in the middle of nowhere."

"This is where we stop. You pay for only half the trip. You want to get to town, you pay me double..." he said calmly.

I looked over at Sam, "What the fuck are these idiots talking about."

Sam tried to argue with the driver through the window. The truck door opened and slammed shut again. The driver walked around back and started grabbing our bags. "What the hell are you doing?" Sam asked.

I interjected, "Fuck it Sam, just give him the fucking money. I don't want to find out what this place looks like after dark."

Sam scowled at the driver with his fist wrapped around the strap of his bag and reached into his pocket. The driver snatched the money out his hand and went back to the front seat without saying a word. "I can't believe those fuckers tried to hustle us. I bet you Tip had something to do with this," he scowled.

"You mean Bob?"

"What's the fucking difference!"

The road filled with backpacks on overpowered motorcycles as we got closer to town. They zigzagged back and forth, trying to avoid the gaping holes in the road. We pulled onto a paved stretch of road that pointed toward the ocean. A kid in basketball shorts and white sneakers, came out of nowhere and clipped the truck's rearview mirror with his handlebars. Our driver cursed and put his foot on the gas but the kid pulled out in front of us. We began to chase him down the mountain as the moped sped ahead, weaving between trucks. Our driver put his foot down taking corners at full speed in an attempt to catch up. We passed a truck on a blind turn. A car was coming straight at us on the other side of the road. The driver jammed the clutch in and threw on the brakes at the last second as we swerved into a ditch.

He started screaming manically as he put the car back into gear. We took off down the straightaway into town. The suspension bounced us up and down as we flew over a bridge. He was full of rage and he wasn't going to stop the truck until he had run the white sneakered pimp over.

The poor kid was on a shitty European moped, outfitted with Indonesian tires and a Japanese engine, and soon enough we were neck and neck. As we came into town it looked like he was going to get away. We came screaming around the corner, and the truck lurched forward and cut him off, pinning him against a wall. The mirror was fine but the driver had enough. He got out and started yelling at the kid, pointing at an invisible scratch on his paint. "Look! Look! You give me money! Look what you did!" The kid shrunk back against the wall and tried to argue with him. I went to jump in but Sam grabbed my arm and pulled me away. This wasn't our fight, and even if it was, we probably didn't have a chance in hell.

The town looked different now that it was filled with warm bodies. I could hear wild yelps and disconcerting grunts echoing down the narrow streets. As we made our past the crowds I could hear the entire mess being drowned out by the kind of ominous bluegrass twang that you might hear playing in the background of a Quentin Tarantino B movie.

We knew long ago that we weren't going to survive in the thick of the madness, so before we left we had made to sure to book a room on the far side of the island. It had everything a modern man could ask for: TV, air conditioning, a hammock on a private balcony, and a swimming pool with a view of the sun as it set into the ocean at the edge of an escarpment, 300 feet below. It was a bit of a trek to get there and it was going to cost us a few extra bucks, but at this point we couldn't afford to put a price on our sanity.

We headed up to the pool that overlooked the ocean and the mountains in the distance. It was overcrowded with people sheltering themselves from the influx of middle class refugees. We tried to find some space at the edge of the pool but we were met with a barrage of unwelcome stares. It was clear we were only delaying the inevitable. We both knew the only way we were going to get through the next few days alive was by hiding out on the mountain. I wasn't ready it to admit to Sam but I had actually started to miss the place. And now that circus was finally in town, we at least knew we were in good company.

As we made out way down the hill I began to worry that it might have fallen into the sea; that it had been a figment of our imagination all along, that the entire adventure had just been one long tortuous dream. As soon as we saw the waves throwing themselves recklessly against the boulders at the edge of the beach my fears were wiped away. The mountain was still there, with its concrete slab perched elegantly on metal stilts above the endless rubble of rocks and waves down below.

Every thing was just as we'd left it, except there was no sign of the cold and calculating noise that had kept us warm during the last storm. Instead we were being submitted to the same old *'don't worry be happy'* island jingles, as if the sound of a long-dead drug-addled revolutionary were meant to give us any comfort. Sam was crushed.

"It's not like they can get away with playing this shit all day long. They got to think about their customers," I said trying to console him.

He shook his head, "Look around you... We *are* their fucking customers."

We walked to the shack at the back of the slab and ordered a round of powdery grey cocktails, then went to the bar and grabbed a couple of beers as we waited for the poison to kick. It didn't take long for the sky to give in. The colour in my cheeks drained slowly into my eyes and my retinas became coated in a frothy film. The water down below turned to a finely pixilated shade of turquoise, just like the brochures had promised, and the trees on the hill shimmered like a collage of industrial strength garbage bags stretched tight over thousands of incandescent bulbs. Things were finally back to normal. I let myself be mesmerized by the swimmers dodging through the waves down below. I let the bliss take control and grinned at the ten storey palm trees as they swayed gently in the breeze. The shimmer of their plastic limbs grew more intense until I had to put on my sunglasses to protect my eyes from the glare.

"I found him!"

My concentration snapped and I saw Sam walking towards me with a wide-eyed grin.

"Found who?"

"_____… I thought we'd never see him again!" he said shaking his head. I smiled back at him as he sat down beside me.

"He's just behind the bar cutting limes," he added as if that was somehow some kind of sign. "He says he's playing later tonight!"

"That's great news." I shook my head vigorously and clenched my fist in solidarity before turning back to watch the swimmers get pummelled in the waves. We sat in the same spot for hours as the sun beat down on us. Once the sun sunk out of sight I started to feel restless.

"Man, I need a break, I can't just sit here all night."

Sam stared at me like a spoiled brat who'd rotted out his eyes by watching too much TV, "But what about..."

"Don't worry," I cut him off, "I wouldn't let you miss that for the world. But I need a break."

I stared back at the waves crashing down below, "Why don't we go for a swim. It'll sober us up."

He looked down at the ocean pounding against the rocks. "We can't go down there. We'll fucking get smashed to pieces."

"Let's go to the pool."

He stared at me with his bulging eyes, "What about all those people?"

"It's dark out. I'll take my chances."

The crowds on the beach were overflowing into the streets and alleyways. Everywhere we turned, there were drunken mannequins draped in bright neon schoolboy uniforms. They erupted into choruses of plastic laughter as they fell sideways out of the bars and into the dirt. We made our way past their glazed-over stares until we were on the path leading up to our compound.

I stripped down once we got to the top of the hill and dove in head first, swimming the length of the pool with my eyes open. The white underwater lighting shimmered under the green film of water that was stretched over it like a translucent chameleon. Sam was standing at the other end up to his waist when I came back up. I went back under and held my breath, staring at the lights. The bulging pupilless eyes stared back, floating in the cloud of vapour underneath the surface. When I came up again Sam was gone.

"It's too cold in there," he said from behind me, as he dried himself and lay down on one of the sun chairs.

I stayed in the water until my fingers were dried out and wrinkled. As we headed back down to the other side of the island to meet our fate I could make out a muddle of black silhouettes floating apprehensively in front of the mountain. When we got closer I could see the thin strips of charred ivory hanging out the sides of the thin black cloth. There were five of them all dressed in black, waiting for us at the bottom of the stairs when we got there. They looked like they were dressed for a funeral and I panicked. But before I got the chance to start asking questions Sam walked past them without breaking his stride and pointed up at the stairs. "This way…"

We sprinted up the mountain and they followed close behind. When we got to the top we made sure to keep a comfortable distance from them. I sat in my usual spot and pressed myself against the bars of the cold metal railing. The beach was alive with raging drunks dancing around bonfires, and the light of the miniature blazes cast anthropomorphic silhouettes on the sand as the plastic palm trees swayed back and forth behind them. I turned around and caught a glimpse of a face partially covered by locks of dark salty hair that wound into unruly sun tinted waves. I tried to keep my eyes fixed on the carnage down below but I felt my heart suck up into my throat. I couldn't help myself from staring at her, salivating over the burnt cream of her skin. It wasn't long until the black dress came up to us. "You got us up here…" she paused for a second, before adding with cheerful impatience, "Now what?"

I tried to come up with an answer, but her piercing grey wolf eyes caught me off guard, and spending a few hours away from the mountain had left me feeling dull and sluggish. "I don't know. We weren't exactly expecting company."

She laughed and I laughed too, hoping that I might convince her that I knew what was going on. There was a calming sense of urgency in her eyes. All it took was one look – one depraved look. I wanted to have her. I needed to have her. "So… Now what?" she asked again.

I felt myself fill with shame. *Now what?* I didn't know and Sam certainly didn't have a clue. This was our last refuge – our last remaining sanctuary. So long as we could defend the mountain we would be safe. *Then why the fuck did you invite them up here?*

I stopped mumbling clumsily in my head and turned to her. "Now… We dance."

Sam and I went to the shack at the back to get some more poisoned cocktails. We climbed up the bamboo tower where we he had left Lana and Jasmine just a few days ago. The music was heavy and grinding now. The girls crept around the floor, gradually encircling us as we slipped back into oblivion. Their faces slammed in and out of view as the poison began to take its familiar hold. My eyes swam around looking for something to latch onto. My hands went blind. They were in my veins, clairvoyant. My hands went blind. I could feel the rhythm sake through my bones, and my jaw started to seize up as I shuddered with delight.

The bass! …. The bass! …. The bass! … Every ounce of strength sucked from the tips of my lifeless fingers. I wanted to scream, I wanted to break down and cry. I wanted to just lie down and die on the spot. My arms hung speechless in the sling fed by a cynical monotonous drip. It was pure bliss. The slow drip continued and an orgy of pleasure grew inside my stomach. Pure nothingness. Blissful nothingness. Sweet unpasteurized perfect nothingness.

The girls grew larger, sprouting towards the ceiling like ominous pixies. Their colossal frames moved over us as they passed in and out of focus in short bursts of yellow and crimson flames. The thin veils of black cloth jumped off their skin as they spun around, before gently floating back into thousands of tiny little folds that melted down the sides of their breasts and thighs.

Boom!   Boom!   Boom!

The poison dug deeper. The girl's faces contorted into twisted mazes of thick blue veins, as their laughing waxy grimaces crackled in unison like a mechanical hydra. I tried to pick out the wolf but her eyes had disappeared into a warm abyss of peach fuzz skin and yawning pink smiles. I tipped over a table and almost lost my balance. All of a sudden a Cheshire grin floated into focus and started talking to me. "… 2 p.m… right here… probably won't remember… don't be late...'

I nodded patiently, "...We'll be here… not a second later…"

The pair of wolf eyes bulged out in front of the grin. They blinked, then focused, then blinked again, before disappearing into the abyss.

I grabbed Sam by the arm and looked at his face. There was a menacing nothingness in his eyes. He was finally becoming unhinged. I couldn't look away. I felt the ugliness creep through my veins, then a sharp nagging pang under my ribs. My only choice was to submit. We needed more. I wanted more. Anything to keep me going – anything to keep this feeling from ending. I ran to the bar with Sam and – seconds… minutes… hours, later the headlines began to roll in: *Shots fired! All directions*!

Shots fired. My vision disintegrated into warm clusters of grainy pixels as the stars fired at one another. They spit out concentric circles of silver and yellow in time with the beat. My pupils twitched as they tried to cling to something tangible. I stared down at beach with disdain. I felt empowered, insane and hopelessly out of control. This land was not for the faint-hearted. *Don't tell me you have the right to be here!* There's no such thing as rights… Only privilege!

"Welcome to the land of decadence and privilege! Welcome to paradise. Welcome to the United Fucking States of Chimerica!"

I tried to focus but the bass shook my concentration. My vision went blurry as my eyes tried to catch up with my thoughts. Or maybe it was the other way around. It was too much to take. The pounding of the bass rattled my skull as I tried to concentrate on a couple of girls talking to each other at the bar. Shaking turned to convulsing; and convulsing turned to disorientation. Everything was deteriorating. I was being consumed by flashing imaginary states. My heart sunk and my mind raced, faster and faster – that sickly sinking feeling growing – sinking faster.

Complete guerilla warfare... "Fuck the spoon give me a knife!" Fucking carnage! Absolute fucking carnage...

My thoughts had turned on me. It was a fucking revolution! Or was it a rebellion... Either way I didn't stand a chance in hell. I started thinking thoughts I never thought worth thinking! If only I could stop myself from thinking! What the hell was I thinking? Think goddamnit, think! Think! Think! Bang!

My thoughts were so loud I couldn't hear my mouth...

I crumpled into a heap on the floor. I was exhausted. I felt a crippling sensation creep through my body and I started to panic, then all of a sudden, I started to smile. I could feel the laughter rising from the pit of my stomach. It trickled up my spine and into the dark recesses of my extremities until I was overcome with an unfathomable lust.

When I came to, Sam was standing over me. He was smiling and the bass was pounding away at my heart; keeping track of time with a savage heartless sound.

I lay there motionless, straining my eyes at Sam; trying to keep my heart from beating out of time. He was leading a full on assault. His shirt was off and sweat was pouring from his face and down his chest. The beads of water dripped from his eyes and ears, draped over the sinews of his aching muscles. They twitched every time the bass fired another round into his ears – through his veins and back through the heart, and all the way back to the depths of his bowels.

He spun around in a violent fury, tip-toeing on the heads of the shadows down below. He was a man possessed – every furious stroke was effortless and purposeful. I dissolved into a figment of his imagination as he continued to enchant me with a display of controlled terror.

I wondered how long he could go on like this. Sooner or later he was going to crack, and chances are I was going to lose it long before he did. But every time I looked back at him he was gnarled with a moistened delight, with his feet dug into the ground like the roots of thousand-year-old redwood.

I sat back down on the concrete slab and stared at the land of misfit toys down below. They were marching together under the bright blue light of the moon as miniature bonfires exploded in jungle behind them. They moved in and out of the shadows as the trees bowed monotonously in front of the crashing waves. The water was dark and the waves lapped up the mountain as the tide roared in. The seas had been building for days now and every time the waves pounded down on the jagged rocks near the shore, their fingertips would smash into tiny tinsels of white spume before falling gracefully back into the undertow.

The explosions gradually became less frequent and more sporadic. But I couldn't make the sound go away! I could still hear the steamrolling barrages of the thumping pounding bass rattling through the dark corners of my mind. The noise of the crowds grew louder and louder. Pounding! Nervously pounding away: incessantly, manically pounding away. I smiled and closed my eyes as the beat went on, always pounding on to the beat of a monotonous drum.

My heart laboured on in heavy sighs as my limbs went limp. I opened my eyes forced a heavy grimace. Sam was gritting his teeth as the bass pounded away. More! Louder! Harder! Boom, Boom, Boom. I couldn't take it anymore.

Sam looked up at _____ and grinned, and _____ grinned back at him. He looked like he was about to collapse. Then, at the flip of a switch the music stopped. My gut wrenched tight and I opened my eyes. I was panting heavily and the muscles in my face contorted into a demented smile. There wasn't a girl in sight. We were standing there, all alone, sweating away like creeps in the middle of the cold concrete floor.

Sam screamed, "More! We want more!"

We both wanted more but _____ just shrugged his hands in the air. "No mor," he shouted as he flipped his empty record bag upside down over his head. We both stared at him in disbelief without saying a word. He told us he would play again soon and we said that we would be back tomorrow. He smiled at us and we turned for the stairs as he waved us off into the night.

The World At Large

Twenty-One

The hum of the air conditioner chugged heavily in the background. I felt myself slowly come back to life, gasping for the watered-down fog that had been keeping us alive for the past few weeks. We'd left the window open and I could taste the salt of the ocean, as the machine laboured hard to recycle the fresh air in the room. Once it was spewed back out, it mixed in with the damp salty breeze before being sucked back into our lungs. I lay still for a while, relishing the soothing burn that came with my every single breath. I tried to forget why I was here. Then I remembered the deal we'd made with the girls. I threw myself up and looked over at Sam. He wasn't moving.

"Sam!" I shouted, "You alive?"

He let out an agonising grown and rolled over.

"Thank god!" I turned on the TV and flipped over to CNN. I'd forgotten all about our meeting. "Shit!" It was almost two O'clock! "Shit!" I repeated under my breath. I jumped out of bed, "Fuck…"

Sam rolled onto the other side of his bed, "What the hell is wrong with you?"

"Come on," I said as I searched through my pile of clothes, "We need to get going…"

"What are you talking about?" He was starting to get on my nerves and I wondered if he just playing dumb for the hell of it.

"We said we'd meet those girls on the mountain at 2."

"Are you crazy? I'm in no state to be around other human beings!"

"Bullshit. All you need is a coffee and a few Robaxacet and you'll be good to go." I grabbed my towel and headed for the shower. "Get your shit together!"

Sam was right behind me when I got out. When he was finished we made our way down the hill.

"I don't see what the big deal is," growled Sam.

"It's already quarter past two. We don't want to keep them waiting," I said as I picked up the pace.

"Since when you do you care whether you're a few minutes late?"

"Ever since I started keeping track of time," I said as I walked ahead.

I rushed up to the bamboo turret where the girls had left us in the middle of the night but there was no one there.

"I guess they're not going to show up," I said in a deflated whisper.

"Maybe they forgot," Sam said, trying to console me. "Let's go down and get a beer. I'm sure they'll show up."

He led the way down to the bar. We ordered a couple of beers and sat along the railing overlooking the crescent below. The waves got shorter and choppier as they rolled off the sand and swept back out to sea. The sun worshippers were slowly beginning to fill the beach, gathering up what valuable real estate was still available by the afternoon. For the last 25 days the beach had been a ghost town but now it was becoming overwhelmed with pleasure seeking parasites from around the world. What began as a ritual of independence and freedom had become nothing more than a self-fulfilling prophecy. It didn't matter whether it was low season or high season, if there were tidal waves, earthquakes or even if it was the end of the world. They wouldn't miss this party if their lives depended on it.

Just then, I caught two girls, no longer dressed on black, out of the corner of my eye. They were skipping up the stairs in flower print dresses. The one with the shorter dress and the longer legs was still wearing a single peacock feather earring

"Sorry we're late," she took a deep gulp and wiped her brow, "There's all kinds of drama going down with the girls. Not much of a surprise there I suppose…"

Her cheeks had a frantic glow and her nostrils flared sporadically underneath her stained-glass eyes in between breaths. She was handsome with a head of untamed hair that matched her eyes.

"Don't worry. We were late too," I said, trying my best to sell the sheepishness in my voice, but she didn't seem to notice.

"Ya, one of the girls that's travelling with us was having a shouting match with her boyfriend so we left them alone to work it out. So much goddamn drama for nothing – they'll be here in a bit. They just need to fuck and make up like they always do. Knowing them they'll be here in no time."

"Can we get you girls anything?" Sam asked.

"That's ok," she flashed her canine eyes at me, "We'll get our own."

They came back with beers and sat down with their backs up against the railings.

"So what happened to you last night?" The girl with the wolf eyes flipped a smile back and forth between us. "After we left..."

"We stayed here, just like we said we would," I said.

"To be honest I don't know why we ever left," added Sam.

She kept smiling with her legs crossed against the railing.

"What about you girls?" I asked.

"We all ended up losing one another at the party. It was a zoo, you could barely move down there."

The shorter one with the dusty complexion jumped in. "I had an amazing time. Every night seems to be better than the next."

"You should have seen it last week. It was a fucking ghost town!" I said.

"How long have you two been here?" she asked.

Sam and I shook our heads and gave our usual reply, "Too long."

We told them about our German wives and the happy couple and the disaster on the mountain, followed by our retreat and inevitable return. "I didn't want to come back but he wasn't going to let me take the easy way out." I said as I jerked my thumb towards Sam.

"Well you're lucky you've got a friend like him. You wouldn't want to miss this party for the world."

I disagreed but I couldn't help but warm to her no bullshit enthusiasm. Besides maybe she was right. We may have been reduced to cowardly wretches in a matter of weeks but at this point we couldn't just pack up our bags and pretend like nothing had ever happened. Just then, a girl with broad shoulders and skinny legs came up from behind and sat down beside us.

"You made it!" shouted Daphne.

"So... How was he?" her sister chipped in.

The girl went red in the face and tried to deflect attention away from herself.

"Is this the girl with the boyfriend?" I asked Daphne.

"Boyfriend?" the big-shouldered girl grumbled defensively, while the other two giggled.

"No, this is Lucy," she smiled. "She made a new friend last night."

"Well I won't be seeing that... friend, ever again." They all laughed and the new girl shuffled away to sit beside Daphne. She had high cheekbones and a smile that was plain but not unpleasant. She fancied herself a lady, and a self-respecting one at that. She was too pious to be reduced to the needs of a man and it was clear that she was disappointed with herself for letting her guard down.

"Where are those two anyway?" asked Daphne.

"They're just in the shower, they'll be here soon." Lucy replied.

The rest of their party eventually trolled up the stairs and joined us in the sun. They were joined by a dishevelled boy who came right up to Sam and introduced himself without hesitation. "The name is Rrr oorrr eh...." he announced in a throaty Scottish groan as he extended his hand.

"What was that?" Sam asked.

"Rorry! Sawwrry, muhst bay the ahkssent!" he kept a tight grip on Sam's hand before turning to me.

"Austin," I said as we shook hands, "and this is Sam."

"Fuckkin' plejah!" he added, as he went on to greeting the rest of the group. They were more than accustomed to his presence by now. He had been following them around long enough to have asserted himself as the dominant brotherly figure that they all longed for. The only one that was unenthusiastic about his presence was the girl he was fucking. When we asked why we hadn't seen him with the girls last night, he told us that he had been off having the "fookinh nite of his life wid teh lahds!" They had been hopping back and forth across the Equator ever since they had left home. Their plan was to try and hit every major party in the Third World and this just happened to be the last stop before they returned to the dreary abyss of some sleepy seaside town. "Ay thunk thas miht bey tha bast won yeht!" he said with a grimace. He pulled up his shirt and pointed to 2nd degree burn on his ribs. "Aye, eht toque tha fuckkers lung enuff, bet thee finalleh got meh!" he had a menacing grin. "Bye Buudah hemself, Ay say, eht's a guuhd fuckkin' ohmen!"

He laughed as he continued to fantasize about the most memorable mishaps of the last few months. It was a relief to hear the kind of mess we could have found ourselves in, had it not been for the girls and the happy couple. When he was done holding court, he sat down beside his concubine and threw his arm around her. She turned her head away and rolled her eyes. He only ever showed her any real affection behind closed doors, and even though she pretended it didn't bother her, it was clear that she was tired of being treated as one of the boys. This was the kind of macho bullshit that had lit her panties on fire in the first place but now she was starting to have regrets. But deep down inside she knew she only had herself to blame.

Together the girls were an odd mix of long time friends and casual acquaintances that had been accumulated over time, and they were relieved to be together again after months of being apart.

"We just got back from staying in this secluded village in the North," said Rory's girlfriend. "I would have sent you a message but we didn't have any internet access. We got to ride elephants through the jungle. It was so amazing!" She reflected for a moment gazing quietly at the dense jungle down below and laughed, "There were bats in my room and a bunch of monkeys kept trying to get in and steal our shit. It felt like I was on Survivor without the subtitles!" She laughed as she considered the thought of being stranded on a desert island under constant surveillance, before letting out a sigh, "I would have stayed longer – if only I hadn't been running out of money…"

"I love your shirt where did you get it?" one of the girls asked, pointing at Rory's concubine.

"In Uganda. I play for an ultimate Frisbee team there with a bunch of ex-pats."

"Wow, that must be an amazing experience!" said the shorthaired one with a sympathetic smile.

Everyone now turned their attention to her, as she spilled the juicy details of her complex undertaking. "It is! It's lots of hard work but it's rewarding," she said. "Did you know that you can get the death penalty for being gay there? It's disgusting really. I've tried so hard to reason with some of the people in the village but they just don't get it. They just have a different set of values."

One of the other frumpy ones joined in, "Isn't it horrible what we did to that continent?"

The girl in the Frisbee t-shirt nodded in agreement and continued to spill her thoughts. She was like a child, full of pity and passion and warm devotion, and she had them right where she wanted them as she prepared for the dramatic grand finale.

"It's just so sad because when you look at their faces you can tell that deep down inside they are good people."

The other girls smiled pathetically as she leaned back and reclined on the flattened bones of her forearms.

Sam was still paying attention to Rory as he rambled on in bug-eyed bursts. I started to worry that I might slip up and say something I would regret but Daphne interrupted just in time, "I'm going to the bar, anyone care to join?"

I got up and followed her to the shack at the back of the mountain.

"What's her deal?" I asked Daphne, trying my best not to offend her.

"Who Lucy?"

"No, the one that's with Rory..."

"Oh, Lisa. She's just a friend I met at med school..."

"You're a doctor?" I asked before she could finish.

She let out a whimpering laugh, "No, I'm a veterinarian."

I nodded as if that meant something to me. "I've never met a vet before."

"Ya, it's kind of a funny story really. I wanted to become a doctor, but I couldn't deal with the patients, so I became a vet. And Julie learned the hard way she couldn't stand the sight of blood, so she moved to Africa and started working at an orphanage."

I felt the strange urge to say something to impress her but my brain felt like a wad of jelly squeezed between two paper thin crackers. All I could do was nod and smile at her and hope that she mistook my silence for some kind of profound wisdom.

We spent the rest of the afternoon decomposing on the mountain as we slipped further and further into a sate of blissful indifference. Rory sat beside me with his arms and legs hung underneath the metal railing that was there to stop the junkies from dashing their brains off the rocks on their way into the ocean. He was doing his best to stop himself from choking on his tongue, and his lifeless face clung to a pair of dark rimmed sunglasses to hold back the chalk-white expression that was creeping slowly from his spine to his lips. I glanced over at Daphne. Her wolf eyes were strained vigilantly at the beach. She laughed and giggled and pointed at the miniature stages that were being erected in the white foam below. The muscles in my jaw eased up as she spoke. I stayed in one spot with my arms pressed against the cold metal, watching her face as it contorted with glee.

"I think I could get used to this," interrupted a muff of curly hair. I switched off again and stared at the sun, hoping to go blind. It was bliss. And at this point, it was the only form of pleasure I knew.

The girls stood up and danced around to another Bob Marley tune as the sun fell further down the spiral. Their faces lit up with in bright shades of green and yellow fuzz as they swayed back and forth under the lingering light. After a few songs they lost interest and sat back down. If it hadn't been for Daphne and her wolf eyes I would have just let my eyes roll back into my head for good. But those eyes – those, grey and green and blue canine eyes somehow managed to keep going.

Once the sun disappeared behind the mountain the girls got up and excused themselves. I insisted they stay in the hope of keeping Daphne around but she was the one leading the charge.

"I'm meeting up with some friends I made on the mainland." She looked down at me, "But I'm sure we'll see you later on…"

I stared at her aimlessly, "We'll find you later on."

The ocean spat out a half pregnant moon on the other side of the horizon. It rose into the sky, rupturing the dark green and navy swatches that kept the island cool at night, dragging a purple and yellow shroud behind it until it stood alone in the sky, beaming with confidence. The moon was bright and heavy and it soaked the sky in perfect shades of purple and green and white. The colours danced in flashes as the pink flesh of the sky turned white in the dim wisp of clouds that remained. The chalky pastels of the giant sphere continued to shake with feral electricity until the burning afterglow was finally snuffed out, and it was nothing but an imperfect circle looking down up on us with a blank stare on its face.

Once it was finally dark we went back into to town to eat pizza and drink beer. I sat in silence as I waited for Sam to make a move. I could hear the loudspeaker on the truck getting closer. The same tired refrain crackled over the megaphone in the inviting tone of a late night game show host.

"…lots of drinks specials all night long. Come down and don't forget to bring your friends…"

Out of nowhere, two drunks on scooters collided head on at 10 miles an hour. One of them tripped over the handlebars and landed on top of the other. They both lay on the ground in a heap of metal and bones laughing uncontrollably before picking themselves up and walking away as if nothing had happened.

"…tonight, come down to the beach and experience the world's best pool party this side of the Pacific. World class DJs and free.… "

I kept sipping on my beer and watching the girls walk past the terrace. The town was finally in bloom. I turned to Sam who was still busy soaking up the remnants of olive oil on his plate with a piece of bread. I thought about suggesting that we check out the party but I knew what the answer would be.

We finished up and headed back to the mountain. _____ was nowhere to be seen. We went to the shed at the back and grabbed a batch of mushroom cocktails and went straight up to our usual spot under the bamboo bandstand. It felt good to be back.

As soon as we made it up the spiral staircase, we were greeted by a group of raving madmen. One of them came straight at us with his jaw cocked open and the whites of his eyes were drowning into a sea of black. The pale moonlike slivers that remained were cloudy and bloodshot, and the front of his black V-neck t-shirt was stained grey with sweat. He threw his arms forward and clutched my shoulders, "Welcome to paradise!"

He spoke in emphatic bursts and his eyes bulged out from their large bony sockets every time he forced the words out of his mouth.

The reggae was finally gone and the heavy driving bass was back. Everyone was dancing around in circles, spilling their beer and falling over laughing. One of the lunatics grabbed me by the scruff on my neck.

"Now this is music!" he snarled.

I nodded aggressively in agreement. He grinned back at me. "This is why we're here…"

The techno fiend bobbed up and down, grinning and swinging his arms violently back and forth. His skin was pale and flaccid. It looked like he hadn't slept in days. "We couldn't take any more of that fucking shit on the beach," he shouted. "They shouldn't even be allowed to call it music." He leaned away and then came crashing right back into view, "Listen," he said holding his finger up to his lips. "You know what that is?" He took his hand off my shoulder and pointed towards the beach. "It's the sound of a pathetic man crying out for pussy!"

He let out a maniacal laugh and grabbed me by the arm, "All we need is the beat. Listen to that beat!" he put his index fingers and whispered. "Shhh… Just listen to it," he said as he closed his eyes and pumped his tightly clench fist towards the floor in patient jarring movements.

The bass was throbbing harder now; pounding on in a sweet inaudible warble. He grinned as he continued to pump his fist towards the ground "Techno!" he barked as he gripped my shoulder tight, "Real German techno!" He let go of me and went back to methodically pumping his fist towards the floor with his eyes cocked into the back of his head. The music pounded on, occasionally fading to a rhythmic tingle, before coming back twice as heavy and twice as hard. It was dark and primal, and we all drifted across the floor half-dancing, half twitching as we faded into the darkness.

This is what it had come to; a dozen grown men, prying themselves full of amphetamines and hallucinogens, sweating away in nihilistic desperation. The masquerade was over. We'd retreated to our last refuge and it was about to be run over with pleasure-seeking hedonists. It was only a matter of time until the place was swarming with them. Then the dream would be over for good. There had to be something better than slaving away with a bunch of drug-addled freaks in a wooden turret, hoping that somehow things would be different the next day. I couldn't keep up like this. I couldn't go on pretending to be human in spite of myself. This mindless junky skull-fucking wasn't going to cut it anymore. But the only thing I could to do was put my head down and get on with it.

After a few hours of thrashing around aggressively the mob started to file out. The head techno fiend came up to me on his way out, "We're going to find more drugs and pussy!" He laughed and patted me on the back. "The only thing better than techno is pussy!"

I fell back into a daze, drifting around the floor, focusing on the cold mechanical pounding of the bass.

"Austin?" I heard someone calling in the dark. It was a familiar voice. I opened my eyes and saw Sunny's polished smiled sparkling on the concrete by the mushroom shack at the back of the mountain.

I rushed down the stairs, wondering how long he had trying to get my attention. "Sunny!"

"Hey man, how's it going?"

"Well, you know how it is." I shuffled back and forth on my feet, hoping to diffuse the nervous tension. "I guess I can't complain."

He reassured me by letting out one of his heaving guttural laughs, "That's the spirit." I thought I'd never see him again but he was just what we needed to raise our morale. "This is Jane by the way," he said pointing to the girl who was nervously clinging to his arm. I'd imagined her as a Northern Hollywood porn star with a big pearl necklace and a pair of tits to match, but she couldn't have been any different. She was pretty with colourless eyes and straight brown hair that barely covered her shoulders.

I blurted out the first thing that came into my mouth, "So you must be the lucky girl."

Sunny burst out in his thick made-for-TV chuckle and grinned. "No, I'm the lucky one."

She blushed accordingly and squeezed Sunny's hand. Sunny looked over at Sam with a look of curious disgust. "And this must be the snake charmer!"

I pushed Sam toward Sunny, "That's him."

Sam shook his hand then stepped back again.

"We just thought we'd come up and check out the view," said Sunny as he gazed out over the island. "Not bad...Not bad at all."

"It's even better on shrooms," I added.

He erupted with his usual barrage of laughter. "Oh man, you're back on those things? I thought you guys were going to go away."

I smiled anxiously, "We did. We just got back."

"Jesus! You guys are out of your minds!" he chuckled and his girlfriend giggled behind him.

I felt disheveled and wretched, and I was starting to get sharp pangs in my stomach. I looked over at Sam. His face was gaunt and weathered but he still had that unmistakable grin. I could only imagine what I looked like and I tried hard not to think about it.

I pulled Sunny aside and wiped the sweat off my brow, "Sunny, you got to get us out of here."

He stared at me cockeyed, as if he had seen something deeply troubling, "Well, we were just about to go and check out that pool party on the other side of the island."

The last thing I wanted was to be surrounded by other people but I couldn't bear to see what would happen if I was left on the mountain with Sam. "That sounds like a great idea. When can we leave?"

"I'm ready when you are," he said in a plain voice.

Sam was still sweating away aggressively on the dance-floor. I worried that he would throw a tantrum and refuse to go, but he was too exhausted and deranged to put up a fight. We walked back through town through the tangled maze of trees on the other side of the island and back up to our room to pick up a bottle of vodka. Sunny's girlfriend gasped in horror as the door opened. "You left the A/C on… and your window is open!"

Sam backed away from the fridge with the bottle in his hand, "I guess we forgot to turn that off," he said matter-of factly.

Sunny laughed but his girlfriend gasped in disgust, "But what about the environment?"

Sam laughed as he took a swig from the bottle. "What about it?"

She let out an emphatic huff, "Haven't you heard of global warming?"

Sam laughed, "Sure." He took another swig, "What do you want me to do about it? Close the window?"

"Well it would be a start…" she said trying to make a point.

Sam laughed again, "Sure, but if you really want to make a difference you should think about getting a vasectomy. That's how I'm plan to make this world a better place."

Sunny let out a nervous laugh. I was worried that things were getting out of hand but he soon rolled into his soothing baritone chuckle and diffused the situation. His girlfriend crossed her arms in disapproval. Sunny kept laughing, then put his arm around her, "Don't worry baby," he gave her a kiss on the cheek "I'd never think of it."

Sunny's laugh was reassuring but the last thing we needed was for to make enemies at this time of the night. I grabbed the bottle from Sam and took a swig, "Why don't we go down to the party."

Sunny grabbed the bottle from me and held it up to his lips, "Sounds like a plan to me."

We followed the rusty echo of the megaphone down the hill and into the streets. *"Tonight! ... Come down and bring your friends..."* The entrance to the party was guarded by a carnival clown selling balloons filled with laughing gas in the shape of exotic animals: zebras, elephants, giraffes. Sunny stopped to have a look but I grabbed his arm and pulled him back. "You don't want that shit," I told him, "You might as well jam a pointed stick in your ear and poke your brain until it pops."

The scene inside the gates was terrifying. The party swarmed around the pool, buzzing to the familiar squeal of mindless self-indulgence that was pounding from the speakers. There was barely an item of clothing in sight, and an army of amateur Jackson Pollocks was running around the pool hopped up on pheromones and bestial tendencies. The laughed as they splattered each other with thick wads of fluorescent paint.

A pre-pubescent stoner with a bandana tied around his head bumped into Sam and spilled neon paint all over his shirt. The kid looked up and squinted at him like a feral rat, "Sorry man, I didn't see you there." I expected Sam to cook his fist back and launch him into the pool but he just waved him out of the way and kept walking.

The edge of pool was lined with couples impatiently clutching and humping each other's brains out. A brawny frat boy stood in the shallow end, clad in an ironically skimpy bathing suit. He had a cackling girl propped up on his shoulders and he was tempting the crowd around him to try and knock them over. A challenger appeared from the deep with a flat-chested bimbo wrapped around his neck. They growled and splashed water at each other as they prepared to joust, before charging head on and falling down in a chaotic splash of frothy white water. We sat down across from a table with a dozen girls frolicking on top of it. I scanned the crowds hoping to find Daphne, but all I could see were vomiting heaps of tits and freshly groomed camel toes wedged between thin patches of mass produced fabric. I couldn't bear to think what this place was going to look like when the holiday hunting season was finally unleashed upon the island in a few months time. "This place is out of control!" Sunny blurted out as he turned to his girlfriend. "It kind of reminds me of that Halloween party we went to when we first started dating."

The party was rapidly deteriorating into a second-rate orgy and Sunny's easy going wisecracks were finally starting to wear on my nerves. His attempted rescue had been a failure. If Sam and I were going to make it through the night we would have to do it all by ourselves. We made up a half-assed excuse and shuffled slowly towards the exit, trudging back through the town with our hands in our pockets. I tried to think of a plan. We couldn't go back to bed. It wasn't even midnight yet. The moon was breaking out of the clouds as we made our way down to the water. The party on the beach was even more banal than the one we had left behind. We kept walking, trying to ignore the dry-humping and fire-breathing. The next thing I knew we were at the foot of the mountain. I stopped for a moment to catch my breath. I stared back at the depraved freaks that were coming up for air like rabid minnows, as they tried to escape the sea of polluted bodies that swarmed the beach. I took a deep breath and turned around to follow Sam back up the stairs so we could seek refuge until morning came.

Twenty-Two

The party continued on until long after the sun had come back up. I struggled out of bed and went to the balcony to watch the train of ferries that were already dumping piles of fresh bodies on the pier. The vultures had finally landed. They were a disease – a cancer – infected with a sickly and insatiable wanderlust. As they disembarked they made their way into the narrow streets, occupying every bar and hostel in sight. By the end of the afternoon the entire island would be reduced to a bloated carcass ripe for the picking. It was an ugly sight, but the truth was these parasitic vagabonds were the heart and soul of the island, and without their regularly scheduled monthly feast, the corpse would simply rot into oblivion.

    The sun was high over top of us by the time we went for breakfast. A group of Dutch tourists crowded around the tables, drinking freshly squeezed juice, so we sat on the only two chairs that were left unoccupied by the side of the pool. A girl in a tight fitting crimson bikini scoffed at us as we sat down before turning to the muscled henchmen in the pool. She muttered something in a thick guttural rumble. The only word I could make out as she huffed emphatically was "Australians", which she exclaimed before shooting us a crooked glance. The cabal in the pool replied by turning toward us and letting out a resilient grunt. I was determined to hold our ground but Sam wasn't going to put up with it. He looked over at me, "I didn't come here to be treated like a fucking Australian"

Neither did I but we didn't have a choice. We'd run out of places to hide. It was either this or pack our bags and just swim right off the edge of the cliff. I watched the Israelis in the pool. They were an odd bunch. The scrawny ones and the women all sported unorthodox haircuts: mullets, mohawks dreadlocks and partially shaved heads to match the facial piercings and tongue rings that were on display every time they opened their mouths. It was a natural sign of rebellion against the oppressive state that had conscripted them. They were flanked by broad shouldered specimens with shaved heads and dead eyes. They each had the same matching tattoo scribbled on the lower part of their neck where their shoulders met their spine. They said almost nothing to the rest of the group, and they spent most of their time quietly watching over the girl in the crimson bikini, making sure we didn't try and make a move.

I looked and tried to figure out what they were doing together. None of them had anything in common with the other except for the fact they had been forced to carry the same standard issue weapons and have the same shitty haircuts for the most important years of their lives, and they'd probably seen more friends and even more strangers die than they had ever hoped for. They should have gone their separate ways long ago and tried to get on with their lives. But now that they had their freedom they refused to leave each other's side. The more I thought about it the more I realized that they had all come here together for the same reason as every other lost and lonely soul that was crawling over this island. They had come here to forget.

The sun disappeared behind a shroud of pink and orange clouds and we retreated to our balcony for a drink. The island had been shaking all day long and it was slowly starting to struggle back to life. The water below was dark and green, lit up only by the flicker of a few early rising stars. Every once in a while a new boat would emerge from the darkness. For the last two days there had been an endless parade of traffic, crossing the water and descending from the hills. They came one after another all afternoon and into the night, dropping off revellers at half hour intervals. The afternoon breeze had vanished and the boats landed softly on the pier to the tune of barbaric laughter that rose sharply from the beach.

We went to meet Daphne at her hostel later that night. I was already too drunk and stoned to stand by the time we left the room. The hostel she was staying at was run by two Scandinavian lesbians and they were throwing a massive party in their bar. They had hired a band of Japanese popstars to play through a carefully selected repertoire of angst-ridden grunge anthems to remind us all of our misspent youth and the crowd sung along faithfully, slurring the words in uncoordinated stutters. It wasn't long until a sad looking moshpit kicked up. I lunged at the strangers that were dressed in pink and green neon uniforms trying to shake the boredom from my bones. Sam joined in for a bit but his heart wasn't in it. He told me he was going to head down the beach, but I insisted on staying. The longer I could keep away from the madness the better. Besides, I couldn't leave Daphne behind. But Sam was drunk and anxious and the obnoxious teenage posturing wasn't helping his nerves. "I'll see you down there," I told him.

He patted me on the shoulder and grinned sympathetically before heading out the door. When I turned around, Daphne was talking to some dishevelled castaway, with long blonde hair and corduroy shorts. I went back to dance-floor and sung my arms around as violently as possible. After a few songs Daphne came back to the dance-floor. "Who was that?" I asked trying to catch her off-guard.

She smiled, "Just some creep that I keep bumping into everywhere I go. It doesn't matter where I go, he always seems to find me."

She went back to sweating beside me without mentioning him again.

"Where's Sam?" she asked.

"He went down to the beach."

"Shouldn't you go find him?"

I put my arm around her, "I think he'll be ok."

She smiled and stuck her arm out. "Well, I don't think I really want to stick around here much longer. Why don't we go down to the party and find him?"

I finished off my beer and left it on the bar. "I guess someone should probably check on him."

We stumbled through the ugly wide-eyed crowds. They were dancing along to the same repetitive tracks that had been haunting us since we'd arrived. Just two days ago you could have driven a tank down the beach without knocking over a lamppost. Now the entire island had been transformed into a bohemian nightmare. The nubile barbarians slaved away under the moon, panting and sweating with their flesh glistening under the glow of Christmas lights and blazing fires. There were thousands of them, one hundred deep from the beach to the ocean, armed to the teeth with booze and drugs and not a care in the world. They were like Bedouin descending upon a thirsty oasis – wary, and tired and full of deeply repressed and excitable lust. There wasn't a single sandblasted shit-hole within 2,000 miles of the Tropic Cancer that was safe.

All of a sudden there was a rush towards one of the stages. We went with the flow to avoid being trampled. We got pushed up against one of the platforms and Daphne huddled close to me under the lights. The stage was packed with odd-looking go-go dancers with large plastic breasts and oiled-up locals spitting fire into the crowd. The stench of sex and candy was suffocating. I grabbed Daphne by the arm and dragged her through the crowd. I tripped over a muscle-bound hunk that was thrusting uncoordinatedly into a limp body on the sand. He licked his lips with delight and kept thrusting as I stepped over him. By the time I lifted my head I was standing face to face with the grey rock of the mountain. The concrete monstrosity was lit up like a roller rink and masses of bodies clambered up its slope, seeking refuge from the salty mess below. The secret was out, and our little piece of paradise had disappeared with it.

"Maybe he's up there," Daphne suggested.

Sam had promised me that he was going to stay away from the mountain, but now that I stood face to face with the dark grey rock, I knew there was only one place he could be. I swam through the packs of gruesomely painted bodies that were sweating away insecurely on the ledge. I made my way toward an empty space near a large stack of speakers. I could make out a single moistened body with damp hair, standing proudly in the shadows, shaking mechanically like a rabid bull. He looked wrinkled and weathered, and his face was contorted into a purposeful grimace. The dark green veins underneath his skin rippled under the pressure, and the muscles that ran from the corners of his eyes, all the way down his stocky jaw line, were tense with impotent rage. His eyes bulged out of his skull, straining threateningly at the crowds around him. It had taken three weeks of pointless attrition but Sam was finally in a state of blissful dementia.

He charged majestically across the concrete slab, back and forth, rearing his head like a rhinoceros. The air around him shook as the speaker propelled the heavy monotonous rhythms into the empty space around him. Even in the midst of his manic thrashing, he managed to look calm. After three weeks of wasting away in the sun I finally knew what had brought me here. I could see it in his eyes, and I knew there was no escaping it.

I started to laugh to myself as I watched Sam grab the speaker. He shook it violently, with his mouth contorting into something which he would have hoped looked like a smile. He wanted more... Harder! Faster! Louder!

Boom... Boom... Boom...

Sam soldiered on with the last strands of madness that were left inside him. He saw me laughing and he looked back at me like an aging elephant stranded in a field of forgotten landmines. Then finally, he snapped, and there it was. The thing we'd been looking for all along – rumbling from deep down inside, twinkling with a deranged glint: nihilism with a human face.

Sam continued to parade up and down the concrete slab, clearing a path of bodies everywhere he went. I watched in awe as he shook with delight. I hesitated for a second, before leaving Daphne's side to join in. Sam could barely recognize me, and for a moment I worried that he had gone past the point of no return. I threw my arm around him and tried to get his attention. I squeezed firmly on his shoulders and he squeezed back with a slumbering grip. He strained his eyes at the people that were dancing around him then turned towards me.

"What the hell are these people doing here?" he asked.

I shook my head and tried to get him to focus, but he was in his own world.

He stared at me as if I was a complete stranger, "There's too many of them, this place is fucked. If they don't leave soon we're all going to fall into the fucking ocean."

He stomped up and down to test the foundations. I could tell from the look on his face that he thought he was making the mountain shake, "What the hell are we going to do when this fucking place collapses!"

"We've had a pretty good run so far..." I said, but Sam wasn't listening. I grabbed him by the collar and shook him violently. For a moment he came back to life and he managed to force a smile. "We'll just have to do the honorable thing and go down with our ship."

The refugees scurried desperately along the shore looking for shelter down below. It was only a matter of time until the moon came crashing down on their heads. They were doomed. We were all doomed. But that was the whole point wasn't it. We were filthy rotten specimens. Guilty to the core, every last mother fucking one of us; and we had all come to this rotten paradise so that we could wash away our cares in the presence of perfectly tanned strangers.

Daphne grabbed me by the wrist and dragged me down onto the rocks. We crawled to the edge on our hands and knees, and we perched there in silence, watching the ocean. The water was dark and angry, and the sound of the waves crashing against the rock drowned out the pounding noise that floated above us. The waves crashed hard against the side of the mountain, sending white spittle flying across the sky before it landed by our feet. Part of me prayed that a wave would land on top of us and sweep us off into the ocean. I watched the spume splatter on the rocks, and the tiny drops of sky dribbled back down the slope, slowly evaporating before being engulfed by the crashing nothingness of the charcoal sea.

The next thing I knew the sky had disappeared into a flash of white noise. I opened my eyes and looked all around me. The music was still pummelling away in the background but al the bodies had disappeared. The thin blue gash on the horizon was being slowly stained in bloodthirsty blotches of orange and pink fire. Daphne clasped her fingers around my hand. She stared at me with her wild eyes and pressed her lips against mine. It was finally over.

She peeled me off the rocks and pulled me reluctantly down the mountain. There were still hundreds of hedonists gawking and prostrating before the sun. They danced away on top of small mountains of rubbish that had formed on the dry sand. They leered at us with perverted smiles and dead eyes as we walked past, while teams of stern-faced policemen with dogs on thick silver chains tried to sniff out their quota of jailbait. Bands of hustlers chased after us as we tried to escape the mundane dementia. I pulled my pockets inside out as a sign of surrender and the hustlers shirked in disgust, before turning their attention to their next victim. We pushed through the madness and made it to safety at the top of the hill. Sam was strung up in the hammock with his hands resting on his chest, and his legs dangling carefully over the floor. I went up to make sure he was breathing. He turned his head and lifted his hand to his mouth to take a drag of the joint, which was wedged between his crippled fingers. It wasn't lit and he giggled to himself as he tried to smoke it. I pulled a lighter out and held it up to his face but he pushed me away and let out another laugh.

"Amhh Okayhh," he mumbled with a raspy voice, as he turned his head towards the blue sky that was creeping up behind the mountains. I went inside to grab a blanket to keep him warm. By the time I got back he was out cold.

Daphne was leaning against the door pretending not to look out of place when I came back in. I grabbed her before she could ask how Sam was doing, and I pinned her against the wall. She pushed back and wrapped her arms around me. She dug her nails deep into my spine and smiled. I fumbled around latching onto anything I could – skin, bone, strands of hair. I tore her shirt off and kept her pinned up against the wall, until we were both standing naked with our hips pressed firmly together. She was panting hard. I could feel my eyes throbbing as I wrestled with her against the wall. She laughed and slapped me gently across the face then grabbed me by the hair and pulled my face down towards her chest. I could feel the waves pounding down on me, holding me under. For a second I was awake.

When I came up for air she was still there, smiling at me with her wolf eyes. I grabbed her by the shoulders and threw her down on the bed. I pushed my nose into the nape of her neck. She urged me on with the brittle tips of her fingers, seeking refuge anywhere they could. I fell back on the bed and she jumped on top of me, wrapping her legs around my waist. I swept my hands under the back of her thighs and rolled off the bed and stood up with her cradled in my arms. We swung gently back and forth in the waves for a moment, before I slammed her back against the wall. She sunk her nails in deeper and I dug my teeth into the pale crease of skin where her tangled hair fell over her collarbone. She pulled me closer with her legs. I could feel her thighs shudder as they squeezed tight against my hips. The waves came crashing down on top of me. I clenched my teeth and she clenched back. I thrust into her one last time and the laminated wood behind her cracked as her back slammed into the wall. The sky burst through the window with a gust of wind and we fell back down onto the bed panting in a fit of laughter. I felt the angst slowly slip from my fingers. I wrapped my arm around her shoulder and smiled. It was all over. I took a deep breath and closed my eyes, and I fell back into a violent daze with the air conditioner humming quietly in the background.

Twenty-Three

The sloppy high-pitched trance that had been haunting my dreams for the past week echoed up from the beach as I lay in bed, praying for someone to save my exploding eardrums. The party had started yesterday morning at sunrise. It had shifted to the Western side of the beach where the sun would be setting in just a few hours. It had been going for almost 24 hours straight now, but there was no sign of it stopping anytime soon.

I turned over in bed to put my arms around Daphne but she was gone. No note, no kiss goodbye, not even a black bra to remember her by. I was certain that the last night had been more than just a shot in the dark, but I guess I had it coming. I looked out the window. Sam was still passed out in the hammock on the front porch. I lay back down and waited for the sun to pass over us. My eyes were heavy and dry and it stung every time I tried to close them but after a few minutes of painful blinking I started to slip away.

Bang! Bang! Bang!

Holy fuck! We're under attack! I could see their faces smiling and laughing at us as they fired into the crowd. My eyes felt heavy as I watched them running through the jungle. I tried to focus. All I could make out were shadows lurking between the overgrown vines.

Bang! Bang! Bang!

My feet rustled underneath me until I could finally feel them rubbing against the polyester sheets. It was just another dream. Another horrible dream.

Bang!   Bang!   Bang!

The knocking carried on for a while, then a soft voice rose from behind the noise, "Are you in there?"

"Fuck off!" I groaned, as I pulled the blanket off my chest. "We don't need any more clean sheets..."

There was a short pause and then another voice from behind the door. "It's not the cleaning lady you fucking moron. It's us!"

Right!... Us.... I put on a pair of dirty underwear and went to open the door. They were all there with Daphne leading the pack. She shook her head and smiled. "Is it ok if we come in?"

I scratched my chest and stared at them, thinking for a moment, "Sure, sure... Come in..." I said as I slithered away from the door.

The girls rolled in and scattered themselves around the patio. I went over and sat beside, Sam who was slowly coming to life in the hammock.

"Good night?" one of them asked.

Sam shook his head and mumbled something about being relieved that it was finally over. The girls shook their heads with indifference. I looked around at their faces. Sam's response probably wasn't the most spirited one they'd ever heard but it was clear that something wasn't right. I reluctantly asked how their nights had been. Daphne's sister smiled but the rest of them remained pleasantly subdued.

I didn't want to break the silence. But as the awkward stares continued I began to feel uneasy. "Is everything ok?" I asked.

They all shrugged and stared off in different directions, "Ya..." said one of them. There was a pause and no one said a word.

"We just want to get the hell out of here," muttered the self-conscious frumpy on, as an infectious look of quiet despair crept onto her face.

Of course they did. We all did. I had wanted to get the fuck out of here from the moment we'd stepped on the island. But they were milking it. Their lifeless faces kept inviting me to pry. I couldn't avoid their pitiful stares. "Are you sure everything is ok?"

"Ya," said Lucy.

"Just forget about it," said another as she fidgeted with her hands close to her face.

"Forget what?" I asked.

"Nothing..." another pause, "Nevermind."

"Nevermind what? What the hell are you talking about?" grumbled Sam with what little voice he had left.

"Nothing..." she sighed insincerely.

There was a pause and the girls all looked in different directions, making sure to avoid direct eye contact. But Lucy couldn't hold it in anymore. "Ok..." she said with a big sigh. "We all went to bed this morning sometime after 6. Then, when I was lying in bed, I heard the sound of a girl weeping outside my window so I went to the door and to see what was happening. When I opened up I saw a girl walking around in circles. She was sobbing and she was naked – completely naked – and she kept mumbling to herself and she was bleeding. She was bleeding and she was just standing there naked moving her lips but she wasn't saying a word, just sobbing uncontrollably."

Lucy's cheeks started to puff up. They went white as she continued talking. "I tried talking to her and then she started to break down. She said she couldn't find her friend – she had lost her friend. She was shaking and crying and she didn't know where she was, so I ran inside to grab a towel and I wrapped her up. I kept trying to figure out what had happened. The only thing I could make out through her sobs was 'the men... the men... the devils... they took me... the devils...'"

I turned to Daphne looking for a hint. Her eyes were full and focussed. She knew what was about to come and I soon resigned myself to the fact that so did I.

"I consoled her and tried to figure out what had happened. There were bruises all over her back and her legs and she was too weak to talk. But after a while the pieces started to come together. She had been drugged and raped by a group of men with masks. She couldn't explain how it happened. The last thing she remembered was being shown pictures of five men and being asked whether she knew any of them. The next thing she knew she was on our door step quivering like a lost puppy."

I felt my stomach quiver as my hands began to tremble. I tried to make myself retch but I didn't have it in me. Those fucking bastards! Those fucking animals, I thought to myself. I should have seen it coming. And what the fuck were we going to do about it? We should burn the fucking beach down. Fucking smash the place to bits! But what was the point? It would only be a matter of time until they built it back up again, bigger and stronger than it had been in the first place.

"They came over from one of those other islands and somehow she managed to lose her friend," she continued. "When we found her she was naked, no ID, no phone – nothing. We managed to find a phone number for the hostel she was staying and we were able to get a hold of her friend. She'd panicked and left on the boat in the morning because she was worried that she'd been left behind. So we found her some clothes and put her on the next boat out of here."

She looked like she was about to break down and cry. Her eyes went red with rage but she just kept shaking her head in disbelief.

"It really makes you think," said one of the other girls as she wiped a tear from her eye. "That could have been anyone of us."

They all nodded in agreement. "I can't even begin to imagine…" sighed Lucy before trailing off into a state of disbelief.

"Think of how the friend must feel."

I thought about it for a while. I thought about the girl and her friend and the long and painful plane ride home. All she'd wanted was a brief escape, and now she would be suffocated with guilt for the rest of her life. How could she ever forgive herself? And what about her father? He'd probably tried to stop her from ever leaving home in the first place. He'd seen it all before and he just wanted to protect her from the kind of person that he swore he'd never become. Now he was going to spend the rest of his life drinking himself to sleep because he didn't do everything in his power to stop the inevitable. I struggled to force myself to feel something. I tried to convince myself that I was somehow complicit. But all I felt was a deep and lonely emptiness. At this point all we could do was take the girls advice and get the hell out of here as quickly as possible.

We sat around on the balcony not saying much until I noticed someone was missing.

"Hey, where's Rory?" I asked.

All of a sudden Lisa broke into tears. The girls all rallied around her and through a blanket of arms on her back to console her.

"He didn't come home last night," one of them whimpered. "We don't know what happened. He kind of just – disappeared."

He'd probably got wasted out of his mind and left her for some gormless floozy. Sam couldn't stand the thought of dealing with broken hearts and tried to reassure them. "Don't worry he's probably at the hospital or in jail."

The pack of girls wrenched their heads towards him in disgust and Lisa began to sob even louder. Sam threw his hands up in the air to plead his innocence. "Don't look at me," he said, no longer wanting their attention. "I was just trying to help…"

Lisa wiped her face and the girls filed out the door like a convent of battered nuns. I told Daphne I'd come by and find her later on, and I shut the door behind them. Our flight didn't leave until the next day, but first we were going to have to a ferry to get to the airport on the neighbouring island. Sam was a fucking mess. I left him to wallow in the room and went down the hill to take care of our travel plans. I could hear the party still raging on in the distance. The streets were strewn with drunks passed out in doorways while small armies of bug-eyed zombies stalked up and down the road looking for their next fix.

I went into the travel agency and booked two tickets. As I was paying I realised that it had been at least a week since I'd checked my emails. I couldn't handle the crippling anxiety that would come with bad news and the thought of the good news seemed even worse.

Rule number 1: Don't ask questions you don't know the answer to.

I couldn't handle that kind of pressure. Not now…

I stood at the counter, staring at the big white clock that hung above the colourful spread of a glossy calendar. The thick black hands ticked ominously over the barren background. The lady behind it kept trying to hand me my tickets. I stood for a while, laughing to myself without moving. She waved them in front of my face until I blinked. I snatched them out of her hand and walked out the door to get a drink.

I went across the street to one of the bars that played nonstop reruns of beloved childhood cartoons on big screen TVs, and ordered a beer. *'We interrupt Jassup Rapapalam's prime time Yoga party to bring you this special bulletin.'* The jaundiced Kent Brockman was reporting live from the horror of the infamous summer camp mutiny where Krusty the Klown had been overthrown: *'Ladies and gentleman, I've been to Vietnam, Afghanistan and Iraq, and I can say without hyperbole that this is a million times worse than all of them put together.'* The camera panned to a group of shirtless children painted up like savages, poking the flaming effigy of the once beloved clown.

Just then, I heard a voice call my name. I recognised the tone but I couldn't quite place it. It was familiar enough that I knew I wanted it to disappear. "Austin! Is that you?"

I turned around and there she was; the Swede that we'd met on the beach a few weeks ago.

"I told you we'd run into each other again!" she said.

"Ya, how about that."

The last thing I needed was to have some slaphappy yoga instructor trying to cheer me up. I shrugged, "I guess it is a small world after all…"

I flashed a toothy smile. The sooner I could get through this the better.

The sun glared off her large blue eyes as she smiled, "So how has your trip been?"

"Good," I said without thinking. But that wasn't going to do. "Strange," I added pensively. "But good…"

"What about the girls? Did they finally run away?" she asked proudly.

"No, we had lots of fun. But they had to go back to Germany or Australia or…"

"Awww…" she squealed and let out an overly sympathetic grown, "Did they break your heart?"

I forced out a laugh from deep in my belly, "Ya, something like that…"

She continued rambling on about her trip without caring if I was listening or not, "I came back feeling so cleansed. It was the most amazing place I've ever seen. If things keep going like this I might even head back there for a few more weeks."

I could feel myself cracking up inside. I couldn't take it anymore. This was the last straw. I stood there staring blankly, hoping I was nodding and smiling.

"We're having a bonfire at our place later on. You should swing by if you want. We're just at Lagoona Bungalows, right on the beach. Oh, and bring Sam too. I think I still owe him a drink."

I smiled at her, "I'll see if I can drag him out of bed…"

She smiled back and turned towards the pair of thick-necked all-star quarterbacks that was waiting for her in the street.

I spent the rest of the afternoon at the bar watching cartoons and drinking just enough to keep me hydrated. After a few drinks I walked around town, hoping to bump into Daphne. I couldn't find her anywhere. It started to get dark and I headed back to the room to check on Sam. He was lying in the same place I'd left him, with the remote in one hand and a book in the other. I couldn't bear the sight of him. He was a pathetic excuse of a human being.

I'd lost my appetite for destruction and I had no intention of sitting in a room, grumbling back and forth like two senile old men until the sun came up. After dinner I left Sam behind and went down to the bonfire on my own.

Ophelia's beach hut was tucked away on a small strip of sand, as far as possible from the deafening carnage.

"You can get some pretty good deals if you're willing to pay the price of a 20 minute walk," said Ophelia.

A small fire burned away in the little cove. I sat down on a log and took my shirt off. The two football players sat outside their tents mixing drinks with a twig. They offered me a cocktail but I settled for a warm beer. It was muggy, almost too hot for a fire. I watched the flicker of the yellow flame and smiled. After three weeks this is how it was going to end. Alone with three strangers on a beach watching the stars cling hopelessly to the sky.

Ophelia came up to me with an immovable smile painted across her face. "How are you doing?" I started to sigh but she continued on before I got the chance to answer. "Are you going to come to the rave with us?"

"No, I think I'll just head to bed."

She smiled at me with her over-sized eyes, "I know how you feel. But you only live once right!"

I shuddered and eked out a smile, "Sure."

I thanked Ophelia for the beer and left her sweating around the campfire, with the two sophomores fighting over her mountainous wealth of affection.

I walked back from the beach with my head hung low. I could hear the mangy dogs barking at me in the distance. I turned through a maze of dark alleys until I came to a bright-lit street. There was a girl with a tangled knot of hair smoking under the flashing white light of a 24-hour clinic. It was Daphne. I walked up to her.

"I didn't know you smoked…"

"I don't," she said half smiling.

"I came looking for you today but… Well at least I found you."

She dropped the cigarette in the dirt and stopped slumping against the wall. "All's well that ends well," she smiled and looked me in the eye. "Although I don't know if Rory would agree,"

"What the hell happened?"

She threw her hands up in the air, "I don't know, he just woke up in a pool of blood on the bridge. He doesn't remember a thing. Now he's got 60 stitches in his head."

I shook my head trying to act shocked, but she wasn't paying attention. We both knew he probably had it coming. Hell, we probably all had it coming. I asked her if she was going to stay behind to take care of him but she shook her head.

"That's Lisa's problem now. I just came down here to try and support her." She was clearly frustrated, "I don't know what the hell she sees in him anyways."

She went back inside to check on Rory. She came back five minutes later and we trekked back up the hill together one last time. The moon was still burning bright and the noise of the island throbbed up the mountainside behind us. We got undressed and jumped into bed. I closed my eyes and held her sweaty body against mine, as we counted down the hours until sunrise.

Twenty-Four

I woke up to the sound of thousands of anxious revellers being herded onto the ferry. The sun was rising for the first time in two days, and I listened as they scurried like army ants trying to escape a giant magnifying glass before it went down one last time. I rolled over in bed. Daphne was smiling beside me in her sleep with her head resting delicately on top of a pillow. I flipped on the TV and started to pack my bags. The camera panned to a scenic shot of a newspaper being blown through a deserted city square as a voice announced the news: The occupying forces had been defeated and the city had been liberated, just in time to salvage the march of the annual Santa Claus parade.

"It's finally over," the anchorman explained with a stern slicked back stare, "and now we can all go back to getting on with our lives."

Daphne woke up and stared at me from the bed as I stuffed the last bundle of clothes into my duffel bag.

"We'll be in the capital in two days…" she said as she rolled over, constantly tracking me with her eyes. "Maybe we'll see you there."

I went over to the bed and gave her a kiss and told her that I'd find her. Then, in a flash she was gone again.

As soon as she left I went down to check my emails. It had been almost a week since I'd heard any news, but this time I had a good feeling. This could be just the break I was looking for. Then I'd be able to turn around and kiss this shit-hole goodbye forever. When I was done on the computer I went back up to the pool. Sam was waiting for me with a cold beer and his book. He tracked me as I sat down across from him.

"What's up?" asked Sam.

"Nothing."

"Where were you?"

"I just went to check my emails," I said.

Sam stared at me intently, "And..."

"And nothing."

Sam took a long sip from his bottle, "They finally got back to you didn't they?"

I nodded my head.

"You didn't get it did you?" he said trying to sound consoling.

I shook my head.

He took a sip of his beer and I ordered one for myself. He stared at me and gave me the first piece of hollow advice that popped into his head, "Don't worry, it'll all work itself in the end."

I wasn't worried. I was more shocked than anything. I had been trying to fool myself all along, pretending that somehow it was a sure thing. The only thing left to do now was go home and pick up the pieces and start again.

We kept drinking until our boat pulled into the harbour. We climbed down the hill one last time and headed to the docks. Most of the pilgrims couldn't stand the thought of hanging around to see the mess they had left behind, and the only ones left on the island were the dedicated bands of euro-trash mercenaries with shaved heads and tribal tattoos that thrived on these depleted wastelands. We grabbed some seats on the roof of the boat to soak in the familiar delirious glow one last time before being exiled back to reality. The boat pulled out from the harbour, rolling from side to side as the sun capped the crests of the waves that were preparing to crash down on an unsuspecting island in the distance. The fleshy pink rocks looked grey as the mountains started to fade behind us. The only glimmer of civilisation was the silver radio tower, which poked through the clouds that were hanging reluctantly over the infernal island.

We made it to the airport, and we watched Premiership Football in the lounge as we waited to board our plane. A mousy concubine sat next to us, watching humbly from the sidelines as her benefactor scalded the excess baggage that he'd managed to squeeze out of a previous marriage. A shrill voice squealed to a rabble of new-age frat boys around the corner.

"Is she going to pick you up from the airport?... Amazing!...You're just counting down the hours aren't you…"

Just counting down the hours…

The girl continued to bombast passengers with her polite observations after we boarded the plane. I was just waiting for her to say that this had been the best fucking trip of her life, so that I could put my head between my legs and wait for the plane to quietly go down. But it landed an hour later without incident. We grabbed our bags and rushed through the terminal to catch a taxi. We couldn't face the thought of having lying around in a hotel, so we went straight from the airport to German beer hall bar where Sam had spent his first night. We were greeted by a giant inflatable snowman and a gyrating plastic Santa Claus crammed into some kind of bastardised nativity scene under a plastic manger outside the bar. The scene inside the hall was more bizarre than I had imagined. It was filled with long wooden benches made out of single planks of wood. The place must have fit nearly 800 people and it was almost three quarters full. It was Sunday night and all the tables near the stage were packed with local families that had come for dinner and a show. For the first time all trip we were outnumbered.

The show was already underway, and a team of waiters swarmed our table to fill it with inconsumable amounts of beer and food. We stuffed our faces and watched the bizarre burlesque unfold. A man on the stage dropped to his knees, surrounded by a chorus of dragons and angels covered in white shrouds. The room fell silent as they waited for something to happen. All of a sudden, there was a large explosion and room lit up with green and red fireworks. A pirate strapped up to the ceiling by a harness glided onto the stage from the back of the room. After an extended sword fight, one of the triumphant geishas broke out into a high-pitched rendition of '*My Heat Will Go On*', and the seniors in the crowd got up from their chairs and swayed back and forth as they belted out the words to the song.

For the next four hours we were bombarded with a dystopian schmorgesborg of Hollywood rip-offs and re-enactments, taken from every tragically unwatchable Oscar nominated pieces of shit that had been churned out in the last 25 years. Halfway through the show, the curtain rose and an Asian mariachi band started to strum along to a familiar theme song. The leader of the band grabbed the mic and urged the geriatric horde to get up and dance, and a giant conga line formed on the perimeter of the room. Sam and I were sucked in as they passed our table. Most of the crowd seemed to know the drill as we made our rounds. I shuffled along the floor with my hands on the hips of our waitress as she shook them back and forth. Sam was right. I'd never seen anything like it. The entire spectacle was beyond absurd. But for the locals who came here religiously week after week, it was just another Sunday night in paradise.

 We stumbled out into the street before the show was over and tried to flag a taxi. We told the first driver that stopped to take us somewhere we could sleep. He drove us around the block a few times then dropped us off at the end of a deserted road. Every hotel we stumbled into took one look at us and blurted out some ridiculous price, knowing full well that at this hour, and in our state we would be willing to pay almost anything for a room. We finally settled for a rat-infested hostel that was willing to give us a single bed for the night for under a hundred dollars. We handed over the cash, crawled up to the seventh floor and fell onto the dingy mattress, with the comfort that it would be less than 24 hours until our lives were back to normal.

Twenty-Five

I woke up in a cold sweat with Sam shivering beside me. He looked ill. I snorted aggressively to stop the mucous from running down my nose and onto my upper lip. I felt a chill crawl up and down my spine as I got up to take a piss in the sink. I tried to rinse it out afterward but there was no running water. At least that explained the smell.

Sam had to meet up with Russell at the company's head office before he left the country, so after we checked out we headed across the town, haunted by the manic squeal of idle traffic.

"You want to come up?" Sam asked as we pulled up to the monstrous high-rise.

"Why not?" I laughed, "Maybe they'll take pity on me and offer me a job."

Sam disappeared into the elevator and I went to wait for him at the bar in the lobby. The suits at the table next to me were going over a report before the conference call they had scheduled later that afternoon. They nodded lethargically every time the greying dinosaur across from them opened his mouth. He spoke with a pompous slur and he wore a navy suit with a purple shirt and an even purpler tie. The heavy nodders might even have called him out on it, if it hadn't been for his commanding silver mane. Once upon a time he had been in their shoes – he'd put in his time, and the company brass thanked him for his efforts by shipping him off to some third rate emerging market to waste away the rest of his days. I'd spent the last three weeks pretending that this would never happen to me. But deep down inside this was what I had been waiting for all along. This was the shape of things to come and the sooner I accepted it the better.

Later that night we went to meet Daphne in a dive bar on the main drag. It felt good to see her again. I hadn't even realised how much I had missed staring at her marbled eyes until now. I watched her lips move as she told me about how she had decided to apply for a job on a nature reserve in South America. I thought about dragging her to the bathroom and bending her over the sink. One more romp, one last perverted rush before returning to reality.

"Why don't you come with me," she said, interrupting my train of thought. She was smiling at me with her big canine eyes. I'd always wanted to go to South America.

I chuckled out loud and smiled back, "It's not like I have a job to go back to or anything."

And so we were reduced to reminiscing about shit that had happened just a few days ago, shit that was so fresh in my mind, I couldn't even be sure whether it had happened or not. At least it was better than talking about what was going to happen to us when it was all over. I watched Daphne as the Monday night troubadour on stage strummed along to UB 40's rendition of an old Elvis Presley classic with faithful precision: *"Wise-men say, only fools rush in... But I can't help..."* I began to feel ashamed and depressed. It was all coming to and end and all I had to show for it was a bruised ego, and a creeping fear that I knew exactly what was waiting for me when I got to the other side.

I looked up at the big clock on the wall. Surely this wasn't how it was supposed to end. But I couldn't find the courage or the insanity to rip up my ticket to spend a few extra nights sweating away in a rundown motel. I kissed Daphne and told her that I would let her know if I ever made it out down the Coast. Sam got up from the table and I left the bar with him by my side. We walked past the wooden stalls that were selling cheap Japanese electronics wrapped in cheap Chinese plastic. Sam looked over at me and we both broke out into an awkward laugh. We kept laughing as we walked past the neon lights and the smell of rotting flesh that filled the overcrowded street. The shit hawks were waiting for us at the end of the intersection. They immediately spotted the bags slung over our shoulders and they started to circle.

"Airport... Airport... Taxi to airport... My friend, my friend... Taxi, taxi... I take you to airport."

They reached for our bags and we brushed them off, "Back off you greasy bastards!"

We pushed through but they followed us until we stopped at the side of the road across from a police station. Sam put down his bag and blurted out a price to the pack and the laughs immediately rose amongst them, "Ha! My friend, that is not possible. Price of gas is high!" But as they were all laughing a stubby man in a blue pin stripe shirt jumped out in front of them, "My friend we go."

"Really?" Sam asked.

He nodded.

Sam tossed out the price again, "For both?"

The driver grimaced, "No... For both – double!"

We kept trying to haggle with them but they just laughed at us. They knew there was only one way out of here and it was through them. Finally a lone scavenger in a bright red shirt dragged us into the back of his cab. We threw our bags on the seats and tried to close the doors but the hawks jammed their claws inside.

"Take your hands off us you mangy dogs!" Sam burst out in a fit of rage.

We slammed the doors and pushed the automatic locks down. I looked back in the rear view mirror and watched them as they foamed at the mouth. In a matter of weeks the levy would break and the backpackers would wash over the streets like rabid hyenas. They would multiply and replenish, and feast on the spoils for 7 months, before returning to hibernate in darkness. That's when the real fighting would start. I leaned my head against the window and bit my lip. I could feel their rotten greed brewing in the pit of my stomach. I focused on the flickering lights that lined the highway and sank lower into my seat.

We jumped out of the cab and stood in the terminal, awkwardly grasping to find a suitable way to bring our shit-show to and end. Sam's flight didn't leave until the morning and his check-in didn't open for another six hours. He joked about missing his plane and booking a flight to Australia. I thought about discouraging him from tracking down that good for nothing whore but it didn't need to be said. I threw my arms around him, "I'm sure I'll see you in London soon enough..."

He smiled, "Let me know when you've figured it all out."

I went through the mind-numbing monotony of the routine security check one more time: shoes off, belt in the bucket, empty your pockets, come this way sir, bow, greet, shoes on, smile, repeat. When it was done, I trudged past the gauntlet of bowing salesman that were standing guard at their duty free posts and went straight to the bar. I sat down and ordered a few rounds, and watched the preview of white sneakered pimps and hemp-clad dreadlocks bloating on about their unimagined exploits. The bartender didn't even didn't even look at me. Not even a nod or a glance. A charming colonial voice came over the intercom to announce that the flight was overbooked. It asked if anyone was willing to be bumped to a later flight. They offered free hotels, and meals and flights, but no one budged.

I walked down the tunnel. The hallway was lined with ads for a big financial firm. Their slogan was scrawled across slick white posters in red block letters: *The world belongs to those who see potential. We help you realise those opportunities.*

So succinct, so profound.

I pushed through to the back of the plane and squeezed in between the two bodies that were blocking my way. I listened as the captain came over the speaker, "We're going to be expecting a little turbulence." Nothing to worry about, just another routine procedure. My mind started to wander off. What if something went wrong? What if things didn't go according to plan this time? The engine started up. I felt the dreadful sinking feeling grow inside the pit of my stomach. In just a few minutes we would take off and return to a sad irrelevance. As soon as we left the ground all bets were off. There was only one escape, but it was too early to contemplate such a morbid solution.

I slumped further into my seat. I felt a haunting desperate chill come over me like some kind of long lost primitive defense mechanism. I started to think about the turbulence. I didn't dread it. I was praying for it. The familiar sinking feeling grew deeper inside me. What if the plane went down? No... what if I *wanted* the plane might go down. I felt guilty for a moment, but it was really just a harmless thought. Besides the statistics were stacked against me: you're 200 times more likely to die in an accident on the way to the airport than a plane crash, or something like that. Maybe if I hoped hard enough, maybe if I prayed to the right god, just maybe I could get the plane to fall from the sky. Then my hands would be clean and I'd be just another blameless martyr.

Anything to avoid having to get off the plane and face whatever was waiting for me on the other side. But what about the little girl kicking the seat behind me? And what about her poor single mother? They were innocent. They both deserved a better ending than that. So young and innocent and irresponsible. They must have deserved better.

My mind filled with dread and angst. I could feel my stomach suck further up against my spine, pinning me to the hard cushions of the reclining chair. I could feel the empty rotting feeling growing deep in the pit of my stomach. I thought about Sam and the happy couple, and their happy wedding, and I thought about Patrick and his slicked back hair.

Maybe I'd get lucky and go back home and get diagnosed with some kind of disorder and be declared medically unfit for service. Maybe they could give me some of those pills they gave to Patrick, and then I could turn right around and tell them to go and fuck themselves. Fuck them! I thought. I didn't need their prescription or their diagnosis. But there was just something so comforting about having a complete stranger give your misery the official seal of approval.

Maybe I could give it all up and go to med school like Daphne. They'd probably make me take the Hypocratic oath but that wasn't such a big deal. I'd already memorised it by heart: *"I swear to be a hypocrite first and foremost, and a human being second, so help me god!"*

27 years old – I'd had a pretty good run, and that was one hell of a few weeks. But the thought of having to talk about it over and over again – clinging to those memories and dreaming of the good ol' days... *Hey remember that time...* I couldn't go on like that. I had no desire to remember. I'd come here to forget, and I'd failed.

I grinned and gripped the armrests with my sweaty palms. I thought about the advertisement in the tunnel. That was it. All I need to do was realise my potential. Capitalising on opportunities – realising potential. The answer had been right in front of me all along! All I had to do now was swallow my pride and get on with life just like the rest of them.

I felt a horrible throbbing feeling take over. My bowels sunk further into my seat, as they tried to make subtle suggestions to the pilot. If only the plane would go down and take all these innocent people down with me. Then it would all be ok. No more thinking. No more revolutions, just silence.

The plane started to accelerate, and the woman next to me made the sign of the cross. My mind was moving a thousand miles and hour, and as the wheels licked the final stretch of pavement, a crosswind caught the underside of the wings and tossed us sideways. Just a little turbulence. Nothing to worry about.

The nose pointed towards the sky and the blood rushed to my head. The plane was going to crash. It was just a matter of time. The pilot pushed down hard on the throttle and engaged the autopilot. The humming of the engine faded into the background as we soared above the city, with thousands of revolutions a minute keeping us quietly afloat.

I thought about Sam, and the happy couple, and the girls, and Daphne. They were probably flying around somewhere in the air next to me. Just another routine flight. I'm sure I'd see them all again one day. It was just a matter of time. There was no point thinking about that now. There was no point thinking at all. My head was pounding – throbbing. Just stop thinking about it. Stop thinking and just relax. It's just another harmless thought, another pounding thought. My thoughts were pounding, throbbing. Boom! Boom! Boom! I could feel the bass throbbing, clawing away at my skin. My thoughts were pounding heavily, nagging my conscience with the incessant beating of the drum. A thousand revolutions growing louder, pounding harder every minute. Throbbing harder, pounding faster. My thoughts were growing louder, pounding, throbbing harder, faster. I couldn't take it anymore. I wanted to get up and scream. I couldn't bear the sound of my own thoughts anymore. I wanted it to stop. It had to stop. My thoughts were so loud I couldn't hear my mouth. My thoughts were so loud I couldn't hear my mouth. My thoughts were so loud I couldn't hear my mouth. My thoughts were so loud.

ABOUT THE AUTHOR

Cody Punter was born and raised in Toronto, Canada. The World At Large is his debut novel. He started working as a reporter shortly after writing the manuscript for the book. He currently writes for a newspaper in the Northwest Territories in Northern Canada.

Made in the USA
Charleston, SC
08 June 2014